Rex Stout

REX STOUT, the creator of Nero Wolfe, was born in Noblesville, Indiana, in 1886, the sixth of nine children of John and Lucetta Todhunter Stout, both Quakers. Shortly after his birth, the family moved to Wakarusa, Kansas. He was educated in a country school, but, by the age of nine, was recognized throughout the state as a prodigy in arithmetic. Mr. Stout briefly attended the University of Kansas, but left to enlist in the Navy, and spent the next two years as a warrant officer on board President Theodore Roosevelt's yacht. When he left the Navy in 1908, Rex Stout began to write free-lance articles, worked as a sightseeing guide and an itinerant bookkeeper. Later he devised and implemented a school banking system which was installed in four hundred cities and towns throughout the country. In 1927 Mr. Stout retired from the world of finance and, with the proceeds of his banking scheme, left for Paris to write serious fiction. He wrote three novels that received favorable reviews before turning to detective fiction. His first Nero Wolfe novel, *Fer-de-Lance*, appeared in 1934. It was followed by many others, among them, *Too Many Cooks*, *The Silent Speaker*, *If Death Ever Slept*, *The Doorbell Rang*, and *Please Pass the Guilt*, which established Nero Wolfe as a leading character on a par with Erle Stanley Gardner's famous protagonist, Perry Mason. During World War II Rex Stout waged a personal campaign against Nazism as chairman of the War Writers' Board, master of ceremonies of the radio program "Speaking of Liberty," and member of several national committees. After the war he turned his attention to mobilizing public opinion against the wartime use of thermonuclear devices, was an active leader in the Authors' Guild, and resumed writing his Nero Wolfe novels. Rex Stout died in 1975 at the age of eighty-nine. A month before his death he published his seventy-second Nero W̶o̶l̶f̶e̶ ̶m̶y̶s̶t̶e̶r̶y̶,̶ ̶A̶ ̶F̶a̶m̶i̶l̶y̶ ̶A̶f̶f̶a̶i̶r̶.̶ Ten years later, a seve̶n̶t̶y̶-̶t̶h̶i̶r̶d̶ ̶n̶o̶v̶e̶l̶ was discovered and pub̶l̶i̶s̶h̶e̶d̶.̶

The Rex Stout Library

REX STOUT

Homicide Trinity

Introduction
by Stephen Greenleaf

BANTAM BOOKS
NEW YORK · TORONTO · LONDON · SYDNEY · AUCKLAND

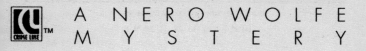

A NERO WOLFE
MYSTERY

HOMICIDE TRINITY

A Bantam Crime Line Book / published by arrangement with
The Viking Press, Inc.

PUBLISHING HISTORY

Viking edition / April 1963
Bantam edition / February 1966
Bantam reissue / August 1993

Acknowledgment is made to ELLERY QUEEN'S MYSTERY MAGAZINE, *in which*
"Eeny Meeny Murder Mo" appeared, and to THE SATURDAY EVENING POST, *in*
which "Death of a Demon" and "Counterfeit for Murder" appeared, the latter
under the title "The Counterfeiter's Knife."

ISBN 0-553-23446-3

Published simultaneously in the United States and Canada

PRINTED IN THE UNITED STATES OF AMERICA

OPM   14 13 12 11 10 9 8 7

Introduction

W hen asked for my thoughts on Rex Stout on the welcome occasion of Bantam's reissue of his work, I wondered what I could possibly add to the existing hagiography. As my mind began to drift toward the world of Wolfe, a world I've visited for more than thirty years, I found myself listing the aspects of Stout's work and person that I envy, not as a reader any longer, but as a laborer in the same field (or at least the same section).

To begin with a minor example, I envy the New York City of the Wolfe novels. Not the imperiled and pitiable cauldron of today, but the mecca of reason and refinement that Stout portrayed so invitingly. That this oasis was occupied in part by men of diabolical design and by Runyonesque rapscallions seemed to add rather than detract from its sheen. That city, so titanic compared to the hinterland I inhabited when I first encountered it, may never have existed outside Stout's novels—I am in no position to say whether it did or didn't—but it was and is a place I would have liked to inhabit.

As for the author himself, I believe I am correct in saying that Nero Wolfe first appeared when his creator was nearly fifty years old. As I approach that decade of my own life, with major upheavals in the recent past and more likely to come, I envy the vigor and confidence Stout demonstrated in launching such an experiment at that age, particularly one so unlikely and problematic as writing mystery novels. It is essential to survival at any age to believe most things are possible. As with other laudable traits—the devotion of copious time and energy to major issues of the day, for example—Rex Stout was an exemplar. I frequently wonder what would happen if suddenly I had no publisher; Stout's career is a template of encouragement, albeit in reverse.

As the months of labor on my current novel accumulate to inevitably total twelve by the time I yield my sovereignty, no matter how ardently I have tried to make gestation briefer, I am reminded that Stout's productivity would shame even a modern Moto. He wrote one of the Wolfe novels in three weeks; the average over the entire oeuvre was not much longer. Envy again, times two to the third power.

So much for the man (space is limited); now for the fiction.

Others have envied Nero Wolfe his passions—the orchids and the cuisine. As my own detective's tastes reflect, I am in large part immune to the charms of nature and the subtleties of gastronomy. (John Marshall Tanner frequently dines on Campbell's soup and Oreo cookies and can label virtually nothing in his environment that isn't man-made). What I coveted was Wolfe's vocabulary. Did I resort to the dictionary in midnovel? Many times, though not as often as I should have. Do I insert words in my protagonist's mouth that would issue more appropriately from Wolfe's? Indeed. A multiple offender.

Wolfe never leaves the brownstone. (Well, hardly ever; his sojourn to Montenegro is an outing of special interest these days, given geopolitical developments. Were he still with us, I'm certain he would go again.) Although my home is not nearly the biosphere that

Wolfe created for himself (or rather that Stout created for Wolfe), I leave it infrequently as well. The solitude that Wolfe demanded is handmaiden to the writing profession, of course, and is a major reason I wanted to become a writer and why I still pursue the art. Initially, writing let me escape the cacophony of litigation. In a more defining sense, it has provided a means to avoid, in large part, the whir of commercial society and the values it suggests.

A word about Archie. Then as now I lacked the chutzpah to identify with Wolfe, so Archie was my alter ego. What I coveted was his savoir faire—always a step ahead, always with the coup de grace for the repartee, always managing the unmanageable: Archie was who I aspired to be. But at best I performed such feats only after the fact, in daydreams and psychodramas and hours of rueful reverie. Which suggests another reason I became a writer, I suppose: the sense that my untimely talents were more suited to the world of fiction, where I, or at least my hero, could deliver on demand. Luckily, demand for Mr. Tanner's savoir faire, such as it is, comes only once a year.

(Addendum: Although Archie was my favorite, he did not suggest the form my own detective would later take. That distinction belongs to Saul Panzer, who for me remains Stout's best creation. Amazingly, our knowledge of Saul is largely once removed—we know him best through Archie's deft descriptions of his genius.)

A final note. Several years ago, when Orson Welles was appearing with disappointing frequency on *The Tonight Show*, it occurred to me (as no doubt to others) that Welles had actually *become* Nero Wolfe, in both physical and intellectual dimensions, and that Hollywood should build a film around that metamorphosis. Hardly a brilliant insight, but that was only a subordinate impulse. The capper was, Why not Carson as Archie? Johnny as Goodwin? Indeed.

Sadly, the two stars had a falling out, for reasons unknown to me; Welles became a butt of Carson's jibes, and the film remains unmade. But the books survive, and thrive, and another generation has the pleasure of meeting Nero and Archie and Fritz and Theodore (and Saul and Orrie and Fred and Doll).

What could be more satisfactory?

—Stephen Greenleaf

Contents

Homicide
Trinity

EENY MEENY
MURDER MO

Chapter 1

I was standing there in the office with my hands in my pockets, glaring down at the necktie on Nero Wolfe's desk, when the doorbell rang.

Since it would be a different story, and possibly no story at all, if the necktie hadn't been there, I had better explain about it. It was the one Wolfe had worn that morning—brown silk with little yellow curlicues, A Christmas gift from a former client. At lunch Fritz, coming to remove the leavings of the spareribs and bring the salad and cheese, had told Wolfe there was a drop of sauce on his tie, and Wolfe had dabbed at it with his napkin; and later, when we had left the dining room to cross the hall to the office, he had removed the tie and put it on his desk. He can't stand a spot on his clothes, even in private. But he hadn't thought it worth the effort to go up to his room for another one, since no callers were expected, and when four o'clock came and he left for his afternoon session with the orchids in the plant rooms on the roof, his shirt was still unbuttoned at the neck and the tie was still on his desk.

It annoyed me. It annoyed Fritz too when, shortly after four, he came to say he was going shopping and would be gone two hours. His eye caught the tie and fastened on it. His brows went up.

"*Schlampick*," I said.

He nodded. "You know my respect and esteem for him. He has great spirit and character, and of course he is a great detective, but there is a limit to the duties of a chef and housekeeper. One must draw the line somewhere. Besides, there is my arthritis. You haven't got arthritis, Archie."

"Maybe not," I conceded, "but if you rate a limit so do I. My list of functions from confidential assistant detective down to errand boy is a mile long, but it does not include valeting. Arthritis is beside the point. Consider the dignity of man. He could have taken it on his way up to the plant rooms."

"You could put it in a drawer."

"That would be evading the issue."

"I suppose so." He nodded. "I agree. It is a delicate affair. I must be going." He went.

So, having finished the office chores at 5:20, including a couple of personal phone calls, I had left my desk and was standing to glare down at the necktie when the doorbell rang. That made the affair even more delicate. A necktie with a greasy spot should not be on the desk of a man of great spirit and character when a visitor enters. But by then I had got stubborn about it as a matter of principle, and anyway it might be merely someone with a parcel. Going to the hall for a look, I saw through the one-way glass panel of the front door that it was a stranger, a middle-aged female with a pointed nose and a round chin, not a good design, in a sensible gray coat and a black turban. She had no parcel. I went and opened the door and told her good afternoon. She said she wanted to see Nero Wolfe. I said Mr. Wolfe was engaged, and besides, he saw people only by appointment. She said she knew that, but this was urgent. She had to see him and would wait till he was free.

There were several factors: that we had nothing on the fire at the moment; that the year was only five days old and therefore the income-tax bracket didn't enter into it; that I wanted something to do besides recording the vital statistics of orchids; that I was annoyed at him for leaving the tie on his desk; and that she didn't try to push but kept her distance, with her dark eyes, good eyes, straight at me.

"Okay," I told her, "I'll see what I can do," and stepped aside for her to enter. After taking her coat and hanging it on the rack and escorting her to the office, I gave her one of the yellow chairs near me instead of the red leather one at the end of Wolfe's desk. She sat with her back straight and her feet together—nice little feet in fairly sensible gray shoes. I told her that Wolfe wouldn't be available until six o'clock.

"It will be better," I said, "if I see him first and tell him about you. In fact, it will be essential. My name is Archie Goodwin. What is yours?"

"I know about you," she said. "Of course. If I didn't I wouldn't be here."

"Many thanks. Some people who know about me have a different reaction. And your name?"

She was eyeing me. "I'd rather not," she said, "until I know if Mr. Wolfe will take my case. It's private. It's very confidential."

I shook my head. "No go. You'll have to tell him what your case is before he decides if he'll take it, and I'll be sitting here listening. So? Also I'll have to tell him more about you than you're thirty-five years old, weigh a hundred and twenty pounds, and wear no earrings, before he decides if he'll even see you."

She almost smiled. "I'm forty-two."

I grinned. "See? I need facts. Who you are and what you want."

Her mouth worked. "It's *very* confidential." Her mouth worked some more. "But there was no sense in coming unless I tell you."

"Right."

She laced her fingers. "All right. My name is Bertha Aaron. It is spelled with two A's. I am the private secretary of Mr. Lamont Otis, senior partner in the law firm of Otis, Edey, Heydecker, and Jett. Their office is on Madison Avenue at Fifty-first Street. I'm worried about something that happened recently and I want Mr. Wolfe to investigate it. I can pay him a reasonable fee, but it might develop that he will be paid by the firm. It *might*."

"Were you sent here by someone in the firm?"

"No. Nobody sent me. Nobody knows I'm here."

"What happened?"

Her fingers laced tighter. "Maybe I shouldn't have come," she said. "I didn't realize . . . maybe I'd better not."

"Suit yourself, Miss Aaron, *Miss* Aaron?"

"Yes. I am not married." Her fingers flew apart to make fists and her lips tightened. "This is silly. I've got to. I owe it to Mr. Otis. I've been with him for twenty years and he has been wonderful to me. I couldn't go to him about this because he's seventy-five years old and he has a bad heart and it might kill him. He comes to the office every day, but it's a strain and he doesn't do much, only he knows more than all the rest of them put together." Her fists opened. "What happened was that I saw a member of the firm with our opponent in a very important case, one of the biggest cases we've ever had, at a place where they wouldn't have met if they hadn't wanted to keep it secret."

"You mean with the opposing counsel?"

"No. The client. With opposing counsel it might possibly have been all right."

"Which member of the firm?"

"I'm not going to say. I'm not going to tell Mr. Wolfe his name until he agrees to take the case. He doesn't have to know that in order to decide. If you wonder why I came, I've already said why I can't tell Mr. Otis about it, and I was afraid to go to any of the others because if one of them was a traitor another one might be in it with him, or even more than one. How could I be sure? There are only four members of the firm, but of course there are others associated—nineteen altogether. I wouldn't trust any of them, not on a thing like this." She made fists again. "You can understand that. You see what a hole I'm in."

"Sure. But you could be wrong. Of course that's unethical, a lawyer meeting with an enemy client, but there could be exceptions. It might have been accidental. When and where did you see them?"

"Last Monday, a week ago today. In the evening. They were together in a booth in a cheap restaurant—more of a lunchroom. The kind of place she would never go to, never. She would never go to that part of town. Neither would I, ordinarily, but I was on a personal errand and I went in there to use the phone. They didn't see me."

"Then one of the members of the firm is a woman?"

Her eyes widened. "Oh. I said 'she.' I meant the opposing client. We have a woman lawyer as one of the associates, just an employee really, but no woman firm member." She laced her fingers. "It couldn't possibly have been accidental. But of course it was conceivable, just barely conceivable, that he wasn't a traitor, that there was some explanation, and that made it even harder for me to decide what to do. But now I know. After worrying about it for a whole week I couldn't stand it any longer, and this afternoon I decided the only thing I *could* do was tell him and see what he said. If he had a good explanation, all right. But he didn't. The way he took it, the way it hit him, there isn't any question about it. He's a traitor."

"What did he say?"

"It wasn't so much what he said as how he looked. He said he had a satisfactory explanation, that he was acting in the interest of our client, but that he couldn't tell me more than that until the matter had developed further. Certainly within a week, he said, and possibly tomorrow. So I knew I had to do something, and I was afraid to go to Mr. Otis because his heart has been worse lately, and I wouldn't go to another firm member. I even thought of going to the opposing counsel, but of course that wouldn't do. Then I thought of Nero Wolfe, and I put on my hat and coat and came. Now it's urgent. You can see it's urgent?"

I nodded. "It could be. Depending on the kind of case

involved. Mr. Wolfe might agree to take the job before you name the alleged traitor, but he would have to know first what the case is about—your firm's case. There are some kinds he won't touch, even indirectly. What is it?"

"I don't want . . ." She let it hang. "Does he have to know that?"

"Certainly. Anyhow, you've told me the name of your firm and it's a big important case and the opposing client is a woman, and with that I could—but I don't have to. I read the papers. Is your client Morton Sorell?"

"Yes."

"And the opposing client is Rita Sorell, his wife?"

"Yes."

I glanced at my wrist watch and saw 5:39, left my chair, told her, "Cross your fingers and sit tight," and headed for the hall and the stairs. Two new factors had entered and now dominated the situation: that if our first bank deposit of the new year came from the Sorell pile it would not be hay; and that one of the kind of jobs Wolfe wouldn't touch, even indirectly, was divorce stuff. It would take some doing, and as I mounted the three flights to the roof of the old brownstone my brain was going faster than my feet. In the vestibule of the plant rooms I paused, not for breath but to plan the approach, decided that was no good because it would depend on his mood, and entered. You might think it impossible to go down the aisles between the benches of those three rooms—cool, tropical, and intermediate—without noticing the flashes and banks of color, but that day I did, and then was in the potting room.

Wolfe was over at the side bench peering at a pseudobulb through a magnifying glass. Theodore Horstmann, the fourth member of the household, who was exactly half Wolfe's weight, 137 to 270, was opening a bag of osmundine. I crossed over and told Wolfe's back, "Excuse me for interrupting, but I have a problem."

He took ten seconds to decide he had heard me, then

removed the glass from his eye and demanded, "What time is it?"

"Nineteen minutes to six."

"It can wait nineteen minutes."

"I know, but there's a snag. If you came down and found her there in the office with no warning it would be hopeless."

"Find whom?"

"A woman named Bertha Aaron. She came uninvited. She's in a hole, and it's a new kind of hole. I came up to describe it to you so you can decide whether I go down and shoo her out or you come down and give it a look."

"You have interrupted me. You have violated our understanding."

"I know it, but I said excuse me, and since you're already interrupted I might as well tell you. She is the private secretary of Lamont Otis, senior partner . . ."

I told him, and at least he didn't go back to the pseudo-bulb with the glass. At one point there was even a gleam in his eye. He has made the claim, to me, that the one and only thing that impels him to work is his desire to live in what he calls acceptable circumstances in the old brownstone on West 35th Street, Manhattan, which he owns, with Fritz as chef and Theodore as orchid tender and me as goat (not his word), but the gleam in his eye was not at the prospect of a big fee, because I hadn't yet mentioned the name Sorell. The gleam was when he saw that, as I had said, it was a new kind of hole. We had never looked into one just like it.

Then came the ticklish part. "By the way," I said, "there's one little detail you may not like, but it's only a side issue. In the case in question her firm's client is Morton Sorell. You know."

"Of course."

"And the opposing client she saw a member of the firm with is Mrs. Morton Sorell. You may remember that you made a comment about her a few weeks ago after you had read the morning paper. What the paper said was that she was suing him for thirty thousand a month for a separation allowance, but the talk around town is that he wants a divorce and her asking price is a flat thirty million bucks, and that's probably what Miss Aaron calls the case. However, that's only a detail. What Miss Aaron wants is merely—"

"No." He was scowling at me. "So that's why you pranced in here."

"I didn't prance. I walked."

"You knew quite well I would have nothing to do with it."

"I knew you wouldn't get divorce evidence, and neither would I. I knew you wouldn't work for a wife against a husband or vice versa, but what has that got to do with this? You wouldn't have to touch—"

"No! I will not. That marital squabble might be the central point of the matter. I will not! Send her away."

I had flubbed it. Or maybe I hadn't; maybe it had been hopeless no matter how I handled it; but then it had been a flub to try, so in any case I had flubbed it. I don't like to flub, and it wouldn't make it any worse to try to talk him out of it, or rather into it, so I did, for a good ten minutes, but it neither changed the situation nor improved the atmosphere. He ended it by saying that he would go to his room to put on a necktie, and I would please ring him there on the house phone to tell him that she had gone.

Going down the three flights I was tempted. I could ring him not to say that she was gone but that we were going; that I was taking a leave of absence to haul her out of the hole. It wasn't a new temptation; I had had it before; and I had to admit that on other occasions it had been more attractive. To begin with, if I made the offer she might decline it, and I had done enough flubbing for one day. So as I crossed the hall to the office I was arranging my face so she would know the answer as soon as she looked at me. Then as I entered I rearranged it, or it rearranged itself, and I stopped and stood. Two objects were there on the rug which had been elsewhere when I left: a big hunk of jade which

Wolfe used for a paperweight, which had been on his desk, and Bertha Aaron, who had been in a chair.

She was on her side, with one leg straight and one bent at the knee. I went to her and squatted. Her lips were blue, her tongue was showing, and her eyes were open and popping; and around her neck, knotted at the side, was Wolfe's necktie. She was gone. But if you get a case of strangulation soon enough there may be a chance, and I got the scissors from my desk drawer. The tie was so tight that I had to poke hard to get my finger under. When I had the tie off I rolled her over on her back. Nuts, I thought, she's gone, but I picked pieces of fluff from the rug, put one across her nose and one on her mouth, and held my breath for twenty seconds. She wasn't breathing. I took her hand and pressed on a fingernail, and it stayed white when I removed the pressure. Her blood wasn't moving. Still there might be a chance if I got an expert quick enough, say in two minutes, and I went to my desk and dialed the number of Doc Vollmer, who lived down the street only a minute away. He was out. "To hell with it," I said, louder than necessary since there was no one but me to hear, and sat to take a breath.

I sat and stared at her a while, maybe a minute, just feeling, not thinking. I was too damn sore to think. I was sore at Wolfe, not at me, the idea being that it had been ten minutes past six when I found her, and if he had come down with me at six o'clock we might have been in time. I swiveled to the house phone and buzzed his room, and when he answered I said, "Okay, come on down. She's gone," and hung up.

He always uses the elevator to and from the plant rooms, but his room is only one flight up. When I heard his door open and close I got up and stood six inches from her head and folded my arms, facing the door to the hall. There was the sound of his steps, and then him. He crossed the threshold, stopped, glared at Bertha Aaron, shifted it to me, and bellowed, "You said she was gone!"

"Yes, sir. She is. She's dead."

"Nonsense!"

"No, sir." I sidestepped. "As you see."

He approached, still glaring, and aimed the glare down at her, for not more than three seconds. Then he circled around her and me, went to his oversized made-to-order chair behind his desk, sat, took in air clear down as far as it would go, and let it out again. "I presume," he said, not bellowing, "that she was alive when you left her to come up to me."

"Yes, sir. Sitting in that chair." I pointed. "She was alone. No one came with her. The door was locked, as always. As you know, Fritz is out shopping. When I found her she was on her side and I turned her over to test for breathing—after I cut the necktie off. I phoned Doc—"

"What necktie?"

I pointed again. "The one you left on your desk. It was around her throat. Probably she was knocked out first with that paperweight"—I pointed again—"but it was the necktie that stopped her breathing, as you can see by her face. I cut—"

"Do you dare to suggest that she was strangled with *my* necktie?"

"I don't suggest, I state. It was pulled tight with a slipknot and then passed around her neck again and tied with a granny." I stepped to where I had dropped it on the rug, picked it up, and put it on his desk. "As you see. I do dare to suggest that if it hadn't been here handy he would have had to use something else, maybe his handkerchief. Also that if we had come down a little sooner—"

"Shut up!"

"Yes, sir."

"This is insupportable."

"Yes, sir."

"I will not accept it."

"No, sir. I could burn the tie and we could tell Cramer that whatever he used he must have waited until he was sure she was dead and then removed it and took it—"

"Shut up. She told you that nobody knew she came here."

"Bah," I said. "Not a chance and you know it. We're stuck. I put off calling until you came down only to be polite. If I put it off any longer that will only make it worse because I'll have to tell them the exact time I found her." I looked at my wrist. "It's already been twenty-one minutes. Would you rather make the call yourself?"

No reply. He was staring down at the necktie, with his jaw set and his mouth so tight he had no lips. I gave him five seconds, to be polite, and then went to the kitchen, to the phone on the table where I ate breakfast, and dialed a number.

Chapter 2

Inspector Cramer of Homicide West finished the last page of the statement I had typed and signed, put it on top of the other pages on the table, tapped it with a finger, and spoke. "I still think you're lying, Goodwin."

It was a quarter past eleven. We were in the dining room. The gang of scientists had finished in the office and departed, and it was no longer out of bounds, but I had no special desire to move back in. For one thing, they had taken the rug, along with Wolfe's necktie and the paperweight and a few other items. Of course they had also taken Bertha Aaron, so I wouldn't have to see her again, but even so I was perfectly willing to stay in the dining room. They had brought the typewriter there after the fingerprint detail had finished with it, so I could type the statement.

Now, after nearly five hours, they were gone, all except Sergeant Purley Stebbins, who was in the office using the phone, and Cramer. Fritz was in the kitchen, on his third bottle of wine, absolutely miserable. Added to the humiliation of a homicide in the house he kept was the incredible fact that Wolfe had passed up a meal. He had refused to eat a bite. Around eight o'clock he had gone up to his room, and Fritz had gone up twice with a tray, and he had only snarled at him. When I had gone up at 10:30 with a statement for him to sign, and told him they were taking the rug, he made a noise but had no words. With all that for background in addition to my personal reactions, it was no wonder that when Cramer told me he still thought I was lying I was outspoken.

"I've been trying for years," I said, "to think who it is you remind me of. I just remembered. It was a certain animal I saw once in a cage. It begins with B. Are you going to take me down or not?"

"No." His big round face is always redder at night, making his gray hair look whiter. "You can save the wisecracks. You wouldn't lie about anything that can be checked, but we can't check your account of what she told you. She's dead. Accepting your statement, and Wolfe's, that you have never had any dealings with her or anyone connected with that law firm, you might still save something for your private use—or change something. One thing especially. You ask me to believe that she told—"

"Excuse me. I don't care a single measly damn what you believe. Neither does Mr. Wolfe. You can't name anything we wouldn't rather have done than report what happened, but we had no choice, so we reported it and you have our statements. If you know what she said better than I do, that's fine with me."

"I was talking," he said.

"Yeah. I was interrupting."

"You say that she gave you all those details, how she saw a member of the firm in a cheap restaurant or lunchroom with an opposing client, the day she saw him, her telling him about it this afternoon, all the rest of it, including naming Mrs. Sorell, but she didn't name the member of the firm. I don't believe it." He tapped the statement and his head came forward. "And I'm telling you this, Goodwin. If you use that name for your private purposes and profit, and that includes Wolfe, if you get yourselves hired to investigate this murder and you use information you have withheld from me to solve the case and collect a fee, I'll get you for it if it costs me an eye!"

I cocked my head. "Look," I said. "Apparently you don't realize. It's already been on the radio, and tomorrow it will be in the papers, that a woman who had come to consult Nero Wolfe was murdered in his office, strangled with his necktie, while he was up playing with his orchids and chatting with Archie Goodwin. I can hear the horse laugh from here. Mr. Wolfe couldn't swallow any dinner; he wouldn't even try. We knew and felt all this the second we saw her there on the floor. If we had known which member of the firm it was, if she had told me his name, what would we have done? You ought to know, since you claim you know us. I would have gone after him. Mr. Wolfe would have left the office, shut the door, and gone to the kitchen, and would have been there drinking beer when Fritz came home. When he went to the office and discovered the body would have depended on when and what he heard from me. With any luck I would have got here with the murderer before you and the scientists arrived. That wouldn't have erased the fact that she had been strangled with his necktie, but it would have blurred it. I give you this just to show you that you don't know us as well as you think you do. As for your believing me, I couldn't care less."

His sharp gray eyes were narrowed at me. "So you would have gone and got him. So he killed her. Huh? How did he know she was here? How did he get in?"

I produced a word I'll leave out, and added, "Again? I have discussed that with Stebbins, and Rowcliff, and you. Now again?"

"What the hell," he said. He folded the statement and stuck it in his pocket, shoved his chair back, got up, growled at me, "If it costs me both eyes," and tramped out. From the hall he spoke to Stebbins in the office. It will give you some idea of how low I was when I say that I didn't even go to the hall to see that they took only what belonged to them. You might think that after being in the house five hours Purley would have stepped to the door to say good night, but no. I heard the front door close with a bang, so it was Purley. Cramer never banged doors.

I slumped further down in my chair. At twenty minutes to midnight I said aloud, "I could go for a walk," but apparently that didn't appeal to me. At 11:45 I arose, picked up the carbons of my statement, went to the office, and put them in a drawer of my desk. Looking around, I saw that they had left it in fairly decent shape. I went and brought the typewriter and put it where it belonged, tried the door of the safe, went to the hall to see that the front door was locked and put the chain bolt on, and proceeded to the kitchen. Fritz was in my breakfast chair, humped over with his forehead on the edge of the table.

"You're pie-eyed," I said.

His head came up. "No, Archie. I have tried, but no."

"Go to bed."

"No. He will be hungry."

"He may never be hungry again. Pleasant dreams."

I went to the hall, mounted one flight, turned left, tapped on the door, heard a sound that was half growl and half groan, opened the door, and entered. Wolfe, fully clothed, wearing a necktie, was in the big chair with a book.

"They've gone," I said. "Last ones out, Cramer and Stebbins. Fritz is standing watch in the kitchen expecting a call for food. You'd better buzz him. Is there any alternative to going to bed?"

"Can you sleep?" he demanded.

"Probably. I always have."

"I can't read." He put the book down. "Have you ever known me to show rancor?"

"I'd have to look in the dictionary. What is it exactly?"

"Vehement ill will. Intense malignity."

"No."

"I have it now, and it is in the way. I can't think clearly. I intend to expose that wretch before the police do. I want Saul and Orrie and Fred here at eight o'clock in the morning. I have no idea what their errands will be, but I shall know by morning. After you reach them sleep if you can."

"I don't have to sleep if there's something better to do."

"Not tonight. This confounded rancor is a pimple on the brain. My mental processes haven't been so muddled in many years. I wouldn't have thought—"

The doorbell was ringing. Now that the army of occupation was gone, that was to be expected, since Cramer had allowed no reporters or photographers to enter the house. I had considered disconnecting the bell for the night, and now, as I descended the stairs, I decided that I would. Fritz, at the door to the kitchen, looked relieved when he saw me. He had switched on the stoop light.

If it was a reporter he was a veteran, and he had brought a helper along, or maybe a girl friend just for company. I was in no hurry getting to the door, sizing them up through the one-way panel. He was a six-footer in a well-cut and well-fitted dark gray overcoat, a light gray woolen scarf, and a gray homburg, with a long bony face with deep lines. She could have been his pretty little granddaughter, but her fur coat fastened clear up and her matching fur cloche covered everything but the little oval of her face. I removed the chain bolt and swung the door open and said, "Yes, sir?"

He said, "I am Lamont Otis. This is Mr. Nero Wolfe's house?"

"Right."

"I would like to see him. About my secretary, Miss Bertha Aaron. About information I have received from the police. This is Miss Ann Paige, my associate, a member of the bar. My coming at this hour is justified, I think, by the circumstances. I think Mr. Wolfe will agree."

"I do too," I agreed. "But if you don't mind—" I crossed the sill to the stoop and sang out, "Who are you over there? Gillian? Murphy? Come here a minute!"

A figure emerged from the shadows across the street. As he crossed the pavement I peered, and as he reached the curb on our side I spoke. "Oh, Wylie. Come on up."

He stood at the foot of the seven steps. "For what?" he demanded.

"May I ask," Lamont Otis asked, "what this is for?"

"You may. An inspector named Cramer is in danger of losing an eye and that would be a shame. I'll appreciate it if you'll answer a simple question: were you asked to come here by either Mr. Wolfe or me?"

"Certainly not."

"Was your coming entirely your own idea?"

"Yes. But I don't—"

"Excuse me. You heard him, Wylie? Include it in your report. It will save wear and tear on Cramer's nerves. Much obliged for—"

"Who is he?" the dick demanded.

I ignored it. Backing up, I invited them in, and when I shut the door I put the bolt on. Otis let me take his hat and coat, but Ann Paige kept hers. The house was cooling off for the night. In the office, sitting, she unfastened the coat but kept it over her shoulders. I went to the thermostat on the wall and pushed it up to 70, and then went to my desk and buzzed Wolfe's room on the house phone. I should have gone up to get him, since he might balk at seeing company until he had dealt with the pimple on his brain, but I had had enough for one day of leaving visitors alone in the office, and one of these had a bum pump.

Wolfe's growl came, "Yes?"

"Mr. Lamont Otis is here. With an associate, Miss Ann Paige, also a member of the bar. He thinks you will agree that his coming at this hour is justified by the circumstances."

Silence. Nothing for some five seconds, then the click of his hanging up. You feel foolish holding a dead receiver to your ear, so I cradled it but didn't swivel to face the company. It was even money whether he was coming or not, and I put my eyes on my wrist watch. If he didn't come in five minutes I would go up after him. I turned and told Otis, "You won't mind a short wait."

He nodded. "It was in this room?"

"Yes. She was there." I pointed to a spot a few inches in front of Ann Paige's feet. Otis was in the red leather chair near the end of Wolfe's desk. "There was a rug but they took it to the laboratory. Of course they—I'm sorry, Miss Paige. I shouldn't have pointed." She had pushed her chair back and shut her eyes.

She swallowed, and opened the eyes. They looked black in that light but could have been dark violet. "You're Archie Goodwin," she said.

"Right."

"You were—you found her."

"Right."

"Had she been . . . Was there any . . ."

"She had been hit on the back of her head with a paperweight, a chunk of jade, and then strangled with a necktie that happened to be here on a desk. There was no sign of a struggle. The blow knocked her out, and probably she—"

My voice had kept me from hearing Wolfe's steps on the stairs. He entered, stopped to tilt his head an eighth of an inch to Ann Paige, again to Otis, went to his chair behind his desk, sat, and aimed his eyes at Otis.

"You are Mr. Lamont Otis?"

"I am."

"I owe you an apology. A weak word; there should be a better one. A valued and trusted employee of yours has died by violence under my roof. She was valued and trusted?"

"Yes."

"I deeply regret it. If you came to reproach me, proceed."

"I didn't come to reproach you." The lines of Otis's face were furrows in the better light. "I came to find out what happened. The police and the District Attorney's office have told me how she was killed, but not why she was here. I think they know but are reserving it. I think I have a right to know. Bertha Aaron had been in my confidence for years, and I believe I was in hers, and I knew nothing of any trouble she might be in that would lead her to come to you. Why was she here?"

Wolfe, rubbing his nose with a fingertip, regarded him. "How old are you, Mr. Otis?"

Ann Paige made a noise. The veteran lawyer, who had probably objected to ten thousand questions as irrelevant, said merely, "I'm seventy-five. Why?"

"I do not intend to have another death in my office to apologize for, this time induced by me. Miss Aaron told Mr. Goodwin that the reason she did not go to you with her problem was that she feared the effect on you. Her words, Archie?"

I supplied them. "'He has a bad heart and it might kill him.'"

Otis snorted. "Bosh! My heart has given me a little trouble and I've had to slow down, but it would take more than a problem to kill me. I've been dealing with problems all my life, some pretty tough ones."

"She exaggerated it," Ann Paige said. "I mean Miss Aaron. I mean she was so devoted to Mr. Otis that she had an exaggerated idea about his heart condition."

"Why did you come here with him?" Wolfe demanded.

"Not because of his heart. Because I was at his apartment, working with him on a brief, when the news came about Bertha, and when he decided to see you he asked me to come with him. I do shorthand."

"You heard Mr. Goodwin quote Miss Aaron. If I tell Mr. Otis what she was afraid to tell him, what her problem was, will you take responsibility for the effect on him?"

Otis exploded. "Damn it, *I* take the responsibility! It's *my* heart!"

"I doubt," Ann Paige said, "if the effect of telling him would be as bad as the effect of *not* telling him. I take no responsibility, but you have me as a witness that he insisted."

"I not only insist," Otis said. "I assert my right to the information, since it must have concerned me."

"Very well," Wolfe said. "Miss Aaron arrived here at twenty minutes past five this afternoon—now yesterday afternoon—uninvited and unexpected. She spoke for some twenty minutes with Mr. Goodwin and he went upstairs to confer with me. He was away half an hour. She was alone on this floor. You know what greeted him when he returned. He has given the police a statement which includes his conversation with her." His head turned. "Archie, give Mr. Otis a copy of the statement."

I got it from my desk drawer and went and handed it to him. I had a notion to stand by, in case Bertha Aaron had been right about the effect it would have on him and he crumpled, but from up there I couldn't see his face, so I returned to my chair; but after half a century of practicing law his face knew how to behave. All that happened was that his jaw tightened a little, and once a muscle twitched at the side of his neck. He read it clear through twice, first fast and then taking his time. When he had finished he folded it neatly, fumbling a little, and was putting it in the breast pocket of his jacket.

"No," Wolfe said emphatically. "I disclose the information at my discretion, but that's a copy of a statement given the police. You can't have it."

Otis ignored him. He looked at his associate, and his neck muscle twitched again. "I shouldn't have brought you, Ann," he said. "You'll have to leave."

Her eyes met his. "Believe me, Mr. Otis, you can trust me. On anything. Believe me. If it's that bad you shouldn't be alone with it."

"I must be. I couldn't trust you on *this*. You'll have to leave."

I stood up. "You can wait in the front room, Miss Paige. The wall and door are soundproofed."

She didn't like it, but she came. I opened the door to the front room and turned the lights on, and then went and locked the door to the hall and put the key in my pocket. Back in the office as I was crossing to my desk Otis asked, "How good is the soundproofing?"

"Good for anything under a loud yell," I told him.

He focused on Wolfe. "I am not surprised," he said, "that Miss Aaron thought it would kill me. I am surprised that it hasn't. You say the police have this statement?"

"Yes. And this conversation is ended unless you return that copy. Mr. Goodwin has no corroboration. It is a dangerous document for him to sign except under constraint of police authority."

"But I need—"

"Archie. Get it."

I stood up. The heart was certainly getting tested. But as I took a step his hand went to his pocket, and when I reached him he had it out and handed it over.

"That's better," Wolfe said. "I have extended my apology and regret, and we have given you all the information we have. I add this: first, that nothing in that statement will be revealed to anyone by Mr. Goodwin or me without your consent; and second, that my self-esteem has been severely injured and it would give me great satisfaction to expose the murderer. Granted that that's a job for the police, for me it is my job. I would welcome your help, not as my client; I would accept no fee. I realize that at the moment you are under shock, that you are overwhelmed by the disaster in prospect for the firm you head; and when your mind clears you may be tempted by the possibility of minimizing the damage by dealing with your intramural treachery yourself, and letting the culprit escape his doom. If you went about it with sufficient resourcefulness and ingenuity it is conceivable that the police could be cheated of their prey, but not that I could be."

"You are making a wholly unwarranted assumption," Otis said.

"I am not making an assumption. I am merely telling you my intention. The police hypothesis, and mine, is the obvious one: that a member of your firm killed Miss Aaron. Though the law does not insist that the testimony against him in court must include proof of his motive, inevitably it would. Will you assert that you won't try to prevent that? That you will not regard the reputation of your firm as your prime concern?"

Otis opened his mouth and closed it again.

Wolfe nodded. "I thought not. Then I advise you to help me. If you do, I'll have two objectives, to get the murderer and to see that your firm suffers as little as possible; if you don't, I'll have only one. As for the police, I doubt if they'll expect you to cooperate, since they are not nincompoops. They will realize that you have a deeper interest than the satisfaction of justice. Well, sir?"

Otis's palms were cupping his knees and his head was tilted forward so he could study the back of his left hand. His eyes shifted to his right hand, and when that too had been properly studied he lifted his head and spoke. "You used the word 'hypothesis,' and that's all it is, that a member of my firm killed Miss Aaron. How did he know she was here? She said that nobody knew."

"He could have followed her. Evidently she left your office soon after she talked with him. Archie?"

"She probably walked," I said. "Between fifteen and twenty-five minutes, depending on her rate. At that time of day empty taxis are scarce, and crosstown they crawl. It would have been a cinch to tail her on foot."

"How did he get in?" Otis demanded. "Did he sneak in unseen when you admitted her?"

"No. You have read my statement. He saw her enter and knew this is Nero Wolfe's address. He went to a phone booth and rang this number and she answered. Here." I tapped my phone. "With me not here that would be automatic for a trained secretary. I had not pushed the button so it didn't ring in the plant rooms. It would ring in the kitchen, but Fritz wasn't there. She answered it, and he said he wanted to see her at once and would give her a satisfactory explanation, and she told him to come here. When he came she was at the front door and let him in. All he was expecting to do was stall for time, but when he learned that she was alone on this floor and she hadn't seen Mr. Wolfe he had another idea and acted on it. Two minutes would have been plenty for the whole operation, even less."

"All that is mere conjecture."

"Yeah, I wasn't present. But it fits. If you have one that fits better I do shorthand."

"The police have covered everything here for fingerprints."

"Sure. But it was below freezing outdoors and I suppose the members of your firm wear gloves."

"You say that he learned she hadn't seen Wolfe, but she had talked with you."

"She didn't tell him that she had told me. It wouldn't take many words for him to learn that she was alone and hadn't seen Mr. Wolfe. Either that, or she did tell him but he went ahead anyhow. The former is more probable and I like it better."

He studied me a while, then he closed his eyes and his head tilted again. When his eyes opened he put them at Wolfe. "Mr. Wolfe. I reserve comment on your suggestion that I would be moved by personal considerations to balk justice. You ask me to help you. How?"

"By giving me information. By answering questions. Your mind is trained in inquiry; you know what I will ask."

"I'll know better when I hear you. Go ahead and we'll see."

Wolfe looked at the wall clock. "It's nearly an hour past midnight, and this will be prolonged. It will be a tiresome wait for Miss Paige."

"Of course," Otis agreed. He looked at me. "Will you ask her to step in?"

I got up and crossed to the door to the front room. As I entered, words were at the tip of my tongue, but that

was as far as they got. She wasn't there. Through a
wide-open window cold air was streaming in. As I went
to it and stuck my head out I was prepared to see her
lying there with one of my neckties around her throat,
though I hadn't left one in the room. It was a relief to
see that the areaway, eight feet down, was unoccupied.

Chapter 3

A roar came from the office. "Archie! What the
devil are you up to?"
I shut the window, glanced around to see if
there were any signs of violence or if she had left a note,
saw neither, and rejoined the conference.

"She's gone," I said. "Leaving no message. When
I—"

"Why did you open a window?"

"I didn't. I closed it. When I took her in there I locked
the door to the hall so she couldn't wander around and
hear things she wasn't supposed to, so when she got
tired waiting the window was the only way out."

"She climbed out a window?" Otis demanded.

"Yes, sir. It's a mere conjecture, but it fits. The
window was wide open, and she's not in the room, and
she's not outside. I looked."

"I can't believe it. Miss Paige is a level-headed and
reliable—" He bit it off. "No. No! I no longer know who
is reliable." He rested his elbow on the chair arm and
propped his head with his hand. "May I have a glass of
water?"

Wolfe suggested brandy, but he said he wanted water, and I went to the kitchen and brought some. He got
a little metal box from a pocket, took out two pills, and
washed them down.

"Will they help?" Wolfe asked. "The pills?"

"Yes. The *pills* are reliable." He handed me the glass.

"Then we may proceed?"

"Yes."

"Have you any notion why Miss Paige was impelled to leave by a window?"

"No. It's extraordinary. Damn it, Wolfe, I have no notions of anything! Can't you see I'm lost?"

"I can. Shall we put it off?"

"No!"

"Very well. My assumption that Miss Aaron was killed by a member of your firm, call him X, rests on a prior assumption, that when she spoke with Mr. Goodwin she was candid and her facts were accurate. Would you challenge that assumption?"

Otis looked at me. "Tell me something. I know what she said from your statement, and it sounded like her, but how was she—her voice and manner? Did she seem in any way . . . well, out of control? Unbalanced?"

"No, sir," I told him. "She sat with her back straight and her feet together, and she met my eyes all the time."

He nodded. "She would. She always did." To Wolfe: "At this time, here privately with you, I don't challenge your assumption."

"Do you challenge the other one, that X killed her?"

"I neither challenge it nor accept it."

"Pfui. You're not an ostrich, Mr. Otis. Next: if Miss Aaron's facts were accurate, it must be supposed that X was in a position to give Mrs. Sorell information that would help her substantially in her action against her husband, your client. That is true?"

"Of course." Otis was going to add something, decided not to, and then changed his mind again. "Again here privately with you, it's not merely her action at law. It's blackmail. Perhaps not technically, but that's what it amounts to. Her demands are exorbitant and preposterous. It's extortion."

"And a member of your firm could give her weapons. Which one or ones?"

Otis shook his head. "I won't answer that."

Wolfe's brows went up. "Sir? If you pretend to help at all that's the very least you can do. If you're rejecting my proposal say so and I'll get on without you. By noon tomorrow—today—the police will have that elementary question answered. It may take me longer."

"It certainly may," Otis said. "You haven't mentioned a third assumption you're making. You are assuming that Goodwin was candid and accurate in reporting what Miss Aaron said."

"Bah." Wolfe was disgusted. "You are gibbering. If you hope to impeach Mr. Goodwin you are indeed forlorn. You might as well go. If you regain your faculties later and wish to communicate with me I'll be here." He pushed his chair back.

"No." Otis extended a hand. "Good God, man, I'm trapped! It's not my faculties! I have my faculties."

"Then use them. Which member of your firm was in a position to betray its interests to Mrs. Sorell?"

"They all were. Our client is vulnerable in certain respects, and the situation is extremely difficult, and we have frequently conferred together on it. I mean, of course, my three partners. It could have only been one of them, partly because none of our associates was in our confidence on this matter, but mainly because Miss Aaron told Goodwin it was a member of the firm. She wouldn't have used that phrase, 'member of the firm,' loosely. For her it had a specific and restricted application. She could only have meant Frank Edey, Miles Heydecker, or Gregory Jett. And that's incredible!"

"Incredible literally or rhetorically? Do you disbelieve Miss Aaron—or, in desperation, Mr. Goodwin? Here with me privately?"

"No."

Wolfe turned a palm up. "Then let's get at it. It is equally incredible for all three of those men, or are there preferences?"

During the next hour Otis balked at least a dozen times, and on some details—for instance, the respects in which Morton Sorell was vulnerable—he clammed up absolutely, but I had enough to fill nine pages of my notebook.

Frank Edey, fifty-five, married with two sons and a daughter, wife living, got twenty-seven per cent of the firm's net income. (Otis's share was forty per cent.) He was a brilliant idea man but seldom went to court. He had drafted the marriage agreement which had been signed by Morton Sorell and Rita Ramsey when they got yoked four years ago. Personal financial condition, sound. Relations with wife and children, so-so. Interest in other women, definitely yes, but fairly discreet. Interest in Mrs. Sorell casual so far as Otis knew.

Miles Heydecker, forty-seven, married and wife living but no children, got twenty-two per cent. His father, now dead, had been one of the original members of the firm. His specialty was trial work and he handled the firm's most important cases in court. He had appeared for Mrs. Sorell at her husband's request two years ago when she had been sued by a man who had formerly been her agent. He was tight with money and had a nice personal pile of it. Relations with his wife, uncertain; on the surface, okay. Too interested in his work and his hobbies, chess and behind-the-scene politics, to bother with women, including Mrs. Sorell.

Gregory Jett, thirty-six, single, had been made a firm member and allotted eleven per cent of the income because of his spectacular success in two big corporation cases. One of the corporations was controlled by Morton Sorell, and for the past year or so Jett had been a fairly frequent guest at the Sorell home on Fifth Avenue but had not been noticeably attentive to his hostess. His personal financial condition was one of the details Otis balked on, but he allowed it to be inferred that Jett was careless about the balance between income and outgo and was in the red in his account with the firm. Shortly after he had been made a member of the firm, about two years ago, he had dropped a fat chunk, Otis thought about forty thousand dollars, backing a Broadway show that flopped. A friend of his, female, had been in the cast. Whether he had had other expenses connected with a female friend or friends Otis either didn't know or wasn't telling. He did say that he had gathered, mostly from remarks Bertha Aaron had made, that in recent months Jett had shown more attention to Ann Paige than their professional association required.

But when Wolfe suggested the possibility that Ann Paige had left through a window because she suspected, or even knew, what was in the wind, and had decided to take a hand, Otis wouldn't buy it. He was having all he could do to swallow the news that one of his partners was a snake, and the idea that another of his associates might have been in on it was too much. He would tackle Ann Paige himself; she would no doubt have an acceptable explanation.

On Mrs. Morton Sorell he didn't balk at all. Part of his information was known to everyone who read newspapers and magazines: that as Rita Ramsey she had dazzled Broadway with her performance in *Reach for the Moon* when she was barely out of her teens, that she had followed with even greater triumphs in two other plays, that she had spurned Hollywood, that she had also spurned Morton Sorell for two years and then abandoned her career to marry him. But Otis added other information that had merely been hinted at in gossip columns: that in a year the union had gone sour, that it became apparent that Rita had married Sorell only to get her lovely paws on a bale of dough, and that she was by no means going to settle for the terms of the marriage agreement. She wanted much more, more than half, and she had carefully begun to collect evidence of certain activities of Sorell's, but he had got wise and consulted his attorneys, Otis, Edey, Heydecker and Jett, and they had stymied her—or thought they had. Otis had been sure they had, until he had read the copy of my statement. Now he was sure of nothing.

But he was still alive. When he got up to go, at two hours past midnight, he had bounced back some. He wasn't nearly as jittery as he had been when he asked for a glass of water to take the pills. He hadn't accepted

Wolfe's offer in so many words, but he had agreed to take no steps until he had heard further from Wolfe, provided he heard within thirty-two hours, by ten o'clock Wednesday morning. The only action he would take during that period would be to instruct Ann Paige to tell no one that she had read my statement and to learn why she had skedaddled. He didn't think the police would tell him the contents of my statement, but if they did he would say that he would credit it only if it had corroboration. Of course he wanted to know what Wolfe was going to do, but Wolfe said he didn't know and probably wouldn't decide until after breakfast.

When I returned to the office after holding Otis's coat for him and letting him out, Fritz was there.

"No," Wolfe was saying grimly. "You know quite well I almost never eat at night."

"But you had no dinner. An omelet, or at least—"

"No! Confound it, let me starve! Go to bed!"

Fritz looked at me, I shook my head, and he went. I sat down and spoke. "Do I get Saul and Fred and Orrie?"

"No." He took in air through his nose and let it out through his mouth. "If I don't know how I am going to proceed, how the deuce can I have errands for them?

"Rhetorical," I said.

"It is not rhetorical. It's logical. There are the obvious routine errands, but that would be witless. Find the cheap restaurant or lunchroom where they met? How many are there?"

"Oh, a thousand. More."

He grunted. "Or question the entire personnel of that law office to learn which of those three men spoke at length with Miss Aaron yesterday afternoon? Or, assuming that he followed her here, left the office on her heels? Or which one cannot account for himself from five o'clock to ten minutes past six? Or find the nearby phone booth from which he dialed this number? Or investigate their relations with Mrs. Sorell? Those are all sensible and proper lines of inquiry, and by mid-morning Mr. Cramer and the District Attorney will have a hundred men pursuing them."

"Two hundred. This is special."

"So for me to put three men on them, four including you, would be frivolous. A possible procedure would be to have Mr. Otis get them here—Edey, Heydecker, and Jett. He could merely tell them that he has engaged me to investigate the murder that was committed in my house."

"If they're available. They'll be spending most of the day at the DA's office. By request."

He shut his eyes and tightened his lips. I picked up the copy of my statement which Otis had surrendered, got the second carbon from my drawer, went and opened the safe, and put them on a shelf. I had closed the safe door and was twirling the knob when Wolfe spoke.

"Archie."

"Yes, sir."

"Will they tackle Mrs. Sorell?"

"I doubt it. Not right away. What for? Since Cramer warned us that if we blab what Bertha Aaron told me we may be hooked for libel, which was kind of him, evidently he's going to save it, and going to Mrs. Sorell would spill it."

He nodded. "She is young and comely."

"Yeah. I've never seen her offstage. You have seen pictures of her."

"You have a flair for dealing with personable young women."

"Sure. They melt like chocolate bars in the sun. But you're exaggerating it a little if you think I can go to that specimen and ask her which member of the firm she met in a cheap restaurant or lunchroom and she'll wrap her arms around me and murmur his name in my ear. It might take me an hour or more."

"You can bring her here."

"Maybe. Possibly. To see the orchids?"

"I don't know." He pushed the chair back and raised his bulk. "I am not myself. Come to my room at eight o'clock." He headed for the hall.

Chapter 4

At 10:17 that Tuesday morning I left the house, walked north fourteen short blocks and east six long ones, and entered the lobby of the Churchill. I walked instead of flagging a taxi for two reasons: because I had had less than five hours' sleep and needed a lot of oxygen, especially from the neck up, and because eleven o'clock was probably the earliest Mrs. Morton Sorell, born Rita Ramsey, would be accessible. It had taken only a phone call to Lon Cohen at the *Gazette* to learn that she had taken an apartment at the Churchill Towers two months ago, when she had left her husband's roof.

In my pocket was a plain white envelope, sealed, on which I had written by hand:

> *Mrs. Morton Sorell*
> *Personal and Confidential*

and inside it was a card, also handwritten:

> *We were seen that evening in the*
> *lunchroom as we sat in the booth. It would*
> *be dangerous to phone you or for you to*
> *phone me. You can trust the bearer of this*
> *card.*

No signature. It was twelve minutes to eleven when I handed the envelope to the chargé d'affaires at the lobby desk and asked him to send it up, and it still lacked three minutes of eleven when he motioned me to the elevator. Those nine minutes had been tough. If it hadn't worked, if word had come down to bounce me, or no word at all, I had no other card ready to play. So as the elevator shot up I was on the rise in more ways than one, and when I stepped out at the thirtieth floor and saw that she herself was standing there in the doorway my face wanted to grin at her but I controlled it.

She had the card in her hand. "You sent this?" she asked.

"I brought it."

She looked me over, down to my toes and back up. "Haven't I seen you before? What's your name?"

"Goodwin. Archie Goodwin. You may have seen my picture in the morning paper."

"Oh." She nodded. "Of course." She lifted the card. "What's this about? It's crazy! Where did you get it?"

"I wrote it." I advanced a step and got a stronger whiff of the perfume of her morning bath—or it could have come from the folds of her yellow robe, which was very informal. "I might as well confess, Mrs. Sorell. It was a trick. I have been at your feet for years. The only pictures in my heart are of you. One smile from you, just for me, would be rapture. I have never tried to meet you because I knew it would be hopeless, but now that you have left your husband I might be able to do something, render some little service, that would earn me a smile. I had to see you and tell you that, and that card was just a trick to get to you. I made it up. I tried to write something that would make you curious enough to see me. Please—*please* forgive me!"

She smiled the famous smile, just for me. She spoke. "You overwhelm me, Mr. Goodwin, you really do. You said that *so* nicely. Have you any particular service in mine?"

I had to hand it to her. She knew darned well I was a double-breasted liar. She knew I hadn't made it up. She knew I was a licensed private detective and had come on business. But she hadn't batted an eye—or rather, she had. Her long dark lashes, which were home-grown and made a fine contrast with her hair, the color of corn silk just before it starts to turn, also home-grown, had lowered for a second to veil the pleasure I was giving her. She was as good offstage as she was on, and I had to hand it to her.

"If I might come in?" I suggested. "Now that you've smiled at me?"

"Of course." She backed up and I entered. She waited while I removed my hat and coat and put them on a chair and then led me through the foyer to a large living room with windows on the east and south, and across to a divan.

"Not many people ever have a chance like this," she said, sitting. "An offer of a service from a famous detective. What shall it be?"

"Well." I sat. "I can sew on buttons."

"So can I." She smiled. Seeing that smile, you would never have dreamed that she was a champion blood-sucker. I was about ready to doubt it myself. It was pleasant to be on the receiving end of it.

"I could walk along behind you," I offered, "and carry your rubbers in case it snows."

"I don't walk much. It might be better to carry a gun. You mentioned my husband. I honestly believe he is capable of hiring someone to kill me. You're handsome—*very* handsome. Are you brave?"

"It depends. I probably would be if you were looking on. By the way, now that I'm here, and this is a day I'll never forget, I might as well ask you something. Since you saw my picture in the paper, I suppose you read about what happened in Nero Wolfe's office yesterday. That woman murdered. Bertha Aaron. Yes?"

"I read part of it." She made a face. "I don't like to read about murders."

"Did you read who she was? Private secretary of Lamont Otis, senior partner of Otis, Edey, Heydecker, and Jett, a law firm?"

She shook her head. "I didn't notice."

"I thought you might because they are your husband's attorneys. You know that, of course."

"Oh." Her eyes had widened. "Of course. I didn't notice."

"I guess you didn't read that part. You would have noticed those names, since you know all four of them. What I wanted to ask, did you know Bertha Aaron?"

"No."

"I thought you might, since she was Otis's secretary and they have been your husband's attorneys for years and they handled a case for you once. You never met her?"

"No." She wasn't smiling. "You seem to know a good deal about that firm and my husband. You said that *so* nicely, about being at my feet and my pictures in your heart. So they sent you, or Nero Wolfe did, and he is working for my husband. So?"

"No. He isn't."

"He's working for that law firm, and that's the same thing."

"No. He's working for nobody but himself. He—"

"You're lying."

"I only allow myself so many lies a day and I'm careful not to waste them. Mr. Wolfe is upset because that woman was killed in his office, and he intends to get even. He is working for no one, and he won't be until this is settled. He thought you might have known Bertha Aaron and could tell me something about her that would help."

"I can't."

"That's too bad. I'm still at your feet."

"I like you there. You're *very* handsome." She smiled. "I just had an idea. Would Nero Wolfe work for me?"

"He might. He doesn't like some kinds of jobs. If he did he'd soak you. If he has any pictures in his heart at all, which I doubt, they are not of beautiful women—or even homely ones. What would you want him to do?"

"I would rather tell him."

She was meeting my eyes, with her long lashes lowered just enough for the best effect, and again I had to hand it to her. You might have thought she hadn't the faintest idea that I was aware that she was ignoring

anything, and that I was ignoring it too. She was so
damn good that looking at her, meeting her eyes, I
actually considered the possibility that she really
thought I had made up that card from nothing.

"For that," I said, "you would have to make an appointment at his office. He never leaves his house on
business." I got a card from my case and handed it to
her. "There's the address and phone number. Or if
you'd like to go now I'd be glad to take you, and he
might stretch a point and see you. He'll be free until one
o'clock."

"I wonder." She smiled.

"You wonder what?"

"Nothing. I was talking to myself." She shook her
head. "I won't go now. Perhaps . . . I'll think it over."
She stood up. "I'm sorry I can't help, I'm truly sorry,
but I had never met that—what was her name?"

"Bertha Aaron." I was on my feet.

"I had never heard of her." She glanced at the card,
the one I had handed her. "I may ring you later today.
I'll think it over."

She went with me to the foyer, and as I reached for
the doorknob she offered a hand and I took it. There
was nothing flabby about her clasp.

When you leave an elevator at the lobby floor of the
Churchill Towers you have three choices. To the right
is the main entrance. To the left and then right is a side
entrance, and to the left and left again is another. I left
by the main entrance, stopped a moment on the sidewalk to put my coat on and pull at my ear, and turned
downtown, in no hurry. At the corner I was joined by a
little guy with a big nose who looked, at first sight, as if
he might make forty bucks a week waxing floors. Actually Saul Panzer was the best operative in the metropolitan area and his rate was ten dollars an hour.

"Any sign of a dick?" I asked him.

"None I know, and I think none I don't know. You
saw her?"

"Yeah. I doubt if they're on her. I stung her and she
may be moving. The boys are covering?"

"Yes. Fred at the north entrance and Orrie at the south. I hope she takes the front."

"So do I. See you in court."

He wheeled and was gone, and I stepped to the curb and flagged a taxi. It was 11:40 when it rolled to the curb in front of the old brownstone on 35th Street.

After mounting the seven steps to the stoop, using my key to get in, and putting my hat coat on the rack in the hall, I went to the office. Wolfe would of course be settled in his chair behind his desk with his current book, since his morning session in the plant rooms ended at eleven o'clock. But he wasn't. His chair was empty, but the red leather one was occupied, by a stranger. I kept going for a look at his front, and said good morning. He said good morning.

He was a poet above the neck, with deep-set dreamy eyes, a wide sulky mouth, and a pointed modeled chin, but he would have had to sell a lot of poems to pay for that suit and shirt and tie, not to mention the Parvis of London shoes. Having given him enough of a glance for that, and not caring to ask him where Wolfe was, I returned to the hall and turned left, toward the kitchen; and there, in the alcove at the end of the hall, was Wolfe, standing at the hole. The hole was through the wall at eye level. On the office side it was covered by a picture of a waterfall. On this side, in the alcove, it was covered by nothing, and you could not only hear through but also see through.

I didn't stop. Pushing the two-way door to the kitchen, I held it for Wolfe to enter and then let it swing back.

"You forgot to leave a necktie on your desk," I told him.

He grunted. "We'll discuss that some day, the necktie. That is Gregory Jett. He has spent the morning at the District Attorney's office. I excused myself because I wanted to hear from you before talking with him, and I thought I might as well observe him."

"Good idea. He might have muttered to himself, 'By golly, the rug is gone.' Did he?"

"No. Did you see that woman?"

"Yes, sir. She's a gem. There is now no question about Bertha Aaron's basic fact, that a member of the firm was with Mrs. Sorell in a lunchroom."

"She admitted it?"

"No, sir, but she confirmed it. We talked for twenty minutes, and she never mentioned the card after the first half a minute, when she merely said it was crazy and asked me where I got it. She told me I was handsome twice, she smiled at me six times, she said she had never heard of Bertha Aaron, and she asked if you would work for her. She may phone for an appointment. Do you want it verbatim now?"

"Later will do. The men are there?"

"Yes. I spoke with Saul when I left. That's wasted. She's not a fool, anything but. Of course it was a blow to learn that that meeting in the lunchroom is known, but she won't panic. Also of course, she doesn't know how we got onto it. She may not have suspected that there was any connection between that meeting and the murder of Bertha Aaron. It's even possible she doesn't suspect it now, though that's doubtful. If and when she does she will also suspect that the man she was with in the lunchroom killed Bertha Aaron, and that will be hard to live with, but even then she won't panic. She is a very tough article and she is still after thirty million bucks. Looking at her as she smiled at me and told me I was handsome, which may have been her honest opinion in spite of my flat nose, you would never have guessed that I had just sent her a card announcing that her pet secret had been spilled. She's a gem. If I had thirty million I'd be glad to buy her a lunch. What's biting Gregory Jett?"

"I don't know. We shall see." He pushed the door open and passed through and I followed.

As Wolfe detoured around the red leather chair Jett spoke. "I said my business was urgent. You're rather cheeky, aren't you?"

"Moderately so." Wolfe got his mass adjusted in his

seat and swiveled to face him. "If there is pressure, sir,
it is on you, not on me. Am I concerned?"

"You are involved." The deep-set dreamy eyes came
to me. "Is your name Goodwin? Archie Goodwin?"

I said yes.

"Last night you gave a statement to the police about
your conversation with Bertha Aaron, and you gave a
copy of it to Lamont Otis, the senior member of my
firm."

"Did I?" I was polite. "I only work here. I only do
what Mr. Wolfe tells me to. Ask him."

"I'm not asking, I'm telling." He returned to Wolfe. "I
want to know what is in that statement. Mr. Otis is an
old man and his heart is weak. He was under shock
when he came here, from the tragic news of the death of
his secretary, who was murdered here in your office, in
circumstances which as far as I know them were certainly no credit to you or Goodwin. It must have been
obvious that he was under shock, and it was certainly
obvious that he is an old man. To show him that statement was irresponsible and reprehensible. As his associate, his partner, I want to know what is in it."

Wolfe had leaned back and lowered his chin. "Well.
When cheek meets cheek. You are manifestly indomi-
table and I must buckle my breastplate. I choose to
deny that there is any such statement. Then?"

"Poppycock. I know there is."

"Your evidence?" Wolfe wiggled a finger. "Mr. Jett.
This is fatuous. Someone has told you the statement
exists or you would be an idiot to come and bark at me.
Who told you, and when?"

"Someone who—in whom I have the utmost confidence."

"Mr. Otis himself?"

"No."

"Her name?"

Jett set his teeth on his lower lip. After chewing on it
a little he shifted to the upper lip. He had nice white
teeth.

"You must be under shock too," Wolfe said, "to suppose you could come with that demand without disclosing the source of your information. Is her name Ann Paige?"

"I will tell you that only in confidence."

"Then I don't want it. I will take it as private information entrusted to my discretion, but not in confidence. I am still denying that such a statement exists."

"Damn you!" Jett hit the arm of his chair. "She was here with him! She saw Goodwin hand it to him! She saw him read it!"

Wolfe nodded. "That's better. When did Miss Paige tell you about it? This morning?"

"No. Last night. She phoned me."

"At what hour?"

"Around midnight. A little after."

"Had she left here with Mr. Otis?"

"You know damn well she hadn't. She had climbed out a window."

"And phoned you at once." Wolfe straightened up. "If you are to trust my discretion you must give it ground. I may then tell you what the statement contains, or I may not. I reject the reason you have given, or implied, for your concern—solicitude for Mr. Otis. Your explanation must account not only for your concern but also for Miss Paige's flight through a window. You—"

"It wasn't a flight! Goodwin had locked the door!"

"He would have opened it on request. You said your business is urgent. How and to whom? You are trying my patience. With your trained legal mind, you know it is futile to feed me inanities."

Jett looked at me. I set my jaw and firmed my lips to show him that I didn't care for inanities either. He went back to Wolfe.

"Very well," he said. "I'll trust your discretion, since there is no alternative. When Otis told Miss Paige she had to leave, she suspected that Miss Aaron had told Goodwin something about me. She thought—"

"Why about you? There had been no hint of it."

"Because he said to her, 'I couldn't trust you on *this*.' She thought he knew that she couldn't be trusted in a matter that concerned me. That is true—I hope it is true. Miss Paige and I are engaged to marry. It has not been announced, but our mutual interest is probably no secret to our associates, since we have made no effort to conceal it. Added to that was the fact that she knew that Miss Aaron might have had knowledge, or at least suspicion, of a certain—uh—episode in which I had been involved. An episode of which Mr. Otis would have violently disapproved. You said my explanation must account both for my concern and for Miss Paige's leaving through a window. It does."

"What was the episode?"

Jett shook his head. "I wouldn't tell you that even in confidence."

"What was its nature?"

"It was a personal matter."

"Did it bear on the interests of your firm or your partners?"

"No. It was strictly personal."

"Did it touch your professional reputation or integrity?"

"It did not."

"Was a woman involved?"

"Yes."

"Her name?"

Jett shook his head. "I'm not a cad, Mr. Wolfe."

"Was it Mrs. Morton Sorell?"

Jett's mouth opened, and for three breaths his jaw muscles weren't functioning. Then he spoke. "So that was it. Miss Paige was right. I want—I demand to see that statement."

"Not yet, sir. Later, perhaps—or not. Do you maintain that the episode involving Mrs. Sorell had no relation to your firm's interests or your professional integrity?"

"I do. It was purely personal, and it was brief."

"When did it occur?"

"About a year ago."

"When did you last see her?"

"About a month ago, at a party. I didn't speak with her."

"When were you last with her tête-à-tête?"

"I haven't been since—not for nearly a year."

"But you are still seriously perturbed at the chance that Mr. Otis has learned of the episode?"

"Certainly. Mr. Sorell is our client, and his wife is our opponent in a very important matter. Mr. Otis might suspect that the episode is—was not merely an episode. He has not told me of the statement you showed him, and I can't approach him about it because he has ordered Miss Paige not to mention it to anyone, and she didn't tell him she had already told me. I want to see it. I have a right to see it!"

"Don't start barking again." Wolfe rested his elbows on the chair arms and put his fingers together. "I'll tell you this: there is nothing in the statement, either explicit or allusive, about the episode you have described. That should relieve your mind. Beyond that—"

The doorbell rang.

Chapter 5

I was wrong about them. As soon as I got a look at them through the one-way panel I guessed who they were, but I had the labels mixed. My guess was that the big broad-shouldered one in a dark blue chesterfield tailored to give him a waist, and a homburg to match, was Edey, fifty-five, and the compact little guy in a brown ulster with a belt was Heydecker, forty-seven, but when I opened the door and the chesterfield said they wanted to see Nero Wolfe, and I asked for names, he said, "This gentleman is Frank Edey and I am Miles Heydecker. We are—"

"I know who you are. Step in."

Since age has priority I helped Edey off with his ulster, putting it on a hanger, and let Heydecker manage his chesterfield, and then took them to the front room and invited them to sit. If I opened the connecting door to the office Jett's voice could be heard and there was no point in his trusting Wolfe's discretion if he couldn't trust mine, so I went around through the hall, crossed to my desk, wrote "Edey and Heydecker" on my memo pad, tore the sheet off, and handed it to Wolfe. He glanced at it and looked at Jett.

"We're at an impasse. You refuse to answer further questions unless I tell you the contents of the statement, and I won't do that. Mr. Edey and Mr. Heydecker are here. Will you stay or go?"

"Edey?" Jett stood up. "Heydecker? Here?"

"Yes, sir. Uninvited and unexpected. You may leave unseen if you wish."

Evidently he didn't wish anything except to see the statement. He didn't want to go and he didn't want to stay. When it became apparent that he wasn't going to decide, Wolfe decided for him by giving me a nod, and I went and opened the connecting door and told the newcomers to come in. Then I stepped aside and looked on, at their surprise at seeing Jett, their manners as they introduced themselves to Wolfe, the way they handled their eyes. I had never completely squelched the idea that when you are in a room with three men and you know that one of them committed a murder, especially when he committed it in that room only eighteen hours ago, it will show if you watch close enough. I knew from experience that the idea wasn't worth a damn, that if you did see something that seemed to point you were probably wrong, but I still had it and still have it. I was so busy with it that I didn't go to my desk and sit until Jett was back in the red leather chair and the newcomers were on two of the yellow ones, facing Wolfe, and Heydecker, the big broad-shouldered man, was speaking.

His eyes were at Jett. "We came," he said, "for information, and I suppose you did too, Greg. Unless you got more at the DA's office than we did."

"I got damn little," Jett said. "I didn't even see Howie, my old schoolmate. They didn't answer questions, they asked them. A lot of them I didn't answer and they shouldn't have been asked—about our affairs and our clients. Naturally I answered the relevant ones, the routine stuff about my relations with Bertha Aaron and my whereabouts and movements yesterday afternoon. Not only mine, but others'. Particularly if anyone had spoken at length with Bertha, and if anyone had left the office with her or soon after her. Obviously they think she was killed by someone connected with the firm, but they don't say why—at least not to me."

"Nor me," Edey said. He was the compact undersized one and his thin tenor fitted him fine.

"Nor me," Heydecker said. "What has Wolfe told you?"

"Not much. I haven't been here long." Jett looked at Wolfe.

Wolfe obliged. He cleared his throat. "I presume that you gentlemen have come with the same purpose as Mr. Jett. He asks for any information that will give light, with emphasis on the reason for Miss Aaron's coming to see me. He assumes—"

Heydecker cut in. "That's it. What was she here for?"

"If you please. He assumes from the circumstances that she was killed because she was here, to prevent a revelation she meant to make, and that is plausible. But surely the police and the District Attorney haven't withheld *all* of the details from you. Haven't they told you that she didn't see me?"

"No," Edey said. "They haven't told me."

"Nor me," Heydecker said.

"Then I tell you. She came without appointment. Mr. Goodwin admitted her. She asked to see me on a confidential matter. I was engaged elsewhere, upstairs, and Mr. Goodwin came to tell me she was here. We had a matter under consideration and discussed it at some length, and when we came down her dead body was here." He pointed at Heydecker's feet. "There. So she couldn't tell me what she came for, since I never saw her alive."

"Then I don't get it," Edey declared. The brilliant idea man was using his brain. "If she didn't tell you, you couldn't tell the police or the District Attorney. But if they don't know what she came to see you about, why do they think she was killed by someone in our office? It's conceivable that they got that information from someone else, but so soon? They started in on me at seven o'clock this morning. And I conclude from their questions that they don't merely think it, they think they know it."

"They do, unquestionably," Heydecker agreed. "Mr. Goodwin. You admitted her. She was alone?" That was the brilliant trial lawyer.

"Yes." Since we weren't before the bench I omitted the "sir."

"You saw no one else around? On the sidewalk?"

"No. Of course it was dark. It was twenty minutes past five. On January fifth the sun set at 4:46." By gum, he wasn't going to trap me.

"You conducted her to this room?"

"Yes."

"Leaving the outer door open perhaps?"

"No."

"Are you certain of that?"

"Yes. If I have one habit that's totally automatic, it's closing that door and making sure it's locked."

"Automatic habits are dangerous things, Mr. Goodwin. Sometimes they fail you. When you brought her to this room did you sit?"

"Yes."

"Where?"

"Where I am now."

"Where did she sit?"

"About where you are. About three feet closer to me."

"What did she say?"

"That she wanted to see Nero Wolfe about something

urgent. No, she said that at the door. She said her case was private and very confidential."

"She used the word 'case'?"

"Yes."

"What else did she say?"

"That her name was Bertha Aaron and she was the private secretary of Mr. Lamont Otis, senior partner in the law firm of Otis, Edey, Heydecker, and Jett."

"What else did she say?"

Naturally I had known that the time would come to lie, and decided this was it. "Nothing," I said.

"Absolutely nothing?"

"Right."

"You are Nero Wolfe's confidential assistant. He was engaged elsewhere. Do you expect me to believe that you did not insist on knowing the nature of her case before you went to him?"

The phone rang. "Not if you'd rather not," I said, and swiveled, lifted the receiver and spoke. "Nero Wolfe's residence, Archie Goodwin speaking."

I recognized the voice. "This is Rita Sorell, Mr. Goodwin. I have decided—"

"Hold it please. Just a second." I pressed a palm over the transmitter and told Wolfe, "That woman you sent a card to. The one who told me I was handsome." He reached for his receiver and put it to his ear and I returned to mine. "Okay. You have decided?"

"I have decided that it will be best to tell you what you came this morning to find out. I have decided that you were too clever for me, not mentioning at all what you had written on the card, when that was what you came for. Your saying that you made it up, that you tried to write something that would make me curious— you didn't expect me to believe that. You were too clever for me. So I might as well confess, since you already know it. I did sit with a man in a booth in a lunchroom one evening last week—what evening was it?"

"Monday."

"That's right. And you want to know who the man was. Don't you?"

"It would help."

"I want to help. You are *very* handsome. His name is Gregory Jett."

"Many thanks. If you want to help—"

She had hung up.

Chapter 6

I cradled the receiver and rotated my chair. Wolfe pushed his phone back and said, "She is a confounded nuisance."

"Yes, sir."

"I suppose we'll have to humor her."

"Yes, sir. Or shoot her."

"Not a welcome option." He arose. "Gentlemen, I must ask you to excuse me. Come, Archie." He headed for the hall and I got up and followed. Turning left, he pushed the door to the kitchen. Fritz was there at the big table, chopping an onion. The door swung shut.

Wolfe turned to face me. "Very well. You know her. You have seen her and talked with her. What about it?"

"I'd have to toss a coin. Several coins. You have seen Jett and talked with him. It could be that she merely wanted to find out if we already knew who it was, and if so she might have named the right one and she might not. Or it might have been a real squeal; she decided that Jett killed Bertha Aaron, and either she loves justice no matter what it costs her, or she was afraid Jett might break and her spot would be too hot for comfort. I prefer the latter. Or it wasn't Jett, it was Edey or Heydecker, and she is trying to ball it up—and she may be sore at Jett on account of the episode. If it backfires, if we already know it was Edey or Heydecker, what the hell. Telling me on the phone isn't swearing to it on the stand. She can deny she called me. Or she might—"

"That's enough for now. Have you a choice?"

"No, sir. I told you she's a gem."

He grunted. He reached for a piece of onion, put it in his mouth, and chewed. When it was down he asked Fritz, "Ebenezer?" and Fritz told him no, Elite. He turned to me. "In any case, she has ripped it open. Even if she is merely trying to muddle it we can't afford to assume that she hasn't communicated with him—or soon will."

"She couldn't unless he phoned her. They've been at the DA's office all morning."

He nodded. "Then we'll tell him first. You'll have to recant."

"Right. Do we save anything?"

"I think not. The gist first and we'll see."

He made for the door. In the hall we heard a voice from the office, Edey's thin tenor, but it stopped as we appeared. As I passed in front of Heydecker he stuck a foot out, but possibly not to trip me; he may have been merely shifting in his chair.

When Wolfe was settled in his he spoke. "Gentlemen, Mr. Goodwin and I have decided that you deserve candor. That was Mrs. Morton Sorell on the phone. What she said persuaded us—"

"Did you say *Sorell?*" Heydecker demanded. He was gawking and so was Edey. Evidently Jett never gawked.

"I did. Archie?"

I focused on Heydecker. "If she had called twenty seconds earlier," I told him, "I wouldn't have had to waste a lie. I did insist on knowing the nature of Bertha Aaron's case before I went to Mr. Wolfe, and she told me. She said she had accidentally seen a member of the firm in secret conference with Mrs. Morton Sorell, the firm's opponent in an important case. She said that after worrying about it for a week she had told him about it that afternoon, yesterday, and asked for an explanation, and he didn't have one, so he was a traitor. She said she was afraid to tell Mr. Otis because he had a weak heart and it might kill him, and she wouldn't tell another firm member because he might be a traitor too. So she had come to Nero Wolfe."

I had been wrong about Jett. Now he was gawking too. He found his tongue first. "This is incredible. I don't believe it!"

"Nor I," Heydecker said.

"Nor I," Edey said, his tenor a squeak.

"Do you expect us to believe," Heydecker demanded, "that Bertha Aaron would come to an outsider with a story that would gravely damage the firm if it became known?"

Wolfe cut in. "No more cross-examination, Mr. Heydecker. I indulged you before, but not now. If questions are to be asked I'll do the asking. As for Mr. Goodwin's bona fides, he has given a signed statement to the police, and he is not an ass. Also—"

"The police?" Edey squeaked. "Good God!"

"It's absolutely incredible," Jett declared.

Wolfe ignored them. "Also I allowed Mr. Otis to read a copy of the statement when he came here last night. He agreed not to divulge its contents when he came here last night. He agreed not to divulge its contents before ten o'clock tomorrow morning, to give me till then to plan a course—a course based on the natural assumption that Miss Aaron was killed by the man she had accused of treachery—an assumption I share with the police. Evidently the police have preferred to reserve the statement, and so have I, but not now—since Mrs. Sorell has named the member of your firm she was seen with. On the phone just now. One of you."

"This isn't real," Edey squeaked. "This is a nightmare." Heydecker sputtered, "Do you dare to suggest—"

"No, Mr. Heydecker." Wolfe flattened a palm on his desk. "I will not submit to questioning; I will choose the facts I'm willing to share. I suggest nothing; I am reporting. I neglecting to say that Miss Aaron did not name the member of the firm she had seen with Mrs. Sorell. Now Mrs. Sorell has named him, but I am not satisfied of her veracity. Mr. Goodwin saw her this morning and found her devious. I'm not going to tell you whom she named, and that will make the pressure on one of you almost unendurable."

The pressure wasn't exactly endurable for any of them. They were exchanging glances, and they weren't glances of sympathy and partnership. In a spot like that the idea I mentioned might be expected to work, but it didn't. Two of them were really suspicious of their partners and one was only pretending to be, but it would have taken a better man than me to pick him; better even than Wolfe, whose eyes, narrowed to slits, were taking them in.

He was going on. "The obvious assumption is that you—one of you—followed Miss Aaron when she left the premises yesterday after she had challenged you, and when you saw her enter my house your alarm was acute and exigent. You sought a telephone and rang this number. In Mr. Goodwin's absence she answered the phone, and consented to admit you. If you can—"

"It was pure chance that she was alone," Edey objected. The idea man.

"Pfui. If I'm not answering questions, Mr. Edey, neither am I debating trifles. With your trained minds that is no knot for you. Speaking again to one of you: if you could be identified by inquiry into your whereabouts and movements yesterday afternoon the police would have the job already done and you would be in custody. All that they have been told by you and by the entire personnel of your office is being checked by an army of men well qualified for the task. But since they have reserved the information supplied by Mr. Goodwin, I doubt if they have asked you about Monday evening of last week. Eight days ago. Have they?"

"Why should they?" It was Jett.

"Because that was when one of you was seen by Miss Aaron in conference with Mrs. Sorell. I'm going to ask you now, but first I should tell you of an understanding

I had with Mr. Otis last night. In exchange for information he furnished I agreed that in exposing the murderer I would minimize, as far as possible, the damage to the reputation of his firm. I will observe that agreement, so manifestly, for two of you, the sooner this is over the better. Mr. Jett. How did you spend Monday evening, December twenty-ninth, say from six o'clock to midnight?"

Jett's eyes were still deep-set, but they weren't dreamy. They had been glued on Wolfe ever since I had recanted, and he hadn't moved a muscle. He spoke. "If this is straight, if all you've said is true, including the phone call from Mrs. Sorell, the damage to the firm is done and you can do nothing to minimize it. No one under heaven can."

"I can try. I intend to."

"How?"

"By meeting contingencies as they arise."

Heydecker put in, "You say Mr. Otis knows all this? He was here last night?"

"Yes. I am not a parrot and you are not deaf. Well, Mr. Jett? Monday evening of last week?"

"I was at a theater with a friend."

"The friend's name?"

"Miss Ann Paige."

"What theater?"

"The Drew. The play was *Practice Makes Perfect*. Miss Paige and I left the office together shortly before six and had dinner at Rusterman's. We were together continuously until after midnight."

"Thank you. Mr. Edey?"

"That was the Monday before New Year's," Edey said. "I got home before six o'clock and ate dinner there and was there all evening."

"Alone?"

"No. My son and his wife and two children spent the holiday week with us. They went to the opera with my wife and daughter, and I stayed home with the children."

"How old are the children?"

"Two and four."

"Where is your home?"

"An apartment. Park Avenue and Sixty-ninth Street."

"Did you go out at all?"

"No."

"Thank you. Mr. Heydecker?"

"I was at the Manhattan Chess Club watching the tournament. Bobby Fischer won his adjourned game with Weinstein in fifty-eight moves. Larry Evans drew with Kalme and Reshevsky drew with Mednis."

"Where is the Manhattan Chess Club?"

"West Sixty-fourth Street."

"Did play start at six o'clock?"

"Certainly not. I was in court all day and had things to do at the office. My secretary and I had sandwiches at my desk."

"What time did you leave the office?"

"Around eight o'clock. My secretary would know."

"What time did you arrive at the chess club?"

"Fifteen or twenty minutes after I left the office." Heydecker suddenly moved and was on his feet. "This is ridiculous," he declared. "You may be on the square, Wolfe, I don't know. If you are, God help us." He turned. "I'm going to see Otis. You coming, Frank?"

He was. The brilliant idea man, judging from his expression, had none at all. He pulled his feet back, moved his head slowly from side to side to tell hope good-by, and arose. They didn't ask the eleven-percent partner to join them, and apparently he wasn't going to, but as I was reaching for Edey's ulster on the hall rack here came Jett, and when I opened the door he was the first one out. I stood on the stoop, getting a breath of air, and watched them heading for Ninth Avenue three abreast, a solid front of mutual trust and understanding, in a pig's eye.

In the office, Wolfe was leaning back with his eyes closed. As I reached my desk the phone rang. It was Saul Panzer, to report that there had been no sign of Mrs. Sorell. I told him to hold the wire and relayed it to

Wolfe, and asked if he wanted to put them on the alibis we had just collected. "Pfui," he said, and I told Saul to carry on.

I swiveled. "I was afraid," I said, "that you might be desperate enough to try it, checking their alibis. It's very interesting, the different ways there are of cracking a case. It depends on who you are. If you're just a top-flight detective, me for instance, all you can do is detect. You'd rather go after an alibi than eat. When you ask a man where he was at eleven minutes past eight you put it in your notebook, and you wear out a pair of shoes looking for somebody who says he was somewhere else. But if you're a genius you don't give a damn about alibis. You ask him where he was only to keep the conversation going while you wait for something to click. You don't even listen—"

"Nonsense," he growled. "They have no alibis."

I nodded. "You didn't listen."

"I did listen. Their alibis are worthless. One with his fiancée, one watching a chess tournament, one at home with young children in bed asleep. Bah. I asked on the chance that one of them, possibly two, might be eliminated, but no. There are still three."

"Then genius is all that's left. Unless you have an idea for another card I could take to Mrs. Sorell. I wouldn't mind. I like the way she says *very*."

"No doubt. Could you do anything with her?"

"I could try. She might possibly make another decision—for instance, to sign a statement. Or if she has decided to hire you I could bring her, and you could have a go at her yourself. She has marvelous eyelashes."

He grunted. "It may come to that. We'll see after lunch. It may be that after they have talked with Mr. Otis—yes, Fritz?"

"Lunch is ready, sir."

Chapter 7

I never got to check an alibi, but it was a close shave. Who made it close was Inspector Cramer.

Since Wolfe refuses to work either his brain or his tongue on business at table, and a murder case is business even when he has no client and no fee is in prospect, no progress was made during lunch, but when we returned to the office he buckled down and tried to think of something for me to do. The trouble was that the problem was too damn simple. We knew that one of three men had committed murder, and how and when. Okay, which one? Eeny meeny murder mo. Even the why was plain enough; Mrs. Sorell had hooked him with an offer, either of a big slice of the thirty million she was after or of more personal favors. Any approach you could think of was already cluttered with cops, except Mrs. Sorrell, and even if I got to her again I had nothing to use for a pry. What it called for was a good stiff dose of genius, and apparently Wolfe's was taking the day off. Sitting there in the office after lunch I may have got a little too personal with him or he wouldn't have bellowed at me to go ahead and check their alibis. "Glad to," I said, and went to the hall for my hat and coat, and saw visitors on the stoop, not strangers. I opened the door just as Cramer pushed the bell button, and inquired, "Have you an appointment?"

"I have in my pocket," he said, "a warrant for your arrest as a material witness. Also one for Wolfe. I warned you."

There were two ways of looking at it. One was that he didn't mean to shoot unless he had to. If he had really wanted to haul us in he would have sent a couple of dicks after us instead of coming himself with Sergeant

Purley Stebbins. The other was that here was a good opportunity to teach Wolfe a lesson. A couple of the right kind of impolite remarks would have made Cramer sore enough to go ahead and serve the warrants, and spending several hours in custody, and possibly all night, would probably cure Wolfe of leaving neckties on his desk. But I would have had to go along, which wouldn't have been fair, so I wheeled and marched to the office, relying on Purley to shut the door, and told Wolfe: "Cramer and Stebbins with warrants. An inspector to take you and a sergeant to take me, which is an honor." He glared at me and then transferred it to them as they entered.

Cramer said, "I warned you last night," draped his coat on the arm of the red leather chair, and sat.

Wolfe snorted. "Tommyrot."

Cramer took papers from his pocket. "I'll serve these only if I have to. If I do I know what will happen, you'll refuse to talk and so will Goodwin, and you'll be out on bail as soon as Parker can swing it. But it will be on your record and that won't close it. Held as a material witness is one thing, and charged with interfering with the operation of justice is another. In the interest of justice we were withholding the contents of the statements you and Goodwin gave us, and you knew it, and you revealed them. To men suspected of murder. Frank Edey has admitted it. He phoned an assistant district attorney."

The brilliant idea man again.

"He's a jackass," Wolfe declared.

"Yeah. Since you told them in confidence."

"I did not. I asked for no pledges and got none. But I made it plain that if I put my finger on the murderer before you do I'll protect that law firm from injury as far as possible. If Mr. Edey is innocent it was to his interest not to have me interrupted by you. If he's guilty, all the worse."

"Who's your client? Otis?"

"I have no client. I am going to avenge an affront to my dignity and self-esteem. Your threat to charge me with interference with the operation of justice is puerile. I am not meddling in a matter that does not concern me. I cannot escape the ignominy of having my necktie presented in a courtroom as an exhibit of the prosecution; I may even have to suffer the indignity of being called to the stand to identify it; but I want the satisfaction of exposing the culprit who used it. In telling Mr. Otis and his partners what Miss Aaron said to Mr. Goodwin, in revealing the nature of the menace to their firm, I served my legitimate personal interest and I violated no law."

"You knew damn well we were withholding it!"

Wolfe's shoulders went up an eighth of an inch. "I am not bound to respect your tactics, either by statute or by custom. You and I are not lawyers; ask the District Attorney if a charge would hold." He upturned a palm. "Mr. Cramer. This is pointless. You have a warrant for my arrest as a material witness?"

"Yes. And one for Goodwin."

"But you don't serve them, for the reason you have given, so they are only cudgels for you to brandish. To what end? What do you want?"

A low growl escaped Sergeant Purley Stebbins, who had stayed on his feet behind Cramer's chair. There is one thing that would give Purley more pleasure than to take Wolfe or me in, and that would be to take both of us. Wolfe cuffed to him and me cuffed to Wolfe would be perfect. The growl was for disappointment and I gave him a sympathetic grin as he went to a chair and sat.

"I want the truth," Cramer said.

"Pfui," Wolfe said.

Cramer nodded. "Phooey is right. If I take Goodwin's statement as it stands, if he put nothing in and left nothing out, one of those three men—Edey, Heydecker, Jett—one of them killed Bertha Aaron. I don't have to go into that. You agree?"

"Yes."

"But if a jury takes Goodwin's statement as it stands, it would be impossible to get one of those men convicted. She got here at 5:20, and he was with her in this room until 5:39, when he went up to you in the plant rooms. It was 6:10 when he returned and found the body. All right, now for them. If one of them had a talk with her yesterday afternoon, or if one of them left the office when she did, or just before or just after, we can't pin it down. We haven't so far and I doubt if we will. They have private offices; their secretaries are in other rooms. Naturally we're still checking on movements and phone calls and other details, but it comes down to this. That list, Purley."

Stebbins got a paper from his pocket and handed it over and Cramer studied it briefly. "They had a conference scheduled for 5:30 on some corporation case, no connection with Sorell. In Frank Edey's office. Edey was there when Jett came in a minute or two before 5:30. They were there together when Heydecker came at 5:45. Heydecker said he had gone out on an errand which took longer than he expected. The three of them stayed there, discussing the case, until 6:35. So even if you erase Edey and Jett and take Heydecker, what have you got? Goodwin says he left her here, alive, at 5:39. They say Heydecker joined the conference at 5:45. That gives him six minutes after tailing her here to phone this number, come and be admitted by her, kill her, and get back to that office more than a mile away. Phooey. And one of them couldn't have come and killed her after the conference. On that I don't have to take what Goodwin says; he phoned in and reported it at 6:31, and the conference lasted to 6:35. How do you like it?"

Wolfe was scowling at him. "Not at all. What was Heydecker's errand?"

"He went to three theaters to buy tickets. You might think a man with his income would get them through an agency, but he's close. We've checked that. He is. They don't remember him at the theaters."

"Did neither Edey nor Jett leave the office at all between 4:30 and 5:30?"

"Not known. They say they didn't, and no one says

they did, but it's open. What difference does it make, since even Heydecker is out?"

"Not much. And of course the assumption that one of them hired a thug to kill her isn't tenable."

"Certainly not. Here in your office with your necktie? Nuts. You can take your pick of three assumptions. One." Cramer stuck a finger up. "They're lying. That conference didn't start at 5:30 and/or Heydecker didn't join them at 5:45. Two." Another finger. "When Bertha Aaron said 'member of the firm' she merely meant one of the lawyers associated with the firm. There are nineteen of them. If Goodwin's statement is accurate I doubt it. Three." Another finger. "Goodwin's statement is phony. She didn't say 'member of the firm.' God knows what she did say. It may be *all* phony. I admit that can never be proved, since she's dead, and no matter what the facts turn out to be when we get them he will still claim that's what she said. Take your pick."

Wolfe grunted. "I reject the last. Granting that Mr. Goodwin is capable of so monstrous a hoax, I would have to be a party to it, since he reported to me on his conversation with Miss Aaron before she died—or while she died. I also reject the second. As you know, I talked with Mr. Otis last night. He was positive that she would not have used that phrase, 'member of the firm,' in any but its literal sense."

"Look, Wolfe." Cramer uncrossed his legs and put his feet flat. "You admit you want the glory of getting him before we do."

"Not the glory. The satisfaction."

"Okay. I understand that. I can imagine how you felt when you saw her lying there with your necktie around her throat. I know how fast your mind works when it has to. It would take you two seconds to realize that Goodwin's report of what she had told him could never be checked. You wanted the satisfaction of getting him. It would take you maybe five minutes to think it over and tell Goodwin how to fake his report so we would spend a couple of days chasing around getting nowhere. With your goddamn ego that would seem to you perfectly all right. You wouldn't be obstructing justice; you would be bringing a murderer *to* justice. Remembering the stunts I have seen you pull, do you deny you would be capable of that?"

"No. Given sufficient impulse, no. But I didn't. Let me settle this. I am convinced that when Mr. Goodwin came to the plant rooms and told me what Miss Aaron had said to him he reported fully and accurately, and the statement he signed corresponds in every respect with what he told me. So if you came, armed with warrants, to challenge it, you're wasting your time and mine. Archie, get Mr. Parker."

Since the number of Nathaniel Parker, the lawyer, was one of those I knew best and I didn't have to consult the book, I swiveled and dialed. When I had him Wolfe got on his phone.

"Mr. Parker? Good afternoon. Mr. Cramer is here waving warrants at Mr. Goodwin and me. . . . No. Material witnesses. He may or may not serve them. Please have your secretary ring my number every ten minutes. If Fritz tells you that we have gone with Mr. Cramer you will know what to do. . . . Yes, of course. Thank you."

As he hung up Cramer left his chair, spoke to Stebbins, got his coat from the chair arm, and tramped out, with Purley at his heels. I stepped to the hall to see that both of them were outside when the door shut. When I returned, Wolfe was leaning back with his eyes closed, his fists on his chair arms, and his mouth working. When he does that with his lips, pushing them out and pulling them in, out and in, he is not to be interrupted, so I crossed to my desk and sat. That can last anywhere from two minutes to half an hour.

That time it wasn't much more than two minutes. He opened his eyes, straightened up, and growled, "Did he omit the fourth assumption deliberately? Has it occurred to him?"

"I doubt it. He was concentrating on us. But it soon will."

"It has occurred to you?"

"Sure. From that time-table it's obvious. When it

does occur to him he'll probably mess it up. It's not the kind he's good at."

He nodded. "We must forestall him. Can you get her here?"

"I can try. I supposed that was what you were working at. I can make a stab at it on the phone, and if that doesn't work we can invent another card trick. When do you want her? Now?"

"No. I must have time to contrive a plan. What time is it?" He would have had to twist his neck to look up at the wall clock.

"Ten after three."

"Say six o'clock. We must also have the others, including Mr. Otis."

Though the Churchill number wasn't as familiar to me as Parker's I knew it, and got at the phone and dialed. I asked for Mrs. Morton Sorell, and after a wait had a voice I had heard before.

"Mrs. Sorell's apartment. Who is it, please?"

"This is Archie Goodwin, Mrs. Sorell. I'm calling from Nero Wolfe's office. A police inspector was here for a talk with Mr. Wolfe and just left. Before that three men you know were here—Edey and Heydecker and Jett. There have been some very interesting developments, and Mr. Wolfe would like to discuss them with you before he makes up his mind about something. You were asking this morning if he would work for you, and that's one possibility. Would six o'clock suit you? You have the address."

Silence. Then her voice: "What are the developments?"

"Mr. Wolfe would rather tell you himself. I'm sure you'll find them interesting."

"Why can't he come here?"

"Because as I told you, he never leaves his house on business."

"You do. You come. Come now."

"I would love to, but some other time. Mr. Wolfe wants to discuss it with you himself."

Silence. Then: "Will the policeman be there?"

"Certainly not."

Silence, then: "You say six o'clock?"

"That's right."

"Very well. I'll come."

I hung up, turned, and told Wolfe, "All set. She wants me to come there but that will have to wait. You have less than three hours to cook up a charade, and for two of them you'll be with the orchids. Anything for me?"

"Get Mr. Otis," he muttered.

Chapter 8

I felt then, and I still feel, that it was a waste of money to have Saul and Fred and Orrie there; and since we had no client it was Wolfe's money. When Saul phoned in at five o'clock I could just as well have told him to call it a day. I do not claim that I can handle five people all having a fit at once, even if one of them is seventy-five years old and another one is a woman, but there was no reason to suppose that more than one of them would really explode, and I could certainly handle him. But when Saul phoned I followed instructions, and there went sixty bucks.

They weren't visible when, at eight minutes after six, the bell rang and I went and opened the door to admit Rita Sorell, nor when I escorted her to the office, introduced her to Wolfe, and draped her fur coat, probably milky mink, over the back of the red leather chair. No one was visible but Wolfe. The fact that she gave Wolfe a smile and fluttered her long dark lashes at him didn't mean that she was a snob; I had got mine in the hall.

"I'm not in the habit," she told him, "of going to see men when they send for me. This is a new experience. Maybe that's why I came; I like new experiences. Mr. Goodwin said you wanted to discuss something?"

Wolfe nodded. "I do. Something private and personal. And since the discussion will be more productive if it is frank and unreserved, we should be alone. If you please, Archie? No notes will be needed."

I objected. "Mrs. Sorell might want to ask me—"

"No. Leave us, please."

I went. After shutting the door as I entered the hall, I turned right, went and opened the door to the front room, entered, shut that door too, and glanced around.

All was in order. Lamont Otis was in the big chair by a window, the one Ann Paige had left by, and she was on one side of him and Edey on the other. Jett's chair was tilted back against the wall to the right. On the couch facing me was Heydecker, in between Fred Durkin and Orrie Cather. Saul Panzer stood in the center of the room. Their faces all came to me and Edey started to speak.

I cut him off. "If you talk," I said, "you won't hear, and even if you don't want to hear, others do. You can talk later. As Mr. Wolfe told you, a speaker behind the couch is wired to a mike in his office, and he is there talking with someone. Since you'll recognize her voice I don't need to name her. Okay, Saul."

Saul, who had moved to the rear of the couch, flipped the switch and Wolfe's voice sounded.

". . . and she described her problem to Mr. Goodwin before he came up to me. She said that on Monday evening of last week she saw a member of the firm in a booth in a lunchroom in secret conference with you; that she had concluded that he was betraying the interest of one of the firm's clients to you, the client being your husband; that for reasons she thought cogent she would not tell another member or members of the firm; that she had finally, yesterday afternoon, told the one she was accusing and asked for an explanation, and got none; that she refused to name him until she had spoken with me; and that she had come to engage my services. Mr. Goodwin has of course reported this to the police."

MRS. SORELL: "She didn't name him?"

WOLFE: "No. As I said, Mrs. Sorell, this discussion

should be frank and unreserved. I am not going to pretend that you have named him and are committed. You told Mr. Goodwin on the phone today that you were with a man in a booth in a lunchroom last Monday evening, and you said his name is Gregory Jett; but you could have been merely scattering dust, and at will you can deny you made the call."

Jett had caused a slight commotion by jerking forward in his tilted chair, but not enough to drown the voice, and a touch on his arm by me had stopped him.

MRS. SORELL: "What if I don't deny it? What if I repeat it, it was Gregory Jett?"

WOLFE: "I wouldn't advise you to. If in addition to scattering dust you were gratifying an animus you'll have to try again. It wasn't Mr. Jett. It was Mr. Heydecker."

Heydecker couldn't have caused any commotion even if he wanted to, with Fred at one side of him and Orrie at the other. The only commotion came from Lamont Otis, who moved and made a choking noise, and Ann Paige grabbed his hand.

MRS. SORELL: "That's interesting. Mr. Goodwin said I would find it interesting and I do. So I sat in a booth with a man and didn't know who he was? Really, Mr. Wolfe!"

WOLFE: "No, madam. I assure you it won't do. I'll expound it. I assumed that one of three men—Edey, Heydecker, or Jett—had killed Bertha Aaron. In view of what she told Mr. Goodwin it was more than an assumption, it was a conclusion. But three hours ago I had to abandon it, when I learned that those three were in conference together in Mr. Edey's office at 5:45. It was 5:39 when Mr. Goodwin left Miss Aaron to come up to me. That they were lying, that they were in a joint conspiracy, was most unlikely, especially since others on the premises could probably impeach them. But though none of them could have killed her, one of them could have provoked her doom, wittingly or not. Of the three, only Mr. Heydecker was known to have left around the same time as Miss Aaron—he had said on a personal errand, but his movements could not be checked. My new assumption, not yet a conclusion, was that he had followed her to this address and seen her enter my house, had sought a phone and called you to warn you that your joint intrigue might soon be exposed, and then, no doubt in desperation, had scurried back to his office, fifteen minutes late at the conference."

It was Edey's turn to make a commotion and he obliged. He left his chair, moved to the couch, and stood staring down at Heydecker. Saul and I were there, but apparently he had no brilliant idea beyond the stare.

WOLFE: "Now, however, that assumption is a conclusion, and I don't expect to abandon it. Mr. Heydecker does not believe, and neither do I, that upon receiving his phone call you came here determined to murder. Indeed, you couldn't have, since you could have no expectation of finding her alone. Mr. Heydecker believes that you merely intended to salvage what you could—at best to prevent the disclosure, at worst to learn where you stood. You called this number and she answered and agreed to admit you and hear you. Mr. Heydecker believes that when you entered and found that she was alone and that she had not seen me, it was on sudden impulse that you seized the paperweight and struck her. He believes that when you saw her sink to the floor, unconscious, and saw the necktie on this desk, the impulse carried you on. He believes that you—"

MRS. SORELL: "How do you know what he believes?"

That would have been my cue if I were needed. I had been instructed to use my judgment. If Heydecker's reaction made it doubtful I was to get to the office with a signal before Wolfe had gone too far to hedge. It was no strain at all on my judgment. Heydecker was hunched forward, his elbows on his knees and his face covered by his hands.

WOLFE: "A good question. I am not in his skull. I should have said, he *says* he believes. You might have known, madam, that he couldn't possibly stand the pressure. Disclosure of his treachery to his firm will end his professional career, but concealment of guilty knowledge of a murder might have ended his life. You might have known—"

MRS. SORELL: "If he says he believes I killed that woman he's lying. He killed her. He's a rat and a liar. He phoned me twice yesterday, first to tell me that we had been seen in the lunchroom, to warn me, and again about an hour later to say that he had dealt with it, that our plan was safe. So he had killed her. When Goodwin told me there had been developments I knew what it was, I knew he would lose his nerve, I knew he would lie. He's a rat. That's why I came. I admit I concealed guilty knowledge of a murder, and I know that was wrong, but it's not too late. Is it too late?"

WOLFE: "No. A purge can both clean your conscience and save your skin. What time did he phone you the second time?"

MRS. SORELL: "I don't know exactly. It was between five and six. Around half past five."

WOLFE: "What was the plan he had made safe?"

MRS. SORELL: "Of course he has lied about that too. It was his plan. He came to me about a month ago and said he could give me information about my husband that I could use to make—that I could use to get my rights. He wanted—"

Heydecker jerked his head up and yapped, "That's a lie! I didn't go to her, she came to me!" That added to my knowledge of human nature. He hadn't uttered a peep when she accused him of murder. Edey, who was still there staring down at him, said something I didn't catch.

Mrs. Sorell was going on: "He wanted me to agree to pay him a million dollars for it, but I couldn't because I didn't know how much I would get, and I finally said I would pay him one-tenth of what I got. That was that evening at the lunchroom."

WOLFE: "Has he given you the information?"

MRS. SORELL: "No. He wanted too much in advance. Of course that was the difficulty. We couldn't put it in writing and sign it."

WOLFE: "No indeed. A signed document is of little

value when neither party would dare to produce it. I presume you realize, Mrs. Sorell, that your purge will have to include your appearance on the stand at a murder trial. Are you prepared to testify under oath?"

MRS. SORELL: "I suppose I'll have to. I knew I would have to when I decided to come to see you."

Wolfe (in a new tone, the snap of a whip): "Then you're a dunce, madam."

Again that would have been my cue if I were needed. The whole point of the set-up, having the four members of the firm in the front room listening in, was to get Heydecker committed before witnesses. If his nerve had held it would have been risky for Wolfe to crack the whip. But he was done for. He hadn't written out a confession and signed it, but he might as well have.

MRS. SORELL: "Oh, no, Mr. Wolfe. I'm not a dunce."

WOLFE: "But you are. One detail alone would sink you. After you rang this number yesterday afternoon, and Miss Aaron answered, and you spoke with her, you got here as quickly as possible. Since you were not then contemplating murder, there was no reason for you to use caution. I don't know if you have a car and chauffeur, but even if you have, to send for it would have meant delay, and minutes were precious. There is no crosstown subway. Buses, one downtown and one crosstown, would have been far too slow. Unquestionably you took a cab. In spite of the traffic that would have been much faster than walking. The doorman at the Churchill probably summoned one for you, but even if he didn't, it will be a simple matter to find it. I need only telephone Mr. Cramer, the police inspector who was here this afternoon, and suggest that he locate the cab driver who picked you up at or near the Churchill yesterday afternoon and drove you to this address. In fact, that is what I intend to do, and that will be enough."

Ann Paige stood up. She was in a fix. She wanted to go to Gregory Jett, where her eyes already were, but she didn't want to leave Lamont Otis, who was slumped in his chair, his head sagging and his eyes shut. Luckily Jett saw her difficulty and went to her and put an arm around her. It scored a point for romance that he could have a thought for personal matters at the very moment his firm was getting a clout on the jaw.

WOLFE: "I shall also suggest that he send a man here to take you in hand until the cab driver is found. If you ask why I don't proceed to do this, why I first announce it to you, I confess a weakness. I am savoring a satisfaction. I am getting even with you. Twenty-five hours ago, in this room, you subjected me to the severest humiliation I have suffered for many years. I will not say it gives me pleasure, but I confess it—"

There was a combination of sounds from the speaker: a kind of cry or squeal, presumably from Mrs. Sorell, a sort of scrape or flutter, and what might have been a grunt from Wolfe. I dived for the connecting door and went with it as I swung it open, and kept going, but two paces short of Wolfe's desk I halted to take in a sight I had never seen before and never expect to see again: Nero Wolfe with his arms tight around a beautiful young woman in his lap, pinning her arms, hugging her close to him. I stood paralyzed.

"Archie!" he roared. "Confound it, get her!"

I obeyed.

Chapter 9

I would like to be able to report that Wolfe got somewhere with his effort to minimize the damage to the firm, but I have to be candid and accurate. He tried but there wasn't much he could do, since Heydecker was the chief witness for the prosecution at the trial and was cross-examined for six hours. Of course that finished him professionally. Wolfe had better luck with another effort; the DA finally conceded that I was competent to identify Exhibit C, a brown silk necktie with little yellow curlicues, and Wolfe wasn't called. Evidently the jury agreed with him, since it only took them five hours to bring in a verdict of guilty.

At that, the firm is still doing business at the old stand, and Lamont Otis still comes to the office five days a week, and I hear that since Gregory Jett's marriage to Ann Paige he has quit being careless about the balance between income and outgo. I don't know if his eleven-percent cut has been boosted. That's a confidential matter.

DEATH OF A
DEMON

Chapter 1

The red leather chair was four feet away from the end of Nero Wolfe's desk, so when she got the gun from her handbag she had to get up and take a step to put it on the desk. Then she returned to the chair, closed the bag, and told Wolfe, "That's the gun I'm not going to shoot my husband with."

Sitting facing her with my back to my desk, which was at right angles to Wolfe's, I raised my brows. I hadn't expected her to put on an act. When she had phoned the previous afternoon to ask for an appointment she had of course sounded a little jumpy, as most people do when they call the office of a private detective, but she had been quite matter-of-fact in giving the details. Her name was Lucy Hazen, Mrs. Barry Hazen. She gave her address, on East 37th Street between Park and Lexington. All she wanted was thirty minutes with Nero Wolfe, to tell him something confidential. She didn't want him to do anything, not even give her advice; she merely wanted to tell him something; and she would pay one hundred dollars for the half-hour. She could and would pay more if she had to, but she hoped the hundred would be enough.

In November or December, when Wolfe's income has reached a point where out of a hundred received he can keep only twenty bucks, he will make an appointment only for someone or something very special, but this was January, no big fee was in prospect, and even a measly C would help in the upkeep of his old brownstone on West 35th Street, including staff, particularly since he wouldn't have to work for it. So it was set for 11:30 the following morning, Tuesday.

When the doorbell rang at 11:30 on the dot and I went to let her in, she gave me a smile and said, "Thank you for getting him to see me." Handshakes can be faked and usually are, but smiles can't. It isn't often that a man gets a natural, friendly, straightforward smile from a young woman who has never seen him before, with no come-on, no catch, and no dare, and the least he can do is return it if he has that kind in stock. As I took her to the office and helped her off with her coat, which was mink, I was thinking that you never know, even the good-looking wife of a well-known public relations operator like Barry Hazen could have her feelings on straight. I was pleased to meet her.

So I was disappointed when she put on an act. It is not natural for a woman to open a conversation with a stranger by taking a revolver from her bag and saying that's the gun she isn't going to shoot her husband with. I must have been wrong about the smile, and since I don't like to be wrong I was no longer pleased to meet her. I raised my brows and tightened my lips.

Wolfe, in his oversized chair behind his desk, darted a glance at the gun, returned his eyes to her, and grunted. "I am not impressed," he said, "by histrionics."

"Oh," she said, "I'm not trying to impress you, I'm only telling you. That's what I came for, just to tell you. I thought it would be more—more definite, I guess—if I brought the gun and showed it to you."

"Very well, you have done so." Wolfe was frowning. "I understand that you intend to ask me for no service or advice; you wish only to tell me something in confidence. I should remind you that I am not a lawyer or a priest; a communication from you to me will not be privileged. If you tell me about a crime I can't engage not to disclose it. I mean a serious crime, not some petty offense such as carrying a deadly weapon for which you have no permit."

"I hadn't thought of that, carrying a weapon." She dismissed it with a little gesture. "That's all right. There hasn't been any crime and there isn't going to be, that's just the point. That's what I came to tell you, that I'm not going to shoot my husband."

Wolfe's eyes were narrowed at her. He is convinced that all women are dotty or devious, or both, and here was more evidence to support it. "Just that?" he demanded. "You wanted half an hour."

She nodded. She set her teeth on her lip, nice white teeth, and in a moment released it. "Because I thought it would be better if I told you something about . . . why. If you will regard it as confidential."

"With the reservation I have made."

"Of course. You know who my husband is? Barry Hazen, Public Relations?"

"Mr. Goodwin has informed me."

"We were married two years ago. I was the secretary of a client of his, Jules Khoury, the inventor. My father, Titus Postel, was also an inventor, and he was associated with Mr. Khoury until his death five years ago. That's where I met Barry, at Mr. Khoury's office. I thought I really was in love with him. I have tried and tried to decide what was the real reason why I married him, I mean the *real* one, whether it was only because I wanted to have—"

She stopped and put her teeth on her lip. She shook her head, with energy, as if to chase a fly. "There you are," she said. "I mean there I am. You don't need to know all that. I'm blubbering, fishing for pity. You don't even need to know why I want to kill him."

Wolfe muttered, "It's your half-hour, madam."

"I don't hate him." She shook her head again. "I think I despise him—I know I do—and he won't let me get a divorce. I tried to leave him, I did leave him, but he made such a— There I go again! I don't *need* to tell you all that!"

"As you please."

"It's not as I please, Mr. Wolfe, it's as I must!"

"As you must, then."

"This is what I *must* tell you. He has a gun in a drawer in his bedroom. That's it there on your desk. We have separate bedrooms. You know how there can be something in your mind but you don't know it's there until all of a sudden there it is?"

"Certainly. The subconscious is not a grave; it's a cistern."

"But we don't know what's in it. I didn't. One day a month ago, it was the day after Christmas, I went to his bedroom and took the gun from the drawer and looked to see if it was loaded, and it was, and all of a sudden I was thinking how easy it would be to shoot him while he was in bed asleep. I said to myself, 'You idiot, you absolute idiot,' and put the gun back, and I didn't go near that drawer again. But the thought came back, it kept coming, mostly when I was trying to go to sleep, and it got worse. It got worse this way, it wasn't just going in when he was asleep and getting the gun and shooting him, it was planning how to do it so I wouldn't get caught. I knew it was idiotic, but I couldn't stop. I could *not!* And one night, just two nights ago, Sunday night, I got out of bed trembling all over and went to the shower and turned on the cold water and stood under it. I had found a plan that would work. I don't have to tell you what the plan was."

"As you please. As you must."

"It doesn't matter. I went back to bed, but I didn't sleep. I wasn't afraid I might do something in my sleep, I was afraid of what my mind might do. I had found out that I couldn't manage my mind. So yesterday after-noon I decided I would fix it so my mind would have to quit. I would tell someone all about it and then the plan wouldn't work, and no plan would work so I wouldn't get caught. Telling a friend wouldn't do, not a real friend, because that would leave a loophole. Of course I couldn't tell the police. I have no pastor because I don't go to church. Then I thought of you, and I phoned for an appointment, and here I am. That's all, except this: I want you to promise that if my husband is shot and killed you will tell the police about my coming here and what I said."

Wolfe grunted.

She unlocked her fingers, straightened her shoulders, and took a long deep breath—in with her mouth closed and out with it open. "There!" she said. "That's it."

Wolfe was regarding her. "I engaged only to listen," he said, "but I must offer a comment. Your stratagem should be effective as a self-deterrent, but what if someone else shoots him? And I report this conversation to the police. You'll be in a pickle."

"Not if I didn't do it."

"Pfui. Of course you will, unless the culprit is soon exposed."

"If I didn't do it I wouldn't care." She extended a hand, palm up. "Mr. Wolfe. After I decided to tell you and made the appointment, I had the first good night's sleep I have had for a month. No one is going to shoot him. I want you to promise, so *I* can't."

"I advise you not to insist on a promise."

"I must! I must *know!*"

"Very well." His shoulders went up a quarter of an inch and down again.

"You promise?"

"Yes."

She opened her bag, a large tan leather one, and took out a checkfold and a pen. "I would rather make it a check than cash," she said, "so it will be on record. Is a check all right?"

"Certainly."

"I mentioned a hundred dollars to Mr. Goodwin. Will that be enough?"

He said yes, and she wrote, resting the check on the side of the bag. To save her the trouble of getting up to

hand it over I went and took it, but when she had closed
the bag she arose anyway, and was turning to get her
coat from the back of the chair when Wolfe spoke.

"Ten minutes of your half-hour is left, Mrs. Hazen, if
you have any use for it."

"No, thank you. I just realized that wasn't exactly the
truth, what I told Mr. Goodwin, that I only wanted
to tell you something. I wanted you to promise something too. I *do* thank you and I won't take—oh! You say
I have ten minutes?" She glanced at her wrist. She
turned to me. "I would love to see the orchids—just a
quick look. If you would, Mr. Goodwin?"

"It will be a pleasure," I said, and meant it, but Wolfe
was pushing back his chair. "Mr. Goodwin doesn't owe
you the ten minutes. I do," he said, lifting his bulk.
"Come with me. You won't need your coat." He headed
for the door. She gave me a glance with a suggestion of
a smile, and followed him out. The sound came from the
hall of the elevator door opening and closing.

I had no kick coming. The ten thousand orchids in the
three plant rooms up on the roof of the old brownstone
were his, not mine. He did like to show them off—so
would you if they were yours—but that wasn't why he
had intervened. He had some letters to dictate, and he
thought that if I took her up to look at the orchids
there was no telling when we would come back down.
Years ago he decided, on insufficient evidence, that I
forget about time when I am with an attractive young
woman, and once he has decided something that settles
it.

The phone rang. I got it at my desk and told it, "Nero
Wolfe's office, Archie Goodwin speaking." It was a man
over in Jersey who makes sausage to Wolfe's specifica-
tions, wanting to know if we were ready for a shipment,
and I switched it to Fritz in the kitchen. Thinking there
was no better way for a licensed detective to fill idle
time than by snooping, I picked up the mink coat for an
inspection. When I saw that the label said Bergmann I
decided that inspection would be superfluous and put it
back on the chair. I picked up the gun that she wasn't

going to shoot her husband with. It was a Drexel .32, nice and clean, and the cylinder was full of cartridges, nothing for a lady with no permit to be toting around town. I inspected her check, East Side Bank and Trust Company, signed Lucy Hazen, and went and put it in the safe. After glancing at my watch, I turned on the radio for the noon news, and stood and stretched while I listened to it. Algeria was boiling. A building contractor on Staten Island denied that he had had favors from a politician. Fidel Castro was telling the Cuban people that the people who ran the United States government were a bunch of bums (my translation). Then:

"The body of a man named Barry Hazen was found this morning in an alley between two buildings on Norton Street in the lower West Side of Manhattan. He had been shot in the back and had been dead for some hours. No further details are available at present. Mr. Hazen was a well-known public-relations counselor. The Democratic leaders in Congress have apparently decided to center their fire—"

I turned it off.

Chapter 2

I went and picked up the gun and smelled it, the barrel tip and the sides. That was silly but natural. When you would like to know if a gun has been fired recently you smell it automatically, but it doesn't mean a thing unless it has just been fired, say within thirty minutes, and there has been no opportunity to clean it. I stood with it in my hand, looking at it, and then put it in a drawer of my desk. Her bag was there on the red leather chair, and I opened it and removed the contents. There were all the items you would expect a woman who wore Bergmann mink to have with her, but nothing more. I got the gun from the drawer, removed the cartridges, and examined them with a glass, to see if one of them, or maybe two, was brighter and newer than the others. They all looked alike. As I was returning the gun to the drawer the sound came from the elevator descending, its thud at the bottom, and the door opening. They entered, Mrs. Hazen in front, and she crossed to the red leather chair, picked up her bag, turned to Wolfe's desk, and then turned to me.

"Where's the gun?" she asked. "I'm taking it."

"There has been a development, Mrs. Hazen." I was facing her at arm's length. "I turned on the radio for the news, and he said that—I'll repeat it verbatim. He said, 'The body of a man named Barry Hazen was found this morning in an alley between two buildings on Norton Street in lower Manhattan. He had been shot in the back and had been dead for some hours. No further details are available at present. Mr. Hazen was a public-relations counselor.' That's what he said."

She was gawking at me. "You're m-m-m-m—" She started over. "You're making it up."

"No. That's what he said. Your husband has been shot dead."

The bag slipped from her hand to the floor and her face went white and stiff. I had seen people turn pale before, but I had never seen blood leave skin so thoroughly and so fast. She backed up an unsteady step, and I took her arm and eased her into the chair. Wolfe, who had stopped in the center of the room, snapped at me, "Get something. Brandy."

I moved, but she said, "Not for me. He said that?"

"Yes."

"He's dead. He's *dead?*"

"Yes."

She rammed her fists against her temples and pounded them. Wolfe said, "I'll be in the kitchen," and turned to go. To him a woman overwhelmed, no matter by what, is merely a woman having a fit, and it's too much for him. But I said, "Hold it, she'll be all right in a minute," and he came and looked down at her, let out a growl, went to his chair, and sat.

"I want to phone somebody," she said. "I have to *know*. Who can I phone?" Her fists were in her lap.

"A shot of brandy or whisky wouldn't hurt," I told her.

"I don't want anything. Who can I phone?"

"Nobody." Wolfe was curt. "Not just now."

Her head jerked to him. "Why not?"

"Because he must first consider whether *I* should phone—phone the police to report what you have told me. I promised to. Archie. Where's the gun?"

"In my desk drawer."

"Has it been fired recently?"

"No telling. If so it's been cleaned. It's fully loaded and the cartridges all look alike."

"Did she shoot him?"

That was routine; he merely wanted my opinion as a qualified expert on women. His over-all estimate of me and my relations with females is full of contradictions, but that doesn't bother him. "For a quick guess," I said, "no. To make it final I would need facts."

"So would I. Did you shoot your husband, Mrs. Hazen?"

She shook her head.

"I prefer to hear it if you can speak. Did you shoot him?"

"No." She had to push it out.

"Since my promise was to you, you may of course release me from it. Do you wish me to phone the police?"

"Not now." The blood was beginning to creep back into her skin. "You don't have to now. You won't ever have to. He's dead, and I didn't kill him." She rose to her feet, not very steady, but not staggering. "That's all over now."

"Sit down." It was a command. "It's not so simple. When the police ask you where you were this morning from eleven o'clock on what will you say? Confound it, quit propping yourself on my desk and sit down! That's better. What will you say?"

"Why . . ." She was on the edge of the chair. "Will they ask me that?"

"Certainly. Unless they already have the murderer and the evidence beyond all question, and that's too much to hope for. You will have to account for every minute since you last saw your husband. Did you come here in a cab?"

"Yes."

"Then you'll say so. You'll have to. And when they ask why you came to see me what will you say?"

She shook her head. She looked at me and back at him. "Oh," she said. "You'll have to tell me what to say."

He nodded. "I expected that." His head turned. "Archie. What grounds have you for your guess?"

I was back in my chair. "Partly personal," I told him, "and partly professional. Personal, my general impression of her, and specifically her smile when I let her in. Professional, two points. First, if she shot him last night after making an appointment with you and then came here with that jabber, she is either completely loony or the trickiest specimen I have ever laid eyes on, and I'll buy neither one. Second, and this is really it, her face when she realized he was dead. She might fake a faint or the staggers or even some fancy hysterics, but no woman alive could make her blood go like that. I said I would need facts to make it final, but I should have said I would need facts, and good ones, to make me guess again."

Wolfe grunted and turned to her with a scowl. "Granting that Mr. Goodwin's grounds are valid, what then? When the police learn that the widow of a man murdered last night came to see me this morning they will harass me beyond tolerance. I owe you nothing. You are not my client. You have paid me a hundred dollars for half an hour of my time, now stretched to more than an hour, and released me from my promise, so that incident is closed. You asked me to tell you what to say when they ask you what you came here for, but they will also ask me. What if you fail to follow my advice and my account differs from yours? Why should I take that risk? I can see no alternative— What are you doing now?"

She had opened her bag and was taking out the check-fold and pen. "I'm going to write a check," she said. "Then I'll be your client. What shall I . . . how much?"

He nodded. "I expected that too. It won't do. I am not a blackmailer. I take pay for services, not for forbearance, and you may not need my services. If you do, we'll see. Will you answer some questions?"

"Of course. But I've taken more than my half an hour, and I owe you—"

"No. If you didn't shoot your husband we have both been snared by circumstance. First, instead of a question, a statement: you can't take the gun. The gun stays here. Now. When and where did—"

"But I'm going to put it back where I got it!"

"No. I accept Mr. Goodwin's guess as a hypothesis, but I can't let you take the gun. When and where did you last see your husband?"

"Last night. At home. We had people for dinner."

"Details. How many people? Their names."

"They were clients of Barry's, important clients—all but one. Mrs. Victor Oliver. Anne Talbot, Mrs. Henry Lewis Talbot. Jules Khoury. Ambrose Perdis. Ted—Theodore Weed—he's not a client, he works for Barry. Seven, counting Barry and me."

"When did the guests leave?"

"I don't know exactly. Barry had told me he was going to discuss something with them, and I wouldn't be needed, and after the coffee I left. That's when I last saw him, there with them. I went upstairs to my bedroom."

"Did you hear him when he went up to bed?"

"No. There's a spare bedroom between his room and mine. And I was played out. I told you, I had the first good night's sleep I have had for a month."

"You didn't see him this morning?"

"No. He wasn't there. He rises early. The maid who—oh. Oh!"

"What?"

"Nothing—nothing that matters to you. I am not liking myself, Mr. Wolfe. I said he rises early, but now I can say he rose early, and I wanted to sing it. I did! No one is good enough to have a right to be glad that someone has died. The Lord knows I'm not. What if I never loved him? What if I married him because—"

Wolfe cut her off. "If you please. You'll have plenty of time for that. About the maid?"

She swallowed with her lips pressed tight. "I'm sorry. The maid who sleeps in and gets breakfast said he hadn't come down, and she had gone up and the door of his room was open and his bed hadn't been slept in. He had done that before, not very often, once or twice a month."

"Without telling you where he was going or, afterwards, where he had been?"

"Yes."

"Do you know or can you guess where he went last night, or with whom, or to whom?"

"No. I have no idea."

"I am still assuming that you didn't kill him, but how vulnerable are you? Were you continually in your house—it is a house, not an apartment?"

"Yes."

"Were you in it continually from the time you went to your bedroom last night until you left this morning?"

"Yes."

"Would the maid have heard you if you had gone out during the night? Sneaked out, and later in again?"

"I don't think so. Her room is in the basement."

Wolfe nodded. "You *are* vulnerable. What time did you leave this morning?"

"At five minutes past eleven. I wanted to be sure to get here on time."

"When did you take the gun from the drawer in your husband's room?"

"Just before I left. I didn't decide to bring it until the last minute."

"How many people know that you despised your husband?"

She gazed at him, not blinking, no reply.

"'Despise' is your word, Mrs. Hazen. It is not adequate. No one kills a man, or wants to, merely because she despises him. But I'm not going into that; it could take all day. How many people know that you despised him?"

"I don't think anyone does." It was barely audible, and I have good ears. "I have never told anyone, not even my best friend. She may have suspected, I suppose she did."

"Pfui." Wolfe flipped a hand. "Your maid knows, for one, if she's not a dolt. She is of course being questioned at this moment. Was your husband wealthy?"

"I don't know. He had a large income, he must have, he was free with money. He owned the house."

"Any children?"

"No."

"You will inherit?"

Her eyes flashed. "Mr. Wolfe, this is ridiculous! I don't *want* anything from him!"

"I am merely examining your position. You will inherit?"

"Yes. He told me I would."

"Didn't he know you despised him?"

"He was incapable of believing that anyone could despise him. I suppose he was a psychopath. I looked up psychopathy in the dictionary."

"No doubt that was a help." He looked up at the wall clock. "I presume you will now go home. Since you must tell the police that you were here you might as well say that you learned of your husband's death from my radio; it will save you the bother of feigning surprise and shock." He eyed her. "I said you would be in a pickle, and you are. When I asked what you wanted of me, I shall say that you consulted me in confidence and I will reveal nothing of your conversation. It will be a little ticklish, but until and unless you are arrested on a charge of murder the pressure will not be intolerable. So you may tell them as much about your visit here, or as little, as you please."

She opened her bag. "I'm going to write a check. You must take it. You *must!*"

"No. You may not be in jeopardy. They may get the murderer today or tomorrow. If they do I may send you a bill for the extra hour; it will depend on my mood. If they don't, and you wish to engage my services, and Mr. Goodwin's guess has not been discredited, we'll see." He pushed his chair back and stood up.

She rose to her feet, steady this time, and I went and held her coat for her.

Chapter 3

When I returned to the office after letting her out, Wolfe had straightened up in his chair to lean forward, and, with his head cocked, was sniffing the air. For a second I thought he was pretending that our ex-client had polluted the atmosphere with perfume, but then I realized that he was merely trying to catch an odor from the kitchen, where Fritz was baking scallops in shells—or probably, since I could catch the odor without sniffing, he was deciding whether Fritz had used only shallots in the sauce or had added an onion. By the time I got to my chair he had settled it; anyway, he turned to me.

"I do not intend," he stated, "to serve the convenience of a murderer. What about her face? I was at one side."

"One will get you fifty," I said. "You heard her stutter that I was m-m-making it up. Then when I said no, he had been shot dead and it hit her as a fact, she went white, all white, in three seconds. Maybe she can wiggle her ears, but she can't do that. No one can."

"Very well. Call Mr. Cohen and get details."

"Anything in particular?"

"Whatever he has, but I want to know if the weapon has been found, or a bullet."

"He would appreciate a major scoop, such as that the widow of the deceased visited the office of Nero Wolfe this morning. Why not, since she's going to report it?"

"Very well."

I got at the phone and dialed the number of the *Gazette*, and soon had Lon Cohen. When I tossed him the bone about Mrs. Hazen coming to see Wolfe, naturally he wanted the whole skeleton, not to mention meat, but I told him that would be all for now and how about some reciprocity? He obliged, and gave me the crop, and I thanked him and hung up and turned to Wolfe.

"The body was found by a truck driver at ten-eighteen a.m. It was stiff, so he must have been dead at least five hours and probably more. He was fully dressed, including an overcoat, and his hat was there on the ground. The usual items in his pockets, including a couple of dollars in change, except that there were no keys, and no wallet and no watch. Of course they could have been taken by someone who found him earlier and forgot to mention it. His name was on letters in his pocket, so the wallet wasn't taken to delay identification. Shot once, in the back, and a rib stopped the bullet and they have it. A thirty-two. Weapon not found. If the police have any leads or notions they're saving them, but of course it was found less than three hours ago." I glanced at my wrist. "Two hours and forty-nine minutes. Lon says he would have paid me five grand if I had kept Mrs. Hazen here until he could send a man to take her picture and ask her who shot her husband, and I told him I'll bear that in mind next time."

"They have the bullet?"

"Right."

"When will a policeman come?"

"It will probably be Cramer in person. You know how he'll react when he learns she was here. Say two hours, possibly sooner."

"Will she report what she told me?"

"No."

A corner of his mouth twitched. "That's why I put up with you; you could have answered with fifty words and you did it with one."

"I've often wondered. Now tell me why I put up with you."

"That's beyond conjecture. I want a bullet that has been fired from that gun, and we shouldn't wait until after lunch. You have twenty minutes. If your guess about Mrs. Hazen is correct, that gun is not evidence, unless the murderer stole into that house afterwards, went to Mr. Hazen's room and returned the gun to the drawer, and slipped out again. If it *is* evidence you'll be tampering with it. Shall I do it?"

"No. You might shoot a toe off." I got the gun from the drawer, removed one of the cartridges, unlocked and opened the drawer where we keep the Marleys for which we have permits, and got a .32 cartridge from the box. I put that cartridge in the Drexel where I had made room for it, turned the cylinder so it would be in firing position, went to the hall and downstairs to the storage room in the basement, switched the light on, and crossed to where a discarded mattress was doubled up on a table. I had used it for this operation before. I cocked the revolver, held it three inches from the mattress, and pulled the trigger.

You would suppose that all .32 cartridges would send a bullet the same distance into a mattress, the same mattress, but they don't. It took me a quarter of an hour to find it, and by the time I got back upstairs Wolfe was at table in the dining room, which is across the hall from the office. Before I joined him I removed the shell, returned the Drexel's own cartridge to its place, and put the gun in the safe and the bullet in an envelope in my desk drawer.

* * *

We were back in the office, Wolfe dictating and me taking, when company came. I had been right on both counts: it was Inspector Cramer in person, and it was 2:55 when the doorbell rang and I went to the hall for a look through the one-way glass panel in the front door, and there he was on the stoop, no sign of a sag in the heavy broad shoulders, the round red face framed by his turned-up overcoat collar and the brim of his gray felt which should have been retired long ago. Since he had no appointment it would have been proper to open the door the two inches allowed by the chain bolt and greet him through the crack, but that always annoyed him, and if it turned out that I had tampered with evidence it wouldn't hurt to show him now that I had my good points. So I pulled the door wide open. Without even a nod, let alone a civil greeting, he crossed the sill, tramped down the hall into the office and on to Wolfe's desk, and demanded, "What time did Mrs. Barry Hazen get here this morning?"

Wolfe tilted his head back to look up at him and inquired, "Is that snow on your hat?"

Having entered and detoured around him, I too looked at the hat. There was nothing whatever on it except signs of age, and outdoors the sun was shining. It would fluster any man to have it put to him that one removes one's hat when one enters a house, but Cramer is ready for anything when he faces Wolfe. It didn't faze him. He merely barked, "I asked you a question!"

"Half past eleven," Wolfe said.

"When did she leave?"

"Shortly before one o'clock."

Cramer took his overcoat off, ignored my offer to take it, put it on the arm of the red leather chair, and sat. "An hour and a half," he said, not barking but a little hoarse. He is always a little hoarse when he is dealing with Wolfe. "What did she have to say?" He hadn't touched the hat.

Wolfe swiveled and leaned back. "Mr. Cramer. I know that Mrs. Hazen's husband has been shot and killed. She was with me when the news came on my radio. I know that when I have been consulted by a person who is in any way connected with a death by violence you automatically assume that I have knowledge of evidence that would be useful in your investigation. Sometimes your assumption is valid; sometimes it isn't. This time it isn't; that is my considered opinion. Mrs. Hazen consulted me in confidence. If at any time I have reason to think that by refusing to disclose what she told me I am obstructing justice, I'll communicate with you at once."

Cramer got a cigar from a pocket, rolled it between his palms, stuck it in his mouth, and clamped his teeth on it. He does that instead of counting ten, when he knows that the words that are on his tongue would make things worse instead of better. He took the cigar from his mouth. "Some day," he said, "you're going to fall off and get hurt, and this could be it. If and when you find it gets too hot to hang onto it any longer, and you turn loose, and you have obstructed justice by not telling me now, I'll get your hide. Nothing and no one will stop me. I'm asking you to tell me what Mrs. Barry Hazen said when she came to see you nine hours after her husband was murdered."

Wolfe shook his head. "I decline to tell you because I believe, as matters stand now, that it is not pertinent to your inquiry. Should I have occasion to change my mind—and by the way, I can offer you an opportunity to change it for me. Archie, where's that bullet?"

I got the envelope from my drawer, took the bullet out, and handed it to him. Cramer's sharp gray eyes were on me and followed the bullet back to Wolfe. Wolfe took it in his fingers, barely glanced at it, handed it back to me, and said, "Give it to Mr. Cramer." As I did so he turned to Cramer. "This will be pointless if you have found the weapon that was used to shoot Mr. Hazen. Have you?"

"No."

"It will also be pointless if you have not found the bullet that killed him. Have you?"

"Yes."

"Then I suggest that you have your laboratory compare that bullet with it. If you find that they were shot by the same gun let me know at once and I'll have some information for you. I would want to see the laboratory report, certified."

"You would." Cramer's eyes were slits and his lips tightened. "Where did you get this bullet?"

"I'll tell you, or I won't, when I get your report."

"By God." Cramer was hoarser. "This *is* pertinent. This is evidence. I'll take you down, both of you—"

"Nonsense. Evidence of what? I don't know and neither do you. If it wasn't fired by the gun that killed Mr. Hazen it is evidence of nothing, and I am not obliged to account for it until I know. I'm not indulging in a prank, Mr. Cramer. There is a possibility that the bullets will match, and if so it will indeed be evidence. Let me know."

Cramer opened his mouth to say something, vetoed it, got to his feet, put the bullet in his pocket, threw the cigar at my wastebasket and missed, picked up his coat and put it on, ignoring my offer to help, and marched out. I went to the hall to see that when the door shut he was on the outside. When I returned to the office Wolfe growled. "Confound these interruptions. We have forty minutes. Where were we on that letter to Mr. Hewitt?" I sat, got my notebook, and told him.

At four o'clock, when he left to go up to the plant rooms for his two-hour afternoon session with the orchids, I got busy at the typewriter. On various occasions I have had a little trouble turning out perfect letters to orchid collectors and providers of food specialties when my mind had other interests and concerns, and that day was one of the worst. Cramer had left at 3:20. He would lose no time getting the bullet to the laboratory; they probably had it by 3:50, or four o'clock at the latest. Examining two bullets with a comparison microscope is a simple chore; ten minutes is ample to decide if they were fired by the same gun. 4:10. Allow a quarter of an hour for writing the report, which wouldn't have to be in shape for a judge and jury. 4:25. Cramer would have a man there waiting for it. He should phone by 4:30, or ring the doorbell by 4:45. He didn't.

By 5:15 I had to keep my jaw set to hit the right keys. If you think I was keyed up more than the circumstances warranted, look it over. If the bullets matched I was a sap. It was a million to one that the murderer hadn't sneaked into the house to put the gun back in the drawer in Hazen's room; why would he? Murderers often do crazy things, but not that crazy. Therefore Mrs. Hazen had lied, and she had either killed him or knew who did, and I was a beetlehead. I had to do three of the letters twice.

By six o'clock, when Wolfe came down from the plant rooms, I had begun to relax. He went to his desk and started on the letters I had put there, which he always reads with care. After he had finished a couple and signed them I remarked, "Of course Cramer wouldn't bother to phone if the bullets didn't match."

He grunted.

"And the laboratory got it more than two hours ago, so we might as well—"

The doorbell rang, and the bottom of my spine curled. Cramer had waited until six o'clock, when he knew Wolfe would be available. I went to the hall and switched the stoop light on, and my spine went back to normal. It was a stranger, a man about my age, maybe a little younger, with no hat and a mop of brown hair shuffled by the wind. I had never been so delighted to see a stranger, but had it under control by the time I got to the door and opened it and said, "Yes, sir?"

"I want to see Nero Wolfe. My name's Weed, Theodore Weed."

I should have had him wait there while I went and told Wolfe, that was the routine, but I was so glad to see him that I invited him in and helped him off with his coat. Then I went to the office and announced, "Theodore Weed to see you. One of the dinner guests. The one who—"

"What does he want?"

He knew damn well I hadn't had time to ask what he wanted. I said, "You."

"No. I've been pestered enough on a matter in which I have no interest. Tell him so and don't—"

Weed was there. He crossed to the red leather chair, plumped into it as if he owned it, and said, "I'm not going to pester you. I'm going to hire you."

Wolfe glared at me. I had let a man in without consulting him; he would have something to say about that when we were alone. Weed was going on. "I know you come high, but I pay my bills. Do you want a retainer?"

Wolfe had transferred the glare to him. "No. You not only intrude, you presume. Archie, show him the door."

"Now wait a minute. I'm not very . . ." He let it hang and started to work his jaw. He had plenty of jaw, a little bony but not out of proportion. He got it under control. "All right, I started wrong. I'll try again. Mrs. Barry Hazen came to see you this morning and left a gun with you. Where is it?"

"Intrusion and presumption," Wolfe said, "and now effrontery. I must insist—"

"Damn it, I know she did! She told me so! She was here when she heard about it, that they had found his body! And she wanted to hire you, she wanted to give you a check, and you wouldn't take it!" He paused to control his jaw. "So I want to hire you, and I'll pay your bill. I just left the District Attorney's office and she's still there. They wouldn't let me see her, but she's there and they're going to charge her with murder. I can't see why it's presumption for me to want to hire you— you're in the detective business and my money is as good as anybody's. All right, I got ahead of myself asking you about the gun, but when I'm your client there's no reason why you shouldn't tell me where it is." He stuck a hand in his pocket and brought out a wad of bills, not a thick one, and unfolded it.

I was trying to decide. Either he thought that Lucy Hazen had killed her husband, and was being chival-

rous, or he didn't think she had but was selling Wolfe
the idea that he did think so. Whichever it was, he was
willing to spend money on it, for he got up from his chair
to put the bills on Wolfe's desk.

As Wolfe started to speak the phone rang, and I
turned and got it. It was Lucy Hazen. She asked for
Wolfe, and I told her to hold it and turned to him. "The
woman that brought the sausage this morning wants to
know if it will do. If you want to ask Fritz you can talk
on the kitchen extension."

He got up and went, and I held on. In a moment
his voice was in my ear. "This is Nero Wolfe. Mrs.
Hazen?"

"Yes. You said this morning that if I need your services you would see." Her voice was shaky. "I do need
them. I'm going to be arrested, and I—"

"Where are you?"

"At the District Attorney's. I don't know any—"

"Say only what you must say on the telephone."

"I'm in a booth with the door closed."

"Pfui. It is probably not only heard but also recorded.
Say only what you must."

"All right." A little pause. "He said I could phone a
lawyer, and I don't know any except my husband's, and
I don't want him. Will you get one for me?"

"I'll send one to you. After speaking with him you can
decide whether to engage him."

"I will. Of course. But I want to engage you too. You
said you would if I needed you."

"I said I would see." A pause, longer than hers. If he
committed himself he would have to work, and he
would rather eat than work. "Very well." He growled
it. "I am engaged. One question: have you disclosed any
of your conversation with me? Yes or no."

"No."

"Satisfactory. One instruction: if you have an intention to reject property left you by your husband you
will neither declare it nor indicate it. You're going to
have some bills to pay."

"But I don't want anything from him! I told you—"

"We're on the phone. The lawyer will join me in that instruction. His name is Nathaniel Parker. Archie, get Mr. Parker. I'll talk from here."

Chapter 4

I pushed the button down, released it, dialed Parker's home number, got him, buzzed the kitchen, and Wolfe got on. He gave Parker the necessary facts, and not much more—nothing of what Mrs. Hazen had told us that morning, nothing about the gun. He did say that I had formed the conclusion that she had not shot her husband, and that he had accepted it. Parker was to arrange for bail if she was bailable, if they held her on the big charge he was to get what he could at the DA's office. I waited to hang up until Wolfe was at the office door. He went to his desk, sat, leveled his eyes at Theodore Weed, and spoke.

"Now sir. That was timely. It was Mrs. Hazen on the phone. I have sent—"

"Where is she?"

"At the District Attorney's office. She thinks she is going to be held. I have sent a lawyer to her, and I have agreed to act in her behalf. You were assuming that I declined her offer of a check because I thought she was guilty of murder or at least was implicated, but you were wrong. She is now my client." He wiggled a finger at the bills on the desk. "Your money. Take it."

Weed's jaw was hanging, his lips parted. He found words. "But you—I don't see why you—I'm—"

"You're not obliged to see and I'm not obliged to explain. Why do you think Mrs. Hazen killed her husband? Was it merely surmise?"

"I don't—I don't think she killed him. She didn't!"

"If I had taken your money what were you going to ask me to do?"

"I don't know exactly. I was going . . . to consult you. I wanted to know what you did with the gun. Have the police got it?"

Wolfe shook his head. "I am acting for her now, Mr. Weed. You are the enemy—one of them. What if you killed Mr. Hazen, or know who did, and would like to see it imputed to her, and suspecting, for whatever reason, that she left a gun with me this morning, you want to find out? What if you are indeed the enemy?"

Weed sat and stared at him. His jaw started to work again and he stopped it. "Look here," he said. "I want to know something. I know your reputation, I know about you. Is that straight, Mrs. Hazen phoned you just now and you're working for her?"

"It is."

"All right, then this is straight too." He stuck an arm out. "You can cut off this arm if it will help her any. And the other one. If that's corny, okay, that's where I stand."

Wolfe regarded him with narrowed eyes. So did I. He looked as if he meant it, but even if he did, that didn't make him our pal. If he would give an arm to help her, and if he had known how she felt about her husband, he might have taken steps to get rid of him for her, which wouldn't cost him even a finger if he was lucky.

Wolfe made a tent with his fingers, the tips together, his elbows on the chair arms. "Indeed," he said. "I have no use for your arm, but some information might be helpful. When did you last see Mr. Hazen?"

"I want to know where that gun is. I know she left it here, she told me so."

"When did she tell you?"

"This afternoon. I was there when she came home."

"What else did she tell you?"

"Not much—there wasn't time. We were interrupted. I knew Hazen had a gun in a drawer in his room, and I had looked to see if it was there and it wasn't, and I asked her if she knew where it was. Have the police got it?"

"No. I'll indulge you further, Mr. Weed. The bullet

that killed Mr. Hazen wasn't fired by that gun. If you already knew that it's no news for you; if you didn't, it should relieve—"

"How do you know it wasn't?"

"Enough for you that I do. Now you indulge me. When did you last see Mr. Hazen?"

"This morning. At the morgue. I went there to identify him, by request. Alive, I saw him last at his house, last night."

"At what hour?"

"Around half past nine. Five or ten minutes either way. The police wanted it more exact, but that's as close as I can come."

"The circumstances?"

"There were people there for dinner. Do you want their names?"

"Yes."

"They were clients of Hazen's. Mrs. Victor Oliver, a widow. Mrs. Henry Lewis Talbot, the wife of the banker. Ambrose Perdis, the shipping tycoon. Jules Khoury, the inventor. And Mr. and Mrs. Hazen and me. Seven. After dinner Hazen told Lucy—his wife—that we were going to discuss a business matter and she left. I left soon after that, and that was the last I saw him alive, there with them."

"How did you spend the next six hours?"

"I walked to the Overseas Press Club—it's a short walk—and was there until around midnight, and then I went home and went to bed. And stayed in bed."

"You were associated with Mr. Hazen in his business?"

"I was in his employ."

"In what capacity?"

"Mostly I write stuff. Handouts, plugs, the usual junk. Also I was supposed to use my contacts. I was a newspaperman when Hazen hired me a little more than a year ago."

"If they were going to discuss a business matter why did you leave?"

"I wasn't needed. Or wanted."

"Then why were you there at all?"

Weed put his hands on the chair arms, levered his fanny up, settled farther back, and took a breath. He rubbed his chair arms with his palms. "You don't think Lucy killed him," he said. "Or you wouldn't be working for her. But even if she didn't she's in one hell of a jam. If you're half as good as you're supposed to be . . . I don't know. Maybe I ought to give you a different answer than the one I gave the District Attorney when he asked why I was there. The right answer. Even if it makes you think *I* killed him. I didn't."

"If you did, Mr. Weed, you're doomed in any case, no matter what answers you give."

"Okay, then here's why I was there. Exclusive for you. Hazen liked to have me in the same room with his wife because he knew how I felt about her. God only knows how he knew, I certainly tried not to show it and I thought I did pretty well, and I'm sure she doesn't know, but he did. He was a remarkable man. He had a sixth sense about people, and maybe a seventh and an eighth, but he also had blind spots. He actually didn't know how his wife felt about him, or if he did he was even more remarkable than I thought."

"Did you know?"

"Of course."

"She told you?"

"My God, no. I doubt if she even told her best friend. Don't think that the way I feel about her made me imagine it. I saw her when he touched her, how she tried to cover up. So that's why I was invited to dinner last night. I don't think he expected or hoped to see me squirm, he didn't have to, he knew how I felt. Of course he was a sadist, but he was a damned subtle one. I was onto him, in a way, after I had been with him a couple of months, but I didn't leave because I . . . I had met her."

"And your feeling for her was returned?"

"Certainly not. I was just a guy that worked for her husband."

"Rather a forlorn situation for you."

"Yeah. That's the right word, forlorn. I told you

because you asked why I was there, and I've got a little idea how you work, and you're working for her. Another thing you might want to know, I think there was something screwy about his business. I know the public-relations game is mostly just a high-grade racket, but even so. Take the four people who were there last night. Why did Mrs. Victor Oliver, the sixty-year-old widow of a millionaire broker, pay him two thousand dollars a month? She needs public relations like I need a hole in the head. The same for Mrs. Talbot—twenty-five hundred a month. Maybe her husband, the banker, could use a P.R. expert, granted that there is one, but why her? Jules Khoury's amounts vary, sometimes a couple of thousand, sometimes more. Possibly an inventor likes to stand in well with the public, though I don't see why, and during the time I've been there Khoury has got damn little for his money. Ambrose Perdis is the screwiest of all. For his business, his shipping corporations, he uses one of the big P.R. operators, the Codray Associates, but personally he has paid Hazen more than forty thousand dollars this past year. I'm not supposed to know all this. I got curious and I got at the records one day."

Wolfe grunted. "A man who hires another man to forge distinction for him deserves as little as he gets. Are you suggesting that Mr. Hazen extorted those sums?"

"I don't know, but he didn't earn them. I admit that very few P.R. operators do earn what they get. If any."

"Did he have any clients other than those four?"

"Sure, about a dozen. Fifteen altogether, as of yesterday. His total take was over a quarter of a million a year."

Wolfe looked up at the clock. "It will be my dinner time in five minutes. If my assumption that Mrs. Hazen didn't kill her husband is correct, and if you didn't, who did?"

That question gets a helpful answer about once in a hundred times. It was obvious that Weed had given it no brain room at all before he rang our doorbell, because he had either thought that Lucy had done it or known that he had, so he had no guesses ready. He was more than willing; the idea appealed to him; but he had to start from scratch, and five minutes wasn't enough. He thought that Wolfe should forget about dinner, though he didn't say so, which was just as well. He said he would return after dinner, but Wolfe said no, if he would leave his phone number he would hear from us. He would have left the bills there on Wolfe's desk if I hadn't handed them to him.

By the time we had finished dinner and were back in the office, with coffee, I had no personal worry. If the bullets had matched we would have heard from Cramer by then. Wolfe got at the letters to sign, still on his desk, and as he finished the last one and I took it he spoke. "Did Mr. Weed shoot him?"

I shook my head. "No comment. I'd have to flip a coin. He cleared up one point, anyway, about her. You said that no one wants to kill a man merely because she despises him. Sure. So what was eating her? Weed. He says she doesn't know how he feels about her and the feeling is not returned. Nuts. Either he lies or he's simple. Of the ten thousand women I have fallen in love with, every single one of them knew it before I did. As for Weed shooting him, I am split. It would be tough to send her a bill for nailing him, but if he didn't you've got a job. Where do you start? Apparently Hazen was the kind of specimen—"

The doorbell rang. Could Cramer possibly have held off so long? No. It would be Weed, to help some more. No. It was a more familiar figure, a tall thin middle-aged man in a dark gray overcoat that had been cut to give him more shoulder, but not overdoing it. Nathaniel Parker had his clothes made by Stover. When I opened the door and greeted and admitted him he headed for the office, keeping his coat on and his homburg in his hand, and I followed.

He was one of the eight men, not counting me, that Wolfe shook hands with. He declined Wolfe's invitation to be seated, saying that he was an hour and a half late for a dinner appointment. "I stopped in instead of phoning," he said, "because I had to deliver this." He took a key from his pocket and handed it to me. "That's the key to Mrs. Hazen's house. Also this." From his inside pocket he took a folded paper. "That's authority from her to enter and get something. What you're to get, if you want to, is an iron box—she said iron but I suppose it's tin or steel—that is under the bottom drawer of the chest in Hazen's bedroom. You remove the drawer and pry up the board that it slides in on, and the box is underneath. She doesn't know what's in it. One day about a year ago Hazen lifted the board and showed her the box, and told her that if he died she was to get the box, have it opened by a locksmith, and burn the contents without looking at them. I thought you might want to have a look, and she is willing. You'll be acting for her, through her attorney."

Wolfe grunted. "I'll use my discretion."

"I know you will. If you don't want to tell me what was in it you'll say it was empty. I'd like to be present when it's opened, but I have an appointment. As for her, what did she tell you this morning?"

"Ask her."

"I did. She wouldn't tell me. She said she would disclose it only if you told her to. If she is charged with homicide I'll want to know that or I'll step out. She has been there more than five hours, and they'll probably keep her another five. If she is held as a material witness I can do nothing about bail until morning. I have an appointment with Hazen's lawyer at nine-thirty. He has the will. Anything else now?"

Wolfe said no, and he went. I escorted him out, returned to the office, and asked, "Any special instructions?"

"No. Will the police be there?"

"I shouldn't think so. It's only where he lived, he wasn't shot there. Do I wear gloves?"

"No. You have her authority."

Ever since a difficulty I got into some years ago I

have made it a practice to have a gun along when I am on an errand that may interfere with a murderer's program. I took off my jacket, got a shoulder holster and a Marley, which I loaded, from the drawer, put them where they belonged, put the jacket back on, checked that Lucy's key was in a pocket and her authority in another one, and went to the hall for my coat and hat.

Chapter 5

I stood across the street from the Hazen house, on 37th Street between Park and Lexington, for a look. It was brick, painted gray with green trim, four stories, narrower than Wolfe's brownstone, with the entrance three steps down from the sidewalk. I noted those details just for the record, but they weren't important. What was important was that there was a tiny sliver of light at the lower part of the right edge of one of the three windows on the third floor—a sliver that you might leave if you weren't quite thorough enough when you arranged a drape.

I didn't know where Hazen's room was; that could be it. It could be a Homicide man looking things over, but it wasn't probable; they had had ten hours. It could be the maid who slept in, but why, at 9:30 at night? Her room certainly wasn't third floor front. Whoever it was and whatever he was doing, I decided not to interrupt him by ringing. I crossed over, descended the three steps, used the key, opened the door with care, entered, closed it with more care, and stood and listened while my eyes adjusted to the dark. For half a minute there was no sound from any direction; then there was something like a bump from up above, followed by a voice, male, very faint. Unless he was talking to himself there was more than one. Thinking there might be occasion for activity, I took off my overcoat and put it on the floor, and my hat, and then tiptoed along the hall, feeling my way, found the stairs, and started up.

Halfway up I stopped. Had there been another voice, a soprano? There had. There was. Then the baritone again. I went on up, with more care now and slower, keeping to the end of the steps next the wall. In the hall on the second floor there was a little light coming from above, enough to catch outlines. Up the second flight I went even slower, since each step might bring me within range. The voices had stopped, but there were tapping sounds. On the fourth step I could get my eyes to the level of the floor by stretching. The hall was the same as the floor below, and the light was coming from a half-open door at its front end. All I could see inside was a chair and part of a bed and drapes over a window, and the back of a woman's head over the back of the chair, silvery hair under a black pancake hat.

I might have stayed put until the voices came again, and now I could get words, but a staircase is not a good tactical position, the light was on them, not me, and at the top I would be nearly out of range through the opening. I moved. As I put my weight on the next to last step the tapping stopped and the baritone came. "There's no sense in this." I made the landing and across to the wall. The soprano came. "There certainly isn't, Mr. Khoury." I started along the wall toward the door. Another female voice came, pitched lower. "I don't think it's here. It could be in Lucy's room, that would be like him." Then another man's voice, a deeper one. "All right, we'll try it," and the door swung wide and the man was there, on the move.

I'm not proud of the next two seconds. I was alerted and he wasn't, and I think I am fairly fast. My excuse is that I was in the middle of a careful step, putting my toe down, but anyway he was at me before I was set, and he damn near toppled me. When you're thrown off balance by impact you only make it worse if you try to get purchase on your way down, so I let myself go, brought my knees up to my chin as I hit the floor, rolled to get my feet at his middle, and let him have it. He was plenty heavy, but it tore him loose and sent him bouncing off the wall. As I sprang to my feet another man was through the door and coming. I sidestepped and ducked, jerking my right back, and hooked him in the kidney. He doubled up and hugged himself, and I kept going to the corner, whirled, had the Marley in my hand, and showed it.

"Come right ahead," I said, "if you want your skull cracked."

The first man, the heavy one, was propped against the wall, panting. The smaller one was trying to straighten up. There was a woman in the doorway, the one who had been in the chair, and another one behind her.

"Also," I said, "this thing is loaded, so don't try reaching for a cigarette. Inside, everybody, and take it easy. I would prefer to get you in the shoulder or leg, but I'm not a very good shot."

The heavy man said, "Who are you?"

"Billy the Kid. Come on, into the room, and no gymnastics. Go to the far side and face the wall."

They moved. As they approached the door the women backed off, and they entered and I followed. The woman with silvery hair started to chatter at me, but I wiggled the gun and told her to go to the wall. When they were there I went over the men from behind, felt no weapons, told them to stay put, and sidestepped to the bed. There were coats and hats on it, and the women's bags. I had the men tagged; the husky one was Ambrose Perdis, the shipping magnate, whose picture I had seen here and there, and I had heard the other one called Khoury; but I needed introductions to the women. As I opened one of the bags and dumped its contents on the bed Perdis turned around and I spoke.

"Hold it. I'm giving you a break. Shall I come and slap you with the gun? Turn around."

He turned. A leather case from the bag was stuffed with credentials—driver's license, credit cards, others.

Some of them said Anne Talbot and others Mrs. Henry Lewis Talbot. That was the young woman, whose attractions, both from the front and the rear, were so obvious that they had caught my eye even though my eyes were busy. There was a leather keyfold and I snapped it open to inspect the keys, and compared one of them with the key to the house which I had in my pocket. It didn't match. I returned the items to the bag one by one and picked up the other bag and dumped it. The woman with silvery hair was Mrs. Victor Oliver. There was no key in her bag like the one I had, and nothing of interest. I examined the pockets of the coats, all four of them, and found no key.

As I stepped around the end of the bed I allowed myself a grin at a detail I had observed; they all had gloves on—not rubber ones secured for the occasion, just gloves. "Now that I know your names," I said, "it's only fair that you should know mine. Archie Goodwin. I work for a man you may have heard of, Nero Wolfe, the private detective. He has been hired by Mrs. Barry Hazen, and I have her key to the house and her written authority to enter. I need to know which one of you has a key and I'm going to find out. You may turn around, but stay where you are. You will take off your clothes and pile them on the floor, including your shoes and socks or stockings, but I think not your underwear. I'll see."

They were facing me at four paces. Anne Talbot said, "I won't. It's outrageous." She was extremely easy to look at.

"Pooh," I said. "Pretend you're at the beach or a pool. Do you want me to peel you? Don't think I wouldn't."

"We have no key," Mrs. Oliver said. She was easy to look away from, with her flabby jowl and little yellow eyes set deep. "The maid let us in. She has gone out, but when she comes back you can ask her."

"She'll deny it," Jules Khoury said. He was the baritone, a wiry swarthy specimen with no hips.

"Look," I said, "you're four to one. If you make me do it the hard way it will be rough. I'll give you two minutes to get your clothes off." I raised my wrist to see my watch without dropping my eyes. "Start with the gloves. I want them too."

"Is this necessary?" Perdis demanded. "Is it so important how we got in?"

"Yes. There were no keys in Hazen's pockets. Twenty seconds gone."

I am enough of a gentleman to turn my back or at least avert my eyes when a lady is undressing, but one of those ladies might possibly have had a gun on her leg, so I forgot my manners. It took the men twice as long as the women. I decided to let Anne Talbot keep her bra and panties; she would have had no reason to bury the key as deep as that. Mrs. Oliver's girdle was so tight she couldn't have slipped a key inside even if she had tried. Khoury had jockeys, no undershirt. Perdis had a baby blue silk altogether, to the knees. I had them turn around, and then used a foot to rake Perdis' pile across the rug, out of range of a kick.

It took longer than it should on account of the gun in my hand, and of course I not only looked for the key but for any other item that might be helpful. No soap. Khoury had a keyfold and Perdis a key ring, but no soap. It wasn't much of a letdown because I had expected it when they all shed and turned their backs. If one of them had had Hazen's key he would either have tried to ditch it or produced it and tried to explain it. Now that I was certain none of them had a cannon or a bomb I could relax a little. I told them to dress, went to the stand at the head of the bed, lifted the receiver from the phone, and was dialing a number when Perdis' voice came.

"Wait a minute! One minute!" He had a touch of accent. "I have something to say. You are calling the police?"

"No." I cradled the receiver. "Say it fast and short."

He was handicapped for man-to-man talk, with his shirt on but his pants in his hands. "You are not a policeman," he said.

"No. I told you who I am."

"He's Archie Goodwin," Anne Talbot said. "I've seen him at the Flamingo."

"You are a private detective," Perdis said.

"Right."

"Then you do things for money. We will pay you fifty thousand dollars if you will leave this house and forget that you have been here. Half of it in cash tomorrow morning and the other half later. We will give you a satisfactory guarantee, perhaps something in writing."

"How much later?"

"That's hard to say. It is delicate. We would need to be sure of your forgetting until certain difficulties have ended."

"That's pretty vague. Get your clothes on and we'll see." I picked up the phone and dialed, and he started toward me. I showed the gun, but he kept coming, saying something, and I dropped the phone and moved to meet him, and damned if he didn't swerve around me and dart for the phone. I had intended to tap him with the gun, not caring for bruised knuckles, but his swerve got him on the wrong side, so I took him from behind, with my left arm hooked under his chin and my hip at his rump, and levered him up and over. He landed on his hands and knees nine feet away. I said, "Cut out the horseplay and put your pants on," and went to the phone and dialed. After nine buzzes Wolfe's voice came. "Yes?"

"Me. Could we use fifty grand?"

A grunt. "In the box?"

"No. I haven't got it yet. I'm in Hazen's bedroom. There are four people with me, two men and two women, lined up against the wall. The four that came to dinner last night. They were in this room looking for something and hadn't found it. Perdis just off—"

"One of them has Hazen's key."

"No. I had them strip and went through their clothes. They say the maid let them in. She's not here; of course they greased her. Perdis just offered me fifty grand to go away and forget I was here. I'll split it with you. He would probably double it."

"Pfui. Are you intact?"

"Sure. I'm calling just to tell you to expect us, say in half an hour, maybe less."

Silence. He would have to work, not tomorrow, but now—and two women. Then: "I suppose I must," and he hung up.

Perdis had joined the others at the wall. As I cradled the phone he spoke. "We will double it. One hundred thousand dollars."

"Skip it." I moved to the foot of the bed. "What would I tell my wife if I had one? You heard me tell Nero Wolfe to expect us in half an hour, but you have a choice. You can leave and go your ways and try to forget you were here, and I'll phone Inspector Cramer and report this incident, omitting nothing. Or you can come and talk it over with Nero Wolfe, and he may or may not care to bother Cramer about it. You may have two minutes to consider it." I looked at my wrist.

"Listen, Mr. Goodwin," Anne Talbot said. She had her clothes on, and with or without them she was highly ornamental. "We were looking for something that belongs to us. We're not thieves. We're respectable—"

I cut her off. "Sorry, but don't waste it on me. I just run errands. It's either Nero Wolfe or the police. If you pick Nero Wolfe there will be a slight delay because I have a little chore to do in this room. You will take your things and go downstairs and on out, and get two taxis. You will get into one of the taxis and wait there in front of the house, and have the other one there for me. I'll be down soon, probably in a couple of minutes. There's one complication: if you split and one or two of you prefer to go somewhere else, I'll phone the police immediately. I would rather not, but I'd have to."

Two of them, Perdis and Mrs. Oliver, started to speak, but I shut them off and moved away from the bed. Anne Talbot went to the bed and got her coat, and Khoury went and held it for her, and then got his own. Anne Talbot said to Perdis and Mrs. Oliver, "Is there any alternative?" Perdis went and got Mrs. Oliver's coat and took it to her, and she went to the bed for her bag.

Perdis was the last one out. When he had started down the stairs I shut the door, put a chair against it, went to the chest of drawers, a big heavy piece at the left wall, and took out the bottom drawer. There was a folded blanket in it. I squatted at the opening. The board that the drawer slid on, solid, not a plywood panel, was flush and snugly fitted, no play to it. I tried to get its edge with my thumbnails; nothing doing. I got out my pocketknife, stuck the point of the blade in the crack at the center, just barely in, pried gently, and up it came. The front edge of the board was beveled. Very neat. I put my hand in, felt metal, got a finger under, and here came the box. It was steel, anything but flimsy, twelve inches by six and about two inches deep, and weighed a good four pounds, with a lock not to be opened with a nail file. I shook it and heard no movement, which didn't prove anything. With the board down, I replaced the drawer, moved the chair away from the door and opened it, and went to the head of the stairs. No sound of voices from below. If I had gone down and joined them in the hall carrying a steel box which I must have found in Hazen's room they would have made quite a party of it. I descended a flight, stood to listen half a minute, and went on down. They had turned on the light in the lower hall. My hat and coat were there on the floor. I put the Marley in the holster, put on the hat and coat, slipped the box under the coat, with my hand in my pocket holding it, turned out the light, and opened the door.

They had followed instructions to a T. Two taxis were there, and they were in the one in the rear, all four of them. After glancing in I told the driver to follow my taxi, went and got in and gave the driver the address, and we rolled.

Chapter 6

When you mount the seven steps to the stoop and enter the hall of the old brownstone on West 35th Street, the first door on your left is to what we call the front room, with the office door farther along on that side. The walls and doors of the front room and office are soundproofed. After convoying the company to the front room and telling them they wouldn't have to wait long, I returned to the hall, put my hat and coat on the rack, proceeded to the office, and put the box on Wolfe's desk pad.

"Good timing," I said. "In another hour or two they would probably have found it."

He reached to pass his fingertips along its edge. "You haven't opened it."

"No. It's a good lock. They're in the front room, all four. I gave them their pick, you or the cops, and they preferred you. There's nothing to add to what I told you on the phone. Before I open it I want to register a guess. Not that it's what Hazen had on them, that's a cinch. My guess is specifically what he had on Mrs. Oliver. She murdered her husband. Wait till you see her."

He made a face. "This will be distasteful. Bring keys."

I went to the cabinet at the far wall, opened a drawer, and made selections. Although I couldn't qualify on the witness stand as a lock expert, I know a Hotchkiss from a Euler, and I can open your suitcase with a paper clip if you'll be patient. Moving the box to my desk, I sat and started in. I had selected four types, little boxes of assortments. In three minutes I eliminated the first type, and in another three the second one. The third seemed more promising, and I was getting hot when Wolfe growled, "Get a hammer and screwdriver."

As he spoke it clicked and I had it. I raised the lid. The box was empty. I upended it for Wolfe to see. "Yeah," I said. "It sure is distasteful."

He took in air, about a bushel, and let it out again. "It's just as well. It would probably have presented us with a problem. More than one. I presume he decided it was a mistake to tell his wife of it and removed the contents. Elsewhere in the house?"

"I doubt it."

"So do I." He leaned back, closed his eyes, and pushed his lips out. In a moment he pulled them in, and then out and in, out and in. He was working. A minute passed, two minutes, three. . . . He opened his eyes and straightened up. "Lock the box and leave it on your desk. Put the keys away. Have a gun in your hand when you admit them, and go to your desk and stay there. Proceed."

I proceeded. After locking the box and returning the keys to the cabinet, I moved four of the yellow chairs up, in a row facing Wolfe's desk, got the gun out, opened the door to the front room, and invited them to enter. The gentlemen followed the ladies. I went to my desk and pronounced names, and when they were seated I sat, with the gun in my hand resting on my thigh.

Wolfe's eyes went right and then left. "This shouldn't take long," he said. "First the situation. I shall not resort to euphemism. You were being blackmailed by Mr. Hazen, either collectively—please don't interrupt. Either collectively or separately. He had other victims, but you four alone were paying him around a hundred and fifty thousand dollars a year, ostensibly for professional services, but that was merely a subterfuge. I don't know whether the police know that or not, probably not, but I do. If there was any doubt it was removed when Mr. Goodwin found you in that house surreptitiously, looking for something, and you offered him a large sum of money. So much—"

"I didn't," Mrs. Oliver blurted. "Mr. Perdis did."

"Pfui. You were there. Did you object? So much for that. I am acting for my client, Mrs. Hazen. She is being held under suspicion of killing her husband, and has given me certain information. This is one item: one day about a year ago her husband showed her a box, a metal box, he had in his bedroom. To show it to her he removed the bottom drawer of a chest and pried up the board the drawer slid on, and the box was underneath the board. He told her that if he died she should get the box, have it opened by a locksmith, and burn the contents without looking at them. It was to get that box that Mr. Goodwin went there this evening, with Mrs. Hazen's key and authority. After you left the room he removed the drawer and lifted the board, and got it. It's there on his desk."

That was like him. I hadn't told him that I had sent them from the room before I got it, and that they hadn't seen it; he took it for granted. I appreciate his compliments, but some day he may overestimate me. I had no idea where or what he was headed for, but I thought a little gesture wouldn't hurt, so I got the box with my left hand, the gun being in my right, and displayed it. Four pairs of eyes were on it, glued to it. Anne Talbot mumbled something. Perdis started up, thought better of it, and sank back. Jules Khoury muttered, "So it was there." I had the gun, but there were four of them, so I got up, detoured around them to the safe, opened the safe door, put the box in, closed the door, and spun the knob. As I returned to my chair Wolfe was speaking.

"I have a proposal to make, but first a question or two. My objective, of course, is to demonstrate that Mrs. Hazen did not kill her husband. Yesterday evening you dined at her table. After dinner she went to her room, and soon after that Mr. Weed left. I'm not going to ask about the sequence and the times of your departures, or where you went and what you did; the police have got all that from you, and if the matter can be resolved by such details they are extremely competent at that sort of thing, and they are ahead of me, with an army. But I want to know about your conversation

with Mr. Hazen after his wife and Mr. Weed left. What
was said?"

"Nothing," Khoury declared.

"Nonsense. Mr. Hazen had told his wife he was going
to discuss something with you. What?"

"Nothing of any importance. He opened champagne.
We discussed the stock market. He asked Mrs. Talbot
what plays she had seen. He got Perdis talking about
ships."

"He talked about poisons," Perdis said.

"He talked about his wife's father," Mrs. Oliver said.
"He said his wife's father was a great inventor, a genius."

Wolfe scowled at them. "This is egregious. If he
discussed some aspect of his peculiar relations with
you, naturally you didn't tell the police about it. But I
know of those relations and the police don't. I intend to
know what was said."

"You don't understand, Mr. Wolfe." It was Anne
Talbot. She was leaning forward, appealing to him.
"You didn't know him. He was a monster. He was a
demon. He didn't want to discuss anything, he just
wanted to have us there together, and we had to go. It
was his special kind of torture. He wanted each of us to
know about the others and to know that the others
knew about us. He liked to see us trying to act as if it
were just a . . . just a dinner party. You didn't know
him."

"He was a devil," Perdis said.

Wolfe surveyed them. "Did he reveal to any of you
the nature of his hold on the others, last evening or any
other time? Or hint at it?"

Anne Talbot and Khoury shook their heads. Mrs.
Oliver said, "No, oh, no." Perdis said, "I think he hinted.
For instance, poison. I thought he hinted."

"But no particulars?"

"No."

"I must concede that he was not an estimable man.
Very well, he is dead, and here we are. As I said, I have
a proposal. It is highly likely, all but certain, that he

kept in that box whatever support he had for his demands on you. The box is in my safe. I don't desire or intend to inspect its contents. But Mrs. Hazen is my client and I am committed to protect both her person and her property. She is not bound to follow her husband's instructions to burn the contents of the box, and it would be quixotic to destroy anything so valuable. I will surrender it to you, you four, for one million dollars."

They gawked at him.

"That's a large sum, but it is not exorbitant. In another seven years, if Mr. Hazen had lived, you would have paid him more than that, and that wouldn't have ended it. This will; this will be final. If I left it to you to apportion the burden you would probably haggle, and time is short, so I shall expect one quarter of the million from each of you, either in currency or certified checks, within twenty-four hours. There is no question of extortion by Mrs. Hazen or me; we haven't seen the contents of the box; I only say, as her agent, you may have them at that price if you want them."

"You haven't opened the box," Perdis said.

"No, I haven't."

"What if it's empty?"

"You get nothing and you pay nothing." Wolfe looked up at the clock. "The box will be opened here tomorrow at midnight, with all of you present, or earlier if and when you meet the terms. If it is empty, so much for that. If it isn't, there will of course be a difficulty. None of you will want the others to inspect the items that pertain to him. I don't want to look at any of them. I suggest that Mr. Goodwin, who is thoroughly discreet, may remove the items singly, examine each one only enough to determine whom it applies to, and hand it over. If you have a better procedure to suggest, do so."

Mrs. Oliver was licking her lips and swallowing, by turns. Perdis was hunched over, his lips tight, his heavy broad shoulders rising and falling with his breathing. Khoury had his chin up, his narrowed eyes aimed at Wolfe past the tip of his long thin nose. Anne Talbot's eyes were closed, and a muscle at the side of her pretty neck was twitching.

"I realize," Wolfe said, "that it may not be easy to produce so large a sum in so short a time, but it is not impossible, and I dare not give you longer. While it is true that the box and its contents are the property of Mrs. Hazen, the police would no doubt regard it as evidential in their investigation of a murder, and I can't undertake to withhold my knowledge of it longer than twenty-four hours." He pushed his chair back and rose. "I shall await your pleasure."

But if he was through they weren't. Mrs. Oliver wanted the box opened then and there, and a display of its contents by me. Khoury said that there *was* a question of extortion, that they were being told to fork over a million dollars in twenty-four hours or else. Perdis demanded that they be given the time and opportunity to talk with Mrs. Hazen, but of course she was in the coop. Anne Talbot was the only one who had nothing to say; she was on her feet, gripping the back of the chair, the muscle in her neck still twitching. Thinking it might help if I went and brought their coats, I did so, and it took Anne Talbot three tries to find the armhole.

When they were out, and the door shut, and I returned to the office, Wolfe was out from behind his desk. "A notion," I said. "Mrs. Hazen may be out on bail by the middle of the morning and accessible to them, and you're up in the plant rooms until eleven o'clock, not to be disturbed. Even if she's locked up, those people have lawyers and connections, Perdis especially. He may play poker with the DA. I could phone Parker to see her in the morning and tell her that no matter what she hears you're not loony, you're just a genius, and you know where you're headed for even when nobody else does, including me."

"Not necessary." He went to the door and turned. "Make sure that the safe's locked. I'm tired. Good night."

He knows darned well that I always make sure the safe's locked, but of course it doesn't often have something in it that's supposed to be worth a million bucks. Up in my room on the third floor, as I undressed I made assorted tries at deciding what was next on his program, and didn't like any of them.

As it turned out the next thing on the program wasn't decided either by me or by him, but by Inspector Cramer. In the morning Wolfe came down from the plant rooms at eleven o'clock as usual, and also as usual I had the mail opened and the dusting done and fresh water in the vase on his desk. He went first to the front of the desk to put a spray of orchids in the vase, Odontoglossum pyramus, then circled around to his chair. As he sat the doorbell rang. I went to the office door for a look and told him it was Cramer. He slapped a palm on the desk, glared at me, and said nothing, and I went to the front and opened up. I didn't like the look on Cramer's face as he entered and let me take his coat and hat. He almost grinned at me, and he didn't stride to the office, he just walked. He sat in the red leather chair, crossed his legs comfortably, and told Wolfe, "I haven't got much time. I want to hear it from you, what Mrs. Hazen came to you for yesterday, just the substance, and then Goodwin will come downtown and get it down in a statement, all of it. With his wonderful memory."

Wolfe was glowering at him. "Mr. Cramer. It shouldn't be—"

"Save it. She's booked for murder. We have the gun. Hazen got his car from the garage Monday night. It has been found parked on Twenty-first Street. There was a gun in the dashboard compartment, and it fired the bullet that killed him. We have traced it. It was bought by Hazen six years ago and he had a permit for it. He kept it in a drawer in his bedroom, and the maid saw it there yesterday morning when she went up to see why he hadn't come down for breakfast. Don't ask me why Mrs. Hazen took it from there afterwards and went to where she had parked the car on Twenty-first Street and put it in the car. I don't know, but maybe you do. So let's hear you."

Chapter 7

I squeezed my eyes shut because if I had kept them open they would have popped, and I didn't want to give Cramer that satisfaction. But I am supposed to help Wolfe when he needs it, and right then he sure could use a few seconds to arrange his mind, so I opened my eyes and asked Cramer, just curious, "What kind of a gun?"

He ignored it. He was having too good a time looking at Wolfe to bother with me. Wolfe was paying me another compliment. I was responsible for our assumption that Mrs. Hazen was innocent, but he didn't glance at me. He lowered his chin, scratched the tip of his nose, regarded Cramer for ten seconds, and then turned to me.

"Archie. It may be desirable to have a record of what Mr. Cramer just said. Type it. Verbatim. Double-spaced, one carbon."

As I got at the typewriter Cramer said, "I don't object. Naturally you've got to stall while you try to figure a way to climb down without breaking your neck."

No comment from Wolfe. I put in paper and hit the keys. Since I had had years of practice reporting long and involved conversations that had had time to fade, that one was no trick at all. As I rolled the paper out Wolfe said, "Initial the original," and I did so, and handed it to him. He read it through, in no hurry, took his pen and initialed it, handed it back to me, and turned to Cramer.

"I'm not stalling," he said. "If what you just told me is true, your demand for information is warranted. If it

·isn't true you're gulling me into disclosing a confidential communication from a client, and I want a record—"

"Then she's your client?"

"She is now. She wasn't when you were here yesterday, but she hired me later through Mr. Parker. I want a record of your words, and I have it. I also want more facts, to make sure that those you have given me are not qualified by others. That's a reasonable precaution, I think. What time did Mr. Hazen take his car from the garage Monday evening?"

"A little after eleven o'clock."

"That was after the dinner guests left?"

"Yes. They left at a quarter to eleven."

"Was anyone with him at the garage?"

"No."

"Was anyone else with him anywhere, out of the car or in it, after a quarter to eleven?"

"No."

"Is it assumed that he was shot in that alley where the body was found?"

"No. He was shot in the car."

"Have you any additional facts implicating Mrs. Hazen, of any kind? Not conjectures, facts. For example, was she seen in or near the car, driving it, or when it was parked on Twenty-first Street during the night, or when—as you have it—she went there yesterday to put the gun in the dashboard compartment?"

"No. No more facts. I expect to get some from you."

"You will. Naturally, when you learned that Mrs. Hazen had been to see me you focused on her, but surely not exclusively. Have you inquired into the movements of the dinner guests after they left?"

"Yes."

"Have any of them been conclusively eliminated?"

"No. Not conclusively."

Wolfe closed his eyes. In a moment he opened them. "That seems to cover it." He took a breath. "Of course I don't like this. And you're not squeezing it out of me, though you think you are. I would tell you nothing and take the consequences if it weren't that I need some information that I can get only from you. I have to know where the gun came from that Mrs. Hazen left with me yesterday. If you'll agree—"

"She left a gun with *you?*"

"Yes. I'll tell you about it, and give it to you, if you will give me its history at the earliest possible moment. I want your word."

"You won't get it. Mrs. Hazen is charged with murder. If she left a gun with you it's evidence in a murder investigation."

Wolfe shook his head. "No. It's evidence in my investigation, but not in yours. You have your gun, the one the murderer used. How can it embarrass you to tell me about this one?"

Cramer considered it. "You're going to tell me what she said about it."

"I am."

"Okay. Go ahead."

"I have your word?"

"Yes."

"Get the gun, Archie."

I went to the safe and squatted to twirl the knob. Ordinarily I leave it unlocked when I'm in the office, but with that box in it I was taking no chances, so after I had worked the combination and got the gun I shut the door and turned the knob. As I crossed to Cramer I spoke. "By the way, I asked a question that wasn't answered. What make is your gun? The one that killed him."

"Drexel thirty-two."

"So's this." I handed it to him. "Of course there are millions of Drexel thirty-twos."

He gave it a look, and darned if he didn't sniff it. As I said, that's automatic. Also he flipped the cylinder open for a glance.

"It was fired yesterday," Wolfe said, "by Mr. Goodwin, to get a bullet. The bullet I gave you."

Cramer nodded. "Yeah. There's nothing on God's earth you wouldn't do. It could have been . . . What the hell, it wasn't. Okay, let's hear you."

Wolfe unloaded. He didn't enjoy it and neither did I,

spilling it, but we had to know about the gun and it might have taken us days. He skipped the details, including no quotes, but gave it straight, both parts, before the news came over the radio and after. He didn't include my reasons for deciding that she hadn't shot her husband, but I didn't mind; it might have got Cramer confused and that would have been a pity. He was a little confused anyhow; toward the end he was frowning, pulling at his lip now and then, a wary look in his eyes. When Wolfe finished he sat looking at it before he spoke.

"What have you left out?" he demanded.

Wolfe shook his head. "Nothing material. You said you wanted the substance; you have it. How long will it take to trace the gun?"

"I don't get it. After she came to you with that fairy tale, and the news came about her husband, and you learned that we were holding her, you took her for a client? I don't get it. I have never known you to take a murderer for a client. Whether it's just your goddamn luck, or what, I don't know, but you haven't. Why did you take her?"

A corner of Wolfe's mouth turned up. "I asked Mr. Goodwin's opinion and he said she was innocent. His judgment of women under thirty is infallible. How long will it take to trace the gun?"

"Nuts." Cramer stood up. "Maybe an hour, maybe a week. I'm taking Goodwin. They'll take his statement at the District Attorney's office, a complete report of the conversation. I'll have a man here at two o'clock to take yours. If I took you down you'd only—"

"I shall sign no statement. I am not obliged to. If you send a man he won't be admitted. If you have questions, ask them."

Cramer's round red face got redder. But that was as far as it went; his memory of what had happened on the three occasions he had taken Wolfe downtown was presumably what stopped him. He stuck the gun in his pocket and turned to me. "Come on, Goodwin. We'll see."

As I arose the phone rang and I reached to get it. It was Nathaniel Parker. He was upset. "Archie? Nat Parker. Mrs. Hazen is being held on a charge of homicide, of course without bail. I want to see Wolfe before I see her. I have to know what she told him yesterday. I'll be there in twenty minutes."

"Fine," I said. "He's in a perfect mood for it. Come ahead." I hung up, told Wolfe, "Parker will be here in twenty minutes," and went to the hall for my coat and hat, with Cramer at my heels.

Chapter 8

D uring the next nine hours I had various opportunities to try to sort it out. En route in a police car to the DA's office, later from there to Homicide West on 20th Street, and several waiting periods while assorted officers of the law, including the DA himself at one point, decided what to do next.

It was complicated enough even before an assistant DA kindly permitted me to use a phone, around three o'clock, and I called Wolfe. Of course the game was button, button, who had the gun when and where? Either gun. If Lucy Hazen had lied, how much? Had the gun that the maid had seen in the drawer Tuesday morning been the one that had shot Hazen or the one she had brought to Wolfe? If the former, Lucy was a liar and also either was a murderer or could name him. If the latter, who had put it in the drawer and when? And why? It wasn't that there were no possible answers; there were too many. And too many of them made it too likely that Lucy had made a monkey of me and therefore were not acceptable.

The first hour or so I was entertained by an assistant DA named Mandel, who was not a stranger to me, and a

Homicide Bureau lieutenant, and it was obvious that the gun puzzle was as tough for them as it was for me, though they didn't say so. Then, while we were having sandwiches and coffee, no recess called, at Mandel's desk, a phone call came for him, and he took the lieutenant to another room, and when they returned their attitude was quite different. Apparently they were no longer interested in guns; they concentrated on what Lucy had said to Wolfe and me, her exact words; and finally, a little before three o'clock, Mandel called a stenographer in and told me to start dictating my statement. Of course the room was wired for sound, and they would have fun later comparing my dictated statement with what I had told them. It was then that I insisted on making a phone call and was escorted to a booth.

I got Wolfe. "Me. In a booth at the DA's office, and it may be tapped. They should be finished with me by the end of the week. They were curious about guns, and then a phone call came and they weren't. I thought you might like to know."

"I already know." He didn't sound depressed. "Mr. Cramer phoned shortly after one. The gun we gave him had been traced without difficulty. It was purchased by Mrs. Hazen's father, Titus Postel, in 1953, and he committed suicide with it five years ago, in 1955."

"And she had it?"

"Not established. I have told Mr. Parker to ask her when he sees her this afternoon. Meanwhile I have got Saul and given him an errand."

I would have liked to ask him what errand, but that wasn't advisable since we might have company on the line. Saul Panzer, the first and best man on our list when we need help, charges more than any other freelance operative in New York, and is worth five times as much. I told Wolfe I might or might not be home for dinner.

Dictating my statement to the stenographer, I had to keep jerking my mind back to it. The gun puzzle was okay now for the cops, since they had tagged Lucy; now they didn't have to buy it that she had been nutty enough to take the gun home after she shot him and put it in the drawer, and the next day get it and take it back to the car. It was much neater. She had got the gun from the drawer Monday, put the one she had, that had been her father's, in its place, and left it in the car after she shot him. And Tuesday she had got the gun from the drawer and brought it to Wolfe as a prop for her fairy tale, evidently not knowing that guns have numbers that can be traced. What better could you ask for?

But for me, unless I was ready to give Lucy up as a bad job, it was what worse could I ask for. Before, there had been too many answers; now there weren't any. I had to file it while I dictated my statement, in which I was supposed to include everything Lucy had said to us in Wolfe's office, and while I went over it after it was typed, and it wasn't easy. Then I was taken to the office of the DA himself, and he and Mandel pecked at me for an hour; and when they finished, around 6:30, and I supposed that was all for the day, I was informed that Cramer wanted me at Homicide West. If I had balked they would have booked me as a material witness and Parker couldn't come to the rescue until morning, so I took it.

In one respect it was an improvement. The dick at Homicide West whom Cramer sent for sandwiches happened to be civilized enough to think that even a dog has a right to eat what he likes, and I got what I asked for, corned beef on rye and milk. Except for that, it was just more of the same, for more than two hours with Cramer and Sergeant Purley Stebbins. I didn't even have the satisfaction of getting a chance to break my record with Lieutenant Rowcliff. I once got him stuttering in two minutes and twenty seconds, and I have a bet with Saul Panzer that I can do it in two minutes flat with three more tries.

Cramer and Stebbins finally decided they had had enough of me. It was 9:32 by my watch, and 9:34 by the clock on the wall, which was wrong, as I crossed the reception room of the precinct house to the door, and on out. I stood on the sidewalk for three good breaths of the cold fresh air, giving my lungs a treat and deciding which way to turn. If right, toward Eighth Avenue, it would be for a taxi; if left, toward Ninth, it would be for a fifteen-minute walk. Voting for the walk, I moved, and had taken three steps when my shoulder was grabbed and yanked from behind and a voice came, with feeling: "You dirty rat!"

The yank had turned me some and I turned myself the rest of the way. It was Theodore Weed. His hands were fists, and the right one was back a foot, with the elbow bent. His eyes were blazing and his bony jaw was set.

"Not here, you damn fool," I said. "Even if you drop me with one swing, which is doubtful, I'll yell police as I go down and here they'll come. Besides, I have a right to know why I'm a rat while I'm still conscious. Why?"

"You know why. You're a filthy stool, and Nero Wolfe too. You're working for Lucy? You are like hell. You gave the police the gun."

"How do you know we did?"

"Things they asked me. Do you deny it?"

My brain was a little tired after the long day, but it was doing its best. This character was by no means crossed off. We only had his word for it that he would give both arms to help Lucy; he had said himself that she didn't know how he felt about her. A chat with him wouldn't hurt and might help, but I couldn't take him home with me until I knew what Wolfe had on his program, if anything.

He still had fists. "I'll tell you what," I said. "We'll go around the corner to Jake's and I'll buy you a drink and we'll discuss it. Then if you still want to take a poke at me Jake will let us use the back room provided we let him watch. Afterwards you can comb your hair if you're up to it. It needs it."

It didn't appeal to him, but what would have? A couple of passersby, noticing his stance and his fists, had stopped to see, and a harness bull, emerging from the station, had also stopped. So he came.

At Jake's, when we had sat at a table by the wall and given our orders to the white apron, and I said I had to make a phone call, he got up and came along to the booth. Very bad manners, but I didn't correct him. I even let him stand in the door of the booth so I couldn't close it. I dialed a number and got it.

"Me. In a booth on Eighth Avenue. Theodore Weed is here at my elbow. He stopped me on the sidewalk to tell me that you and I are filthy stools because we gave the gun to the cops. When I asked him how he knew we did he said from things they asked him, which is possible since he had just come from Homicide West, probably from a session with Rowcliff, and you know Rowcliff. I'm buying him a drink, but I thought you might like to apologize to him personally for tossing our client to the wolves. He has blood in his eye."

"No. Come home at once."

"You have Saul."

"Not here. I need you. Mrs. Oliver and Mr. Perdis are in the front room. Mrs. Oliver has been here since seven o'clock. Mr. Khoury will arrive at any moment. I have been pestered by this confounded telephone all day. Mrs. Talbot called for the fifth time half an hour ago to say that she hopes to be here by ten o'clock, and it's nearly that now. On second thought, bring Mr. Weed. I have a question for him."

"You'll have to bulldog him first."

"Pfui. Bring him. How soon will you be here?"

I told him fifteen minutes, and hung up. "No time for a drink," I told Weed. "Nor for a floor show, with me on the floor. Mr. Wolfe wants me. You may came along if you care to."

"I was going there," he said grimly, "when I saw you."

"Good. But take it easy. He has a knife in his belt that he uses to stab people in the back."

On the way out I handed the white apron, whose name was Gil, a couple of ones. Outside, we flagged a taxi, and as it rolled uptown I undertook to straighten him out. "Look at it," I said. "If we're stools and selling

her to the cops there's not much of anything you can do
but shoot us, and even that wouldn't help her any. The
fact is, we're with her and you're not. We know she
didn't kill her husband. Either you thought she had and
probably still do, or you killed him yourself. If the
former, your feeling for her has got a smudge. If
the latter, you did a swell job, handling it so that she
gets the credit for it. Go soak your head."

"Why did you give the police the gun?"

"Soak your head some more. We're working for her,
not you."

No comment until the cab was turning into 35th
Street, then: "I don't think she killed him."

"Good for you. We appreciate it."

"And I didn't."

"That's not so important, but we'll keep it in mind."

At the curb in front of the old brownstone there was
a black limousine with a chauffeur in it. That would be
Mrs. Oliver's. Mounting the seven steps to the stoop, I
used my key, but the chain bolt was on and I had to ring
for Fritz. As he took Weed's coat and I disposed of
mine, he said, "Thank God, Archie, thank God," and I
asked him what for, and he said, "For you. It has been
very bad. Three phone calls during dinner, and that
woman was in the front room."

"I can imagine. How many are in there now?"

"Three. Her and two men."

So Khoury had come. I took Weed to the office. Wolfe
was at his desk with a book. Weed headed for him,
talking. "I want to know why—"

"Shut up!" Wolfe bellowed.

Wolfe's bellow would stop a tiger ready to spring.
Weed stood and glared at him. Wolfe finished a para-
graph, inserted his marker, put the book down, and
issued a command. "Sit down. I prefer eyes at my level.
Sit down! When you arrived at the Hazens' for dinner
Monday evening were the others already there?"

"I want to know why you gave the gun—"

"Bah. Are you a jackass? You must be, to suppose
you can call me to account. Sit down! You said you

would give an arm to help Mrs. Hazen. Keep your arm; I want only some information. Must I repeat my question?"

Five of the yellow chairs were there. Weed took the nearest one. He ran his fingers through his mop of hair, but only a comb and brush could have handled it. "Mrs. Oliver was there," he said. "And Khoury. Perdis and Mrs. Talbot came soon after I did. I don't see why—"

"This is what I want to know. While you were there, was any one of them absent from the gathering long enough to go to Mr. Hazen's bedroom and back? Consider it. Dismiss your fatuous huff for the moment and put your mind on something pertinent."

Weed tried to. To do so he had to take his eyes from Wolfe, so he tilted his head back and looked at the ceiling. He took his time, then lowered his head. "I don't think so. I'm pretty sure none of them left the room at all, either before we went to the dining room or after. Of course they were all there when I left, so—"

The doorbell rang. I went to the hall, but Fritz was there opening the door. When the newcomer had crossed the sill I stepped back into the office and gave Wolfe a nod, and he asked, "Mrs. Talbot?"

"Yes, sir."

"Mr. Weed to the hall, then bring them in, and Mr. Weed to the front room. We may need him later."

"I'm staying right here," Weed declared, "until I—"

"You are not. I have work to do and no time to bicker with you. Out. Out!"

"But damn it—"

"Out."

Weed looked at me, standing at the door. What he met was a stony gaze. He got up and came, past me and into the hall. When he was four paces along I went and opened the door to the front room.

Chapter 9

I put Anne Talbot in the chair nearest me because from her face and the way she moved it seemed likely that she might need smelling salts any minute, and there were some in my drawer. Next to her was Jules Khoury, then Mrs. Oliver, and then Ambrose Perdis. I had expected remarks as they entered, especially from Mrs. Oliver, who had been waiting more than three hours, but there hadn't been a peep from anyone. I felt like an usher at a funeral.

Wolfe took them in. "Since you are here," he said, "I assume that you are prepared to act on my proposal. Mrs. Oliver?"

I had her in profile and couldn't see her deep-set yellow eyes, and from that angle her sagging jowl was even less attractive. She opened her bag and took out a slip of paper. "This is a cashier's check," she said, "on the Knickerbocker Trust Company for two hundred and fifty thousand dollars, made out to me. I'll endorse it. Or I won't."

"That will of course depend. Mrs. Talbot?"

Anne Talbot's lips parted but no sound came. She tried again and got it out. "I have a certified check for sixty-five thousand dollars and forty thousand dollars in cash. I'll pay the rest as soon as I can—I think I can pay it in a month, but it might take longer. Of course you'll want me to sign something, a note, whatever you say, I tried—" She had to swallow. "I tried—" Another swallow. "I did the best I could."

"Mr. Perdis?"

"I have a certified check for my share."

"The full amount?"

"Yes."

"Mr. Khoury?"

"I have nothing."

"Indeed. Then why are you here?"

"I want to know what's in the box. If there's anything worth a quarter of a million to me, I'll buy it."

"The deadline is midnight." Wolfe glanced at the clock. "You would have ninety minutes."

"I don't think so. I don't think Mrs. Hazen knows about this. I think you're putting the screws on us without her knowledge. Whatever you're doing, I want to know what's in the box."

"Well." Wolfe's eyes left him to take in the others. "This situation was not covered by the terms of my proposal. Two of you are prepared to comply with the terms and should not suffer for Mr. Khoury's dissent. As for you, Mrs. Talbot, I am willing to accept your declaration of good faith, that you have done your best. You will of course commit yourself in writing to pay the balance. As for you, Mr. Khoury, if you are willful so am I. Whatever the box contains that relates to you will be turned over to the police at midnight. Archie, get the box and the key." Back to them: "We have procured a key that will serve."

Thinking it desirable to keep up appearances, I first got a Marley from the drawer and loaded it. Then to the cabinet for the key, and then to the safe. As I worked the combination my back was to them, but as I opened the door and took out the box I had an eye on them, not only for appearances. It was conceivable that Perdis or Khoury, or both, had come with the idea of getting something for nothing if a chance offered. All four of them had twisted around in their chairs to follow me, and they twisted back as I circled around to Wolfe's desk. As I was putting the box down the phone rang. It would. I was going to tell Wolfe to take it, but didn't have to.

He lifted the receiver. "Yes? . . . Yes, Saul . . . indeed . . . That isn't necessary. . . . Satisfactory. . . . No, stay there, Archie is here . . . How sure are you? . . . Very satisfactory. . . . No, call again in an hour or so."

As he hung up there was a gleam in his eye. "Open it," he said. I inserted the key, fiddled with it a little, got it, lifted the lid all the way, stared a second for effect, and said, "It's empty," and when Perdis bounced up and came, my hand jerked up with the gun, not having been told that that part of the performance was over. I slipped the gun in my pocket and turned the box on its edge so that all could see the shiny inside. Perdis blurted at Wolfe, "Damn you! You've got it! You had a key!" Mrs. Oliver squawked something. Anne Talbot lowered her head and covered her face with her hands. Jules Khoury stood up, vetoed whatever he had intended, and sat down again. He spoke. "Use your head, Perdis. He didn't even know it was empty. Why would he—"

"You're wrong," Wolfe snapped. "I did know it was empty. I knew it last night when I made my proposal."

They were speechless. Anne Talbot lifted her head. "I made the proposal," Wolfe said, "not out of caprice, to plague you, but for a purpose, and the purpose has been served. You have the gun, Archie? Go and stand at the door. No one is to leave."

I obeyed. Perdis, still on his feet, was in the way, so I detoured around back of the chairs. He was yapping, and Khoury was up again. Of course I hadn't the dimmest idea what was coming next as I shut the door and put my back to it, gun in hand, but apparently Wolfe had. Ignoring them, he had lifted the receiver and was dialing. Since he hadn't consulted the book and there were only three phone numbers he bothered to keep in his head, I knew who he must be getting, even before he spoke and asked for Mr. Cramer. In a moment he had him.

"Mr. Cramer? The situation has developed as I expected. How soon can you be here with Mrs. Hazen? . . . No. I will not. I told you more than half an hour ago that I would almost certainly call you. . . . No. I told you that her presence would be essential. If you come without her you won't be admitted. . . . Yes. I am prepared to suggest a substitute. . . . Yes. . . . Yes!"

Mrs. Oliver was on her feet too; they all were, except for Anne Talbot, and as Wolfe hung up Perdis said through his teeth, "Damn you, you gave it to the police!"

"No," Wolfe said. "Are you a dunce? Would I contrive such a hocus-pocus just to pass the time? Confound it, sit down! I have something to say that you would prefer to hear before Mr. Cramer arrives."

"I'm leaving," Mrs. Oliver said. "This was all a trick and you'll regret it. I'm going."

"No one is going. Mr. Goodwin wouldn't shoot you, but he wouldn't have to. Sit down."

Khoury, with his chair right back of his knees, merely had to bend them. Perdis, going to his chair, jostled Mrs. Oliver and didn't apologize. She turned to face me at the door, decided that Wolfe was right, I wouldn't have to shoot, and sat.

"You heard me on the phone," Wolfe told them. "Mr. Cramer will be here shortly, and Mrs. Hazen will be with him. The nature of your peculiar relations with Mr. Hazen will have to be divulged to him, that can't be helped, but he doesn't have to know of your invasion of that house yesterday evening. It's only fair—don't interrupt me, there isn't much time—"

Perdis persisted. "You have no evidence of our relations with Hazen."

"Pfui. Your bid to Mr. Goodwin? It's only fair that three of you should know about the box. All that I told you about it last evening was true—Mr. Hazen showing it to his wife and telling her that if he died she should get it and burn the contents, and Mr. Goodwin getting it from beneath the drawer after sending you from the room. Asked by Mr. Perdis if I had opened it, I said no. But Mr. Goodwin had, and it was empty."

"I don't believe it," Mrs. Oliver said. "It's a trick."

Wolfe nodded. "I concocted a trick, that's true, but it's a fact that the box was empty. That's what you have a right to know, three of you. It's an understatement to say that you would like to know where the former contents are, but I have no idea and neither has Mr. Goodwin, and I'm sure Mrs. Hazen hasn't. The obvious conjecture is that Mr. Hazen transferred them to some other place which he preferred. If I could offer—"

"She has them," Mrs. Oliver said harshly. "Lucy Hazen. I suppose you don't know it or you wouldn't have had us come ready to pay. She took them after she killed him and now we'll have her. She'll be in prison but we'll have her the rest of our lives."

"I don't believe it," Anne Talbot said. She hadn't spoken since the box had been opened. "Lucy wouldn't do that. But this is even worse than it was. . . . Now we don't know . . . and I tried so hard. . . ."

"I don't believe the box was empty," Khoury told Wolfe. "I think you're lying."

"I don't," Perdis said. "Why would he? There's six hundred and five thousand dollars here ready for him." His eyes went to Wolfe. "But this Cramer—that's Inspector Cramer? You said he has to know about what you call our peculiar relations with Hazen. Why does he?"

The doorbell rang. I was on post and could have let Fritz take it, but they were all in their chairs, so I opened the door to the hall and stepped through. I expected to see Cramer alone, since there hadn't been time for him to get Lucy from the jug, but she was there with him on the stoop, and at her elbow was Sergeant Purley Stebbins. He must have had her brought to 20th Street when Wolfe made his first phone call. And as I dropped the gun in my pocket and moved, the door to the front room opened and Theodore Weed darted out and to the front door. He couldn't possibly have heard through the soundproofed wall and door, so either he had been looking out a window or his feeling for her included some kind of a personal electronic receiver.

Seeing no reason to spoil his fun, I let him open the door. Cramer shot him a glance as he entered. Lucy crossed the threshold, saw him, and stopped. She stared, and he stared back. He lifted a hand and let it drop. Stebbins, back of her, growled, "On in, Mrs. Hazen." She looked at me, and back at Weed, and I said, "Everything's under control, Mrs. Hazen," and Weed backed up a step. I thought, and still think, that he had intended to warn her that Wolfe and I were a pair of Judases, but the mere sight of her paralyzed him. He stood and stared while Cramer and Stebbins got their coats off and I took hers and put it on a hanger. When we headed for the office he followed us, and there was no point in herding him back to the front room. Either Wolfe had the cards or he hadn't.

Three steps in, Cramer stopped to send his eyes around. I didn't envy him any. The four people there weren't a bunch of bums, anything but; they had position and connections and lawyers if necessary, and much wampum. And here he was, in the office of a private detective, with a woman charged with murder. Of course he had a good reason: he suspected he might have stubbed his toe. I hadn't been present when Wolfe had made his previous phone call, but presumably he had said that he expected soon to be ready to offer a substitute for Mrs. Hazen, and Cramer knew Wolfe only too well.

But naturally he didn't care to give that reason to that audience. He faced them. "I'm here because Wolfe told me that you four people would be here and I wanted to know what he had to say to you. I brought Mrs. Hazen because from something Wolfe said I got the idea that it would be in the interest of justice for her to be here. I want to make it plain that as an officer of the law I don't rely on any private detective to do my job for me, and what's more no private detective is going to interfere."

He went to the red leather chair and sat. Stebbins took Lucy to the extra chair, next to Perdis, and stood behind her. That way they had their murderer surrounded, with Cramer in front of her only three paces off. Weed went to a chair over by the big globe. As I circled around to get to my desk Wolfe spoke.

"Mr. Stebbins. Mrs. Hazen is your prisoner, and of course it's your duty to guard her. But I doubt if she intends any outbreak. If you wish to stand by the murderer of Mr. Hazen I suggest that you move to Mr. Khoury."

Silence. Not a sound. For the record, for how people react, four of them—Cramer, Lucy, Mrs. Oliver, and Anne Talbot—kept their eyes at Wolfe. Perdis and Sergeant Stebbins moved theirs to Khoury. Weed, over by the globe, got up, took a step, and stopped. Khoury's head tilted back, slowly, until his eyes were forced on Wolfe past the tip of his long thin nose. "That's my name," he said. "I'm the only Khoury here."

"You are indeed." Wolfe's head turned. "Mr. Cramer. As I said, I am prepared to offer a substitute for your consideration, but that's all. Not only have I no conclusive evidence, I have none at all. I have only some suggestive facts. First, Mr. Hazen was a blackmailer. He extorted large sums, not only from these four people, but also from others, using his public-relations business as a cover. He had in his possession—"

"You can't prove that," Mrs. Oliver blurted.

"But I can," he told her. "Item, you have in your bag a check for two hundred and fifty thousand dollars. For what? Account for it. I advise you, madam, to hold your tongue. I would prefer to tell Mr. Cramer only what I must to support my suggestion, and I'll go beyond that only if you force me to. You shouldn't have challenged me. Now that you have, were the amounts that you paid Mr. Hazen, ostensibly for professional services, actually paid under coercion?"

She looked down at the bag in her lap, looked up again, and said, "Yes."

"Then don't interrupt me." Wolfe returned to Cramer. "Mr. Hazen had in his possession various objects, I don't know what, to substantiate his demands. Last evening I told these four people that I had secured these objects and that I would surrender them for one million dollars, giving them twenty-four hours to meet my terms. They are here. Three of them—"

"The objects are here?" Cramer demanded.

"No. I don't know where they are. I have never seen them. The people are here. This will go better if you keep your questions until I'm through. Three of them—Mrs. Oliver, Mrs. Talbot, and Mr. Perdis—came prepared to pay, and that was what I was after. I was acting on the premise, certainly worth a test, that one of Hazen's victims had killed him, and to kill him might have been futile unless he got the object or objects that had made it possible for Hazen to bleed him. For a moment I abandon fact for surmise. Mr. Khoury did get the object or objects. By some ruse, probably with the promise of a large sum of money as a lure, he induced Hazen to get his car from the garage Monday night and drive somewhere, and to have with him the object or objects. That surmise is not haphazard. The others came here this evening prepared to pay, but not Mr. Khoury. He knew I had nothing to support my threat. Even when I told him that the objects pertaining to him would be given to the police in ninety minutes he was unmoved."

"Get back to facts," Cramer growled. His head turned. "Mr. Khoury, do you want to comment?"

"No." From Khoury's smile you might have thought he was enjoying it. "This is fascinating. I thought I had decided not to bring my share of the million because I didn't believe he had anything that threatened anybody."

Wolfe, ignoring him, stayed at Cramer. "For a fact I submit the conversation at the gathering Monday evening after Mrs. Hazen and Mr. Weed had left. Of course you and your staff have it in detail, but you didn't know that Hazen was a blackmailer and that he not only bled his prey, he was pleased to torment them. In that conversation he introduced topics that obviously referred to the pinch he had them in—for instance, poison. I don't know which of those present that touched, and am not concerned. But one of his topics pointed clearly at Mr. Khoury. He remarked that his wife's father had been a great inventor, a genius; and his wife's father, Titus Postel, had been associated with Mr. Khoury. So it seemed likely that his hold on Mr. Khoury was in some way connected with Titus Postel, but at the time I learned that, yesterday evening, I had no reason to single out Mr. Khoury for special attention, so I merely noted it for possible future application."

Wolfe took a breath. "But two incidents today did single out Mr. Khoury. Shortly after one o'clock you phoned me to say that the gun I had given you had been the property of Titus Postel and that he had committed suicide with it five years ago; and soon after that, on the telephone with Mr. Khoury, he informed me that he would be present this evening but that he was declining my proposal. He didn't put it in those terms, but that was the gist."

Khoury made a noise, a subdued snort. Cramer said, "Yes, Mr. Khoury?"

"Nothing," Khoury said.

Wolfe resumed. "Now the guns. Call them Gun H, Mr. Hazen's, the one he was shot with, left in his car; and Gun P, Mr. Postel's, which I gave you this morning. My account of them is not established fact, but it is more than mere surmise because it is based on a high degree of probability. When Mr. Khoury went to that grotesque dinner party Monday evening he had Gun P with him. During the—"

"You can prove he had it?"

"Certainly not. I'm telling you what happened, not what I can prove. During the evening he found or made an opportunity to go to Mr. Hazen's bedroom, took Gun H from the drawer, and put Gun P in its place. With a double purpose: first, and minor, so that Hazen would find a gun there—they were the same make—if he looked for it. Second, and major, to implicate Mrs. Hazen. He intended to leave Gun H in the car after he killed Hazen. The police would of course learn that it had been Hazen's, kept in that drawer in his room, and when they found Gun P there in its place, the gun that had belonged to Mrs. Hazen's father, they would naturally assume that she had put it there in a witless effort to mislead them. By the way." His head turned. "Mrs. Hazen. The gun that had belonged to your father—was it in your possession?"

Lucy's lips formed a "No," but there was almost no sound where I sat, five steps away.

"When did you see it last?"

She shook her head. "I don't understand." I could hear her now. "When they told me the gun I brought you was the one my father shot himself with I thought they were lying. I don't understand."

"No wonder. Neither do the police. Did you ever have that gun—your father's?"

"I had it for a while. They gave it to me after . . . after he died. I kept it with some of his things. But it disappeared."

"How long after his death did it disappear?"

"I don't know. It was about two years after that I noticed it was gone."

"Had you any idea who took it?"

"I didn't know, but I thought perhaps Mrs. Khoury had. I didn't ask her. She thought I shouldn't keep it because it only reminded me . . ." She let it hang. "Is it true that my husband was a blackmailer?"

"Yes. And your former employer is not only a murderer, he tried to make you his scapegoat. You have been unfortunate in your choice of male associates, but I can relieve your mind about one you didn't choose, your father. He didn't commit suicide; he was murdered. By Mr. Khoury."

"No," Khoury said. "Another one? You're piling it on."

Wolfe leveled his eyes at him. "Your aplomb is admirable, sir," he said, no sarcasm. "Of course you're counting on what I said at the beginning, that I have no evidence. You're too sanguine. The evidence almost certainly exists, but to get it will require authority and a large trained staff, and I have neither. I am obliged to Mr. Hazen for a valuable hint, his remark that Mrs. Hazen's father was a great inventor and a genius. That suggested that you might have cheated him out of the proceeds of his genius, and immediately after talking with you on the phone today I put a man on it."

Wolfe turned to Cramer. "The man was Saul Panzer. You know his capacities. He phoned me about an hour ago, just before I called you, and what he reported was the basis for my statement to Mrs. Hazen, that Khoury killed her father. I don't tell you what he reported because you will get it from him, and also because I don't want Mr. Khoury to know what has been uncovered, and neither do you. As I said, I am only offering a suggestion, but I trust it is cogent enough to persuade you to restrict Mr. Khoury's movements, and to put some men to work. He may have taken Hazen's keys on the chance that they might be useful, and he may still have them, though not on his person. Find them. Ransack his premises. He may even still have the object or objects he certainly took; find them. If you see his wife before he is allowed to communicate with her you may learn something about Gun P." He flipped a hand. "But this is superfluous; you know your job. If I have—"

Khoury had moved. No rush, he wasn't a bit disturbed, but he was on his feet. "Really," he said, "there's a limit." His straight line to the door was in front of Mrs. Oliver and Perdis and Lucy, but it would have been bad manners to cross their bows, so he started around. On past Mrs. Oliver, and Perdis, and Lucy, with Stebbins at her shoulder, before Cramer spoke. "Stop him, Purley." Khoury whirled, saying through his teeth, "Don't touch me."

"Nuts," Purley said, and began going over him for a gun. Gun X, maybe. Anyway, Khoury couldn't have made it to the hall because Theodore Weed was there filling the door.

Chapter 10

I'll have to leave it with two loose ends.

First, the object or objects pertaining to Anne Talbot, Mrs. Oliver, Perdis, and presumably other assorted Hazen clients. They have never turned up. At least, the cops never found them. If one of the clients did, he didn't announce it. So if the hints Hazen scattered around at the dinner party aroused your curiosity, I can't satisfy it.

Second, the fee that Wolfe had certainly earned. Lucy refused to take any of Hazen's leavings; she wouldn't even take the house. That was noble, and even decent, considering how he had got it, but private detectives have to eat. Unquestionably Nero Wolfe has to eat. There's a chance that she'll get a chunk of Khoury's pile eventually, on account of the evidence Cramer dug up that Khoury had stolen a couple of Titus Postel's inventions, but Khoury, who is now in the death house while his lawyers hop around from court to court, has admitted nothing, and neither has his wife. So if you're curious as to how much Wolfe collected for his thirty-six hours' work I can't satisfy you on that either.

As for a third point you might be curious about, whether Lucy and Theodore Weed have found out how they feel about each other, you may have one guess. If you need more than one, what do you suppose makes the world go around?

COUNTERFEIT
FOR MURDER

Chapter 1

My rule is, never be rude to anyone unless you mean it. But when I looked through the one-way glass panel of the front door and saw her out on the stoop, my basic feelings about the opposite sex were hurt. Granting that women can't stay young and beautiful forever, that the years are bound to show, at least they don't have to let their gray hair straggle over their ears or wear a coat with a button missing or forget to wash their face, and this specimen was guilty on all three counts. So, as she put a finger to the button and the bell rang, I opened the door and told her, "I don't want any, thanks. Try next door." I admit it was rude.

"I would have once, Buster," she said. "Thirty years ago I was a real treat."

That didn't help matters any. I have conceded that the years are bound to show.

"I want to see Nero Wolfe," she said. "Do I walk right through you?"

"There are difficulties," I told her. "One, I'm bigger than you are. Two, Mr. Wolfe can be seen only by appointment. Three, he won't be available until eleven o'clock, more than an hour from now."

"All right, I'll come in and wait. I'm half froze. Are you nailed down?"

A notion struck me. Wolfe believes, or claims he does, that any time I talk him into seeing a female would-be client he knows exactly what to expect if and when he sees her, and this would show him how wrong he was.

"Your name, please?" I asked her.

"My name's Annis. Hattie Annis."

"What do you want to see Mr. Wolfe about?"

"I'll tell him when I see him. If my tongue's not froze."

"You'll have to tell me, Mrs. Annis. My name—"

"*Miss* Annis."

"Okay. My name is Archie Goodwin."

"I know it is. If you're thinking I don't look like I can pay Nero Wolfe, there'll be a reward and I'll split it with him. If I took it to the cops they'd do the splitting. I wouldn't trust a cop if he was naked as a baby."

"What will the reward be for?"

"For what I've got here." She patted her black leather handbag, the worse for wear, with a hand in a woolen glove.

"What is it?"

"I'll tell Nero Wolfe. Look, Buster, I'm no Eskimo. Let the lady in."

That wasn't feasible. I had been in the hall with my hat and overcoat and gloves on, on my way for a morning walk crosstown to the bank to deposit a check for $7417.65 in Wolfe's account, when I had seen her through the one-way glass panel aiming her finger at the bell button. Letting her in and leaving her in the office while I took my walk was out of the question. The other inhabitants of that old brownstone on West 35th Street, the property of Nero Wolfe except for the furniture and other items in my bedroom, were around but they were busy. Fritz Brenner, the chef and housekeeper, was in the kitchen making chestnut soup. Wolfe was up in the plant rooms on the roof for his two-hour morning session with the orchids, and of course Theodore Horstmann was with him.

I wasn't rude about it. I told her there were several places nearby where she could spend the hour and thaw out—Sam's Diner at the corner of Tenth Avenue, or the drug store at the corner of Ninth, or Tony's tailor shop where she could have a button sewed on her coat and charge it to me. She didn't push. I said if she came back at a quarter past eleven I might have persuaded Wolfe to see her, and she turned to go, and then turned back, opened the black leather handbag, and took out a package wrapped in brown paper with a string around it.

"Keep this for me, Buster," she said. "Some nosy cop might take it on himself. Come on, it won't bite. And don't open it. Can I trust you not to open it?"

I took it because I liked her. She had fine instincts and no sense at all. She had refused to tell me what was in it, and was leaving it with me and telling me not to open it—my idea of a true woman if only she would comb her hair and wash her face and sew a button on. So I took it, and told her I would expect her at a quarter past eleven, and she went. When I had seen her descend the seven steps to the sidewalk and turn left, toward Tenth Avenue, I shut the door from the inside and took a look at the package. It was rectangular, some six inches long and three wide, and a couple of inches thick. I put it to my ear and held my breath, and heard nothing. But you never know what science will do next, and there were at least three dozen people in the metropolitan area who had it in for Wolfe, not to mention a few who didn't care much for me, so instead of taking it to the office, to my desk or the safe, I went to the front room and stashed it under the couch. If you ask if I untied the string and unwrapped the paper for a look, your instincts are not as fine as they should be. Anyhow, I had gloves on.

Also there had been nothing doing for more than a week, since we had cleaned up the Brigham forgery case, and my mind needed exercise as much as my legs and lungs, so walking crosstown and back I figured out what was in the package. After discarding a dozen guesses that didn't appeal to me I decided it was the Hope diamond. The one that had been sent to Washington was a phony. I was still working on various details, such as Hattie Annis's real name and station and how she had got hold of it, on the last stretch approaching the old brownstone, and therefore got nearly to the stoop before I saw that it was occupied. Perched on the top step was exactly the kind of female Wolfe expects to see when I talk him into seeing one. The right age, the right face, the right legs—what showed of them below the edge of her fur coat. The coat was not mink or sable. As I started to mount she got up.

"Well," she said. "A grand idea, this outdoor waiting room, but there ought to be magazines."

I reached her level. The top of her fuzzy little turban was even with my nose. "I suppose you rang?" I asked.

"I did. And was told through a crack that Mr. Wolfe was engaged and Mr. Goodwin was out. Mr. Goodwin, I presume?"

"Right." I had my key ring out. "I'll bring some magazines. Which ones do you like?"

"Let's go in and look them over."

Wolfe wouldn't be down for more than half an hour, and it would be interesting to know what she was selling, so I used the key on the door and swung it open. When I had disposed of my hat and coat on the hall rack I ushered her to the office, moved one of the yellow chairs up for her, and went to my desk and sat.

"We have no vacancies at the moment," I said, "but you can leave your number. Don't call us, we'll call—"

"That's pretty corny," she said. She had thrown her coat open to drape it over the back of the chair, revealing other personal details that went fine with the face and legs.

"Okay," I conceded. "It's your turn."

"My name is Tammy Baxter. Short for Tamiris. I haven't decided yet which one to use on a theater program when the time comes. What do you think, Tammy or Tamiris?"

"It would depend on the part. If it's the lead in a musical, Tammy. If it packs some weight, O'Neill for instance, Tamiris."

"It's more apt to be a girl at one of the tables in the night-club scene. The one who jumps up and says, 'Come on, Bill, let's get out of here.' That's her big line." She fluttered a gloved hand. "Oh, well. What do you care? Why don't you ask me what I want?"

"I'm putting it off because I may not have it."

"That's nice. I like that. That's a good line, only you threw it away. There should be a pause after 'off.' 'I'm putting it off . . . because I may not have it.' Try it again."

"Nuts. I said it the way I felt it. You actresses are all alike. I was getting a sociable feeling about you and look what you've done to it. What do you want?"

She laughed a little ripple. "I'm not an actress, I'm only going to be. I don't want anything much, just to ask about my landlady, Miss Annis—Hattie Annis. Has she been here?"

I raised a brow. "Here? When?"

"This morning."

"I'll ask." I turned my head and sang out, "Fritz!" and when he appeared, in the doorway to the hall, I inquired, "Did anyone besides this lady come while I was out?"

"No, sir." He always sirs me when there is company, and I can't make him stop.

"Any phone calls?"

"No, sir."

"Okay. Thank you, sir." He went, and I told Tammy or Tamiris, "Apparently not. You say your landlady?"

She nodded. "That's funny."

"Why, did you tell her to come?"

"No, she told me. She said she was going to take something—she was going to see Nero Wolfe about something. She wouldn't say what, and after she left I began to worry about her. She never got here?"

"You heard what Fritz said. Why should you worry?"

"You would too if you knew her. She almost never

leaves the house, and she never goes more than a block away. She's not a loony, really, but she's not quite all there, and I should have come with her. We all feel responsible for her. Her house is an awful dump, but anybody in show business, or even trying to be, can have a room for five dollars a week, and it doesn't have to be every week. So we feel responsible. I certainly hope—" She stood up, letting it hang. "If she comes will you phone me?"

"Sure." She gave me the number and I jotted it down, and then went to hold her coat. My feelings were mixed. It would have been a pleasure to relieve her mind, but of what? What if her real worry was about the Hope diamond, which she had had under her mattress, and she knew or suspected that Hattie Annis had snitched it? I would have liked to put her in the front room, supplied with magazines, to wait until her landlady arrived, but you can't afford to be sentimental when the fate of a million-dollar diamond is at stake, so I let her go. Another consideration was that it would be enough of a job to sell Wolfe on seeing Hattie Annis without also accounting for the presence of another female in the front room. He can stand having one woman under his roof temporarily if he has to, but not two at once.

At eleven o'clock on the nose the sound of the elevator came, and its usual clang as it jolted to a stop at the bottom, and he entered, told me good morning, went to his desk, got his seventh of a ton deposited in the oversized custom-built chair, fingered through the mail, glanced at his desk calendar, and spoke.

"No check from Brigham?"

"Yes, sir, it came." I swiveled to face him. "Without comment. I took it to the bank. Also my weakness has cropped up again, but with a new slant."

He grunted. "Which weakness?"

"Women. One came, a stranger, and I told her to come back at eleven-fifteen. The trouble is, she's a type that never appealed to me before. I hope to goodness my taste hasn't shifted. I want your opinion."

"Pfui. Flummery."

"No, sir. It's a real problem. Wait till you see her."

"I'm not going to see her."

"Then I'm stuck. She has a strange fascination. Nobody believes in witches casting spells any more. I certainly don't, but I don't know. As for what she wants to see you about, that's simple. She has got something that she thinks is good for a reward, and she's coming to you instead of the police because she hates cops. I don't know what it is or where she got it. That part's easy, you can deal with that in two minutes, but what about me? Have I got a screw loose?"

"Yes." He picked up the top item from the little pile of mail, an airmail letter from an orchid hunter in Venezuela, and started to read it. I swung my chair around and started sharpening pencils that didn't need it. The noise of the sharpener gets on his nerves. I was on the fourth pencil when his voice came.

"Stop that," he growled. "A witch?"

"She must be."

"I'll give her two minutes."

You can appreciate what I had accomplished only if you know how allergic he is to strangers, especially women, and how much he hates to work, especially when a respectable check has just been deposited. Besides that satisfaction I had something to look forward to, seeing his expression when I escorted Hattie Annis in. I thought I might as well go and retrieve the package from under the couch and put it in my desk drawer, but vetoed it. It could stay put till she came. Wolfe finished the letter from the orchid hunter and started on a circular from a manufacturer of an automatic humidifier.

Eleven-seventeen and the bell didn't ring. At 11:20 Wolfe looked up to say that he had some letters to give me but didn't like to be interrupted, and I said neither did I. At 11:25 he got up and went to the kitchen, probably to sample the chestnut soup, in which he and Fritz had decided to include tarragon for the first time. At 11:30 I went to the front room and got the package. Nuts to her, if she couldn't be punctual for an appointment. She would get her package back, at the door, and that would be all. I was straightening up after fishing it from under the couch when the bell rang, and had it in my hand when I went to the hall.

It was her all right, but through the one-way glass panel I noticed a couple of changes as I stepped to the door: there was a button on her coat where one had been been missing, and her face needed washing even more than it had before. Her whole right cheek was a dark smudge. Touched by the button, I decided to hear her excuse for being late, if any, but as I opened the door she collapsed. No moan, no sound at all, she just crumpled. I jumped and grabbed her, so she didn't go clear down, but she was out, dead weight. I tightened my right arm around her to free my left to toss the package into the hall and then gathered her up, crossed the sill, and kicked the door shut.

As I was turning to the front room Wolfe's voice came. "What the devil is that?"

"A woman," I said, and kept going. On her feet I would have guessed her at not more than a hundred and fifteen pounds, but loose and sagging she was a good deal heavier. I put her on the couch, on her back, straightened her legs, and took a look. She was breathing shallow, but no gasping. I slipped a hand under her middle and lifted, and stuffed a couple of cushions beneath her hips. As I took her wrist and put a finger on her pulse Wolfe's voice came at my back.

"Get Doctor Vollmer."

I turned my head. He had meant it for Fritz, who had appeared at the door. "Hold it," I said. "I think she just fainted."

"Nonsense," Wolfe snapped. "Women do not faint."

I had heard that one before. His basis for it was not medical but personal; he is convinced that unless she has a really good excuse, like being slugged with a club, any woman who passes out is merely putting on an act—a subhead under his fundamental principle that every woman is always putting on an act. Ignoring it, I checked her pulse, which was weak and slow but not too bad, asked Fritz to bring my overcoat and open a window, and went to the lavatory for the smelling salts. I was waving the bottle under her nose and Fritz was spreading the coat over her when her eyes opened. She blinked at me and started to lift her head, and I put my hand on her brow.

"I know you," she said, barely audible. "I must have made it."

"Only to the door," I told her. "You flopped on the stoop and I carried you in. Lie still. Shut your eyes and catch up on your breathing."

"Brandy?" Fritz asked me.

"I don't like brandy," she said.

"Tea?"

"I don't like tea. Where's my bag?"

"Coffee," I told Fritz. "She must like something." He went. Wolfe had disappeared. "Sniff this," I told her, handing her the bottle, and went to the hall. The package was over by the rack, and her handbag was on the floor near the wall. I didn't know how it got there, and I still don't, but since I reject Wolfe's fundamental principle I assume that a fainting woman can hang onto something. Returning to the patient, I was just in time to keep her from rolling off the couch. She was trying to pull the cushions out from under her middle. When I put a hand on her shoulder she protested, "Pillows are for heads, Buster. Can't you tell my head from my fanny? Give me the bag."

I handed it to her and she turned onto her side, propping on her elbow, to open it. Apparently her concern was for a particular item, for after a brief glance inside she was closing it, but I said, "Here, put this in," and offered the package.

She didn't take it. "So I'm still alive," she said. "I'm froze stiff, but I'm alive. Don't Nero Wolfe believe in heat?"

"It's seventy in here," I told her. "When you faint your blood does something. Here's your package."

"Did you open it?"

"No."

"I knew you wouldn't. I'm still dizzy." Her head went back down. "You're such a detective, maybe you can tell me what he was going to do if he killed me. He would have had to stop the car and get out to get the bag. Wouldn't he?"

"I should think so. If it was the bag he wanted."

"Of course it was." She took a deep breath, and another. "He thought the package was in it. Anyhow, it was your fault I was there, what you said about the button. I've been intending to sew that button on for a month, and when you said to have one put on and charge it to you, that was too much. I hadn't done anything about my clothes on account of a man for twenty years, and here was a man offering to buy me a button. So I went home and sewed it on."

She stopped to breathe. I stuck the package in my pocket. "Where is home?" I asked.

"Forty-seventh Street. Between Eighth and Ninth. So that's why I was there, but you keep your head, Buster. Don't offer to buy me some hair dye. When I left I was going to take a Ninth Avenue bus to come back here, and walking along Forty-seventh Street the car came on the sidewalk behind me and hit me here." She touched her right hip. "Bumping up over the curb must have spoiled his aim. It didn't hit me hard enough to knock me down, so I must have stumbled when I jumped. Anyhow I fell, and I must have rolled over more than once because I was walking near the curb and I came against a building. Is that Nero Wolfe?"

The door to the office had opened and Wolfe was there, scowling at us. I told her yes, and told him. "Miss Hattie Annis. She's telling me why she was late for her appointment. She went to her house on Forty-seventh Street, and coming back a car climbed the curb and hit her. I know there's no chair here big enough for you, but she ought to stay flat a little longer."

"I am capable of standing for two minutes," he said stiffly.

"You don't look it," Hattie said. "You would do fine for Falstaff."

"Finish it," I told her. "And the car went on?"

"It must have. When I got up it was gone. A man and a woman helped me up, and another man stopped, but nothing was broke and I could walk. So I walked. I didn't want to try climbing on a bus. I kept in close to the buildings, and I stopped to rest about every block, and the last two blocks I didn't think I would make it, but I did. How did you know I was there if I fainted?"

"You rang the bell. I caught you before you hit bottom."

"And you carried me in and I missed it. Carried by a man and didn't know it. What's life up to?"

Wolfe came in a step. "Madam. I told Mr. Goodwin I would give you two minutes."

She had lifted her head and I had put a cushion under it. "I appreciate it," she said. "A wonderful day. Buster carries me in and Falstaff gives me two minutes—and here's another one with coffee!"

Fritz coming with the coffee eased the situation. To Wolfe anyone having food or drink in his house is a guest, and guests have to be humored, within reason. He couldn't tell me to bounce her while I was bringing a stand for the tray and Fritz was filling her cup. So he stood and scowled. When she had taken a sip he spoke.

"Mr. Goodwin said you have something that you think is good for a reward. What is it?"

She had sat up and taken off the woolen gloves. She took another sip. "That's good coffee," she said. "First I'll tell you how I got it. I own that house on Forty-seventh Street. I was born in it." Another sip. "Do you happen to know that all stage people are crazy?"

Wolfe grunted. "They have no monopoly."

"Maybe not, but theirs is a special kind. I'm not saying I like them, but they give me a feeling. My father owned a theater. My house is only an eight-minute walk from Times Square, and I only need one room and a kitchen, so they can live there whether they can pay or not. Five of them are living there now—three men and two girls—and they use the kitchen. They're supposed to make their beds and keep their rooms decent, and some of them do. I never go in their rooms. My room is the second floor front—"

"If you please." Wolfe was curt. "To the point."

"I'll get there, Falstaff. Let the lady talk." She took a sip. "Good coffee. The ground floor front is the parlor. Nobody goes in there much since my mother died years ago, but once a week I go in and look around, and when I went in yesterday afternoon a mouse ran out from under the piano and went in back of the bookshelves. Do you believe a mouse could run up a woman's leg?"

"No." Wolfe was emphatic.

"Neither do I. I got my umbrella from the hall and poked behind the shelves, but he didn't come out. There's no back to the shelves, so if I took the books out I'd have him. The bottom shelf has a *History of the Thirteen Colonies* in ten volumes and a set of Macaulay with the backs coming off. I took them all out, but the mouse wasn't there. He must have moved while I was getting the umbrella. But in back of the books was a little package I had never seen before, and I opened it, and that's what I've got. If I took it to the cops, good-by. We can split the reward three ways, you and me and Buster here."

"What's in it?"

Her head turned. "Open it, Buster."

I took it from my pocket, sat on a chair, untied the string, and unwrapped the paper. It was a stack of new twenty-dollar bills. I flipped through it at a corner and then at another corner. All twenties.

"Imagine handing that to the cops," Hattie said. "Of course he knew I had it and he tried to kill me."

Wolfe grunted. "How much, Archie?"

"About two inches thick. Two hundred and fifty to the inch. Ten thousand dollars, more or less."

"Madam. You say he tried to kill you. Who?"

"I don't know which one." She put her cup down and picked up the pot to pour. "It could be one of the girls, but I'd rather not. If he hadn't tried to kill me I would just as soon—"

The doorbell rang. After putting the lettuce and paper and string on the chair, I went to the hall and took a look. It was a medium-sized round-shouldered stranger in a dark gray overcoat and a snap brim nearly down to his ears. Before opening the door I shut the one to the front room.

"Yes, sir?"

He took a leather fold from a pocket, flipped it open, and offered it. I took it, Treasury Department of the United States. Secret Service Division. Albert Leach. In the picture he had no hat on, but it was probably him. I handed it back.

"My name is Albert Leach," he said.

"Check," I said.

"I'd like to speak with Mr. Wolfe and Mr. Goodwin."

"Mr. Wolfe isn't available. I'm Goodwin."

"May I come in?"

It was a little ticklish. Of course I had smelled a rat the second I saw his credentials. The walls and doors on that floor were all soundproofed, but with Wolfe and Hattie in there together there was no telling, and I didn't want him inside. But it had started to snow and the stoop had no roof, and I certainly wanted to know what was on his mind.

I have him room and he stepped in. "I'm sorry," I said, "but Mr. Wolfe is busy and I'm helping him with something, so if you'll tell me—"

"Certainly." He had removed his hat. His hair was going, but it would be a couple of years before he could be called bald. "I want to ask about a woman named Baxter. Tamiris Baxter or Tammy Baxter. Is she here?"

"No. Around twenty-five? Five feet four, light brown hair, hazel eyes, hundred and twenty pounds, fur coat and fuzzy turban?"

He nodded. "That fits her."

"She was here this morning. She came at twenty minutes past ten, uninvited and unexpected, and left at ten-thirty."

"Has she been back?"

"No."

"Has she phoned?"

"No."

"Another woman named Annis, Hattie Annis. Has she been here?"

I cocked my head. "You know, Mr. Leach, I don't mind being polite, but what the hell. Mr. Wolfe is a licensed private detective and so am I, and we don't answer miscellaneous questions just to pass the time. I've heard of Hattie Annis because Miss Baxter asked if she had been here, and I told her no. She asked me to phone her if she came, but I probably won't. What if this Hattie Annis comes and hires Mr. Wolfe to do a job? She might not want anyone to know she had been here. So skip it."

"I'm an officer of the law, Goodwin. I'm an agent of the United States government."

"So you are. And?"

"I want to know if Hattie Annis has been here today."

"Ask her. Miss Baxter gave me the phone number. Do you want it?"

"I have it." He put his hat on. "I know your reputation, Goodwin, and Wolfe's. You may get away with fancy tricks with the New York Police Department, but I advise you not to try any with the Secret Service." He turned and went, leaving the door open.

I shut the door and then went to the office. I got the best glass from a drawer of Wolfe's desk and a new twenty-dollar bill from the safe, and proceeded to the front room. Wolfe was still standing, scowling down at her, and she was talking. She broke off as I entered and turned to me. "You're just in time, Buster. He's trying to tell me there may be no reward, and I never heard of—what are you doing?"

I had picked up the stack of bills and was going to a window. Putting the one on top side by side with the one I had taken from the safe, one minute with the glass settled it. I took the one from the bottom of the stack, and one from the middle, and used the glass on them.

The same. I stuck the good one in my pocket and crossed to them.

"There'll probably be an award," I told her. "Official. They're phonies. Counterfeit."

Chapter 2

I told a friend of mine about this incident one day a few weeks later, and when I got this far I asked her to guess what Hattie's reaction had been. "That's easy," my friend said. "She accused you of taking good bills from the package and substituting bad ones. You should have known she would." My friend couldn't have been more wrong, but I admit it was my fault. I hadn't drawn Hattie true to life. What Hattie actually said was, "Of course they're counterfeit. Why would he hide real money in my parlor? And why would I bring it to Nero Wolfe?"

"You knew they were phonies?" I demanded.

"I knew they must be."

"You didn't mention it."

"Why should I? To you two great detectives? You knew it too or you wouldn't have examined them with a magnifying glass."

I shook my head. "I didn't know it, I only suspected it. I suspected it when I answered the bell just now and found a T-man at the door. A T-man is a Secret Service agent of the Treasury Department. He wanted to know if a woman named Tamiris Baxter was here. I told him no, that she was here this morning for ten minutes and left her—"

"Tammy Baxter? Tammy was here?"

"Right. She wanted to know if you had been here and I told her no. She left her phone number and asked me to ring her if you came. Then the T-man asked if Hattie

Annis had been here, and I told him I was against answering miscellaneous questions, which is true, but the thing was I had got curious about this stack of bills and wanted to take a look. So he left and I came and looked. Now you say you knew they were counterfeit."

"Archie." Wolfe was gruff. "You saw that man's credentials?"

"Of course."

"He asked for Miss Annis?"

"He asked if she had been here."

"Why didn't you bring him in?"

"Because he wanted to look at the bills. If they were okay I saw no reason to let the T-man disturb a guest of yours who appreciates Fritz's coffee."

The trouble was, she had finished with the coffee. "Very well," he said, "you have looked at them. Does the Secret Service have a New York office?"

"Yes." A list of the things any two-bit dick knows and he doesn't would fill a book.

"Call them and report. If Miss Annis leaves before they arrive keep the bills, and of course they will want the wrapping paper. Give her a receipt if she wants one." He turned and made for the office, shutting the door.

It didn't stay shut long. I admit I could have stopped her, by taking a step and stretching an arm, but I thought he might at least have given her a chance to thank him for the coffee. So I didn't take the step until she had the door open, and then went only to the sill. Wolfe was in his chair behind his desk before he knew she was there.

"Did you mean that?" she demanded. "Call the cops and hand it over?"

"Not the cops, madam." He was sharp. "The Secret Service. I have a responsibility as a citizen. Counterfeit money is contraband. I can't let you walk out of my house with it."

She put a hand on the desk edge for a prop. "Bootlicker," she said. "The great detective Nero Wolfe just a flunky for the cops. If Falstaff was here I'd apologize to him. Maybe he wasn't much of a hero, but he was no toady. You can't glare me down, the lady's going to talk.

I found that stuff in my house, and I thought, I'd rather just burn it than turn it over to the cops. I thought the thing to do was find out who put it there and then go to a newspaper. Finding a counterfeiter ought to call for a reward. But I didn't know how to find out because my mind doesn't work like that, so I thought I would get a detective and split the reward with him, and I might as well get the best, so I go to Nero Wolfe, and this is what happens. Counterfeit money may be contraband, but it's not your counterfeit money, it's mine, I found it in my house, but what do you care, you want to suck up to the cops, so you tell him to call them and report, and keep the bills, and swaggle out. I spit at you. I don't spit, but I spit at you." She about-faced. "You too, Buster? Is this what you carried me in for?"

"Madam," Wolfe said.

She whirled back. "Don't madam me!"

"You have a point," Wolfe said. "I reject your charge of servility, but you have a point, and an interesting one. I am not an officer of the law. Has a private citizen the right to confiscate contraband? I doubt it. Even if he has the right, is it a duty? Surely not. That counterfeit money is yours until it is seized by public authority. I confess to error, but I was prompted by expedience, not sycophancy. I merely wanted to get clear of a muddle. Now, confound it, you have raised a point I can't ignore, but neither can I ignore my obligation as a citizen. I offer a suggestion: Mr. Goodwin will put the bills in my safe and go with you to your house and investigate. You say you wanted to engage me to identify and expose the counterfeiter; he will decide if that is feasible without prolonged and expensive inquiry. If it isn't I'll return your property to you, but I shall notify the Secret Service that I am doing so. In either case, I shall expect no fee. You are not my client. I am merely wriggling out of a muddle. Well?"

"We split the reward three ways," she said.

"I have no interest in a reward." He flipped a hand, discarding it. "There probably won't be any."

"There had better be. I don't need it, I've got enough

to go on and then some, but I've never earned any money and this is my chance. Keeping it in your safe, that's all right. I'm not going to apologize for what I said until I see what happens."

"I wouldn't expect you to. Archie?"

I moved. The bills were still in my hand, but the wrapping paper and string were on the chair. I went and brought them, holding the paper by the corner. "A question," I said. "Since he hid it where it might possibly be found he might have had sense enough not to leave prints, but he might not. If not, I've got him right here. I can find out in ten minutes, but it would be tampering with evidence, and the question is, do I?"

"Of course," Hattie said. "I thought of that but I didn't know how."

"You can't test it without leaving traces," Wolfe said.

"No."

"Then don't. That can wait."

Of course my prints were already there, on both the bills and the paper, but there was no point in adding more, so I took care putting them in the safe. I asked Wolfe if he had any instructions, and he said no, I knew what the situation required. I got Hattie's bag and gloves from the front room; she hadn't taken her coat off. I thought I might as well try her pulse, but she wouldn't let me. When I showed her to the lavatory to look in the mirror she had to admit her face could stand some attention, and when she came out the smudge was gone and she had even tucked her hair in some.

Walking to Tenth Avenue for a taxi she limped a little, but she said it was nothing, just that her hip had a sore spot. When we were stopped by a red light at 38th Street the sight of a harness bull on the sidewalk prompted her to explain why she was so down on him and his. I got it that her father had been shot by one without provocation, but she seemed a little hazy about the details, and I was more interested in something else: what did she know of Tammy Baxter? She must be involved somehow, since the T-man wanted her. Hattie said no, it couldn't be Tammy, because she only had one suit, two dresses, three blouses, and two skirts, and her fur coat was rabbit, and if she were a counterfeiter she would have more clothes. I conceded that that was pretty decisive, but why was the T-man interested in her? How long had she been living in Hattie's house? Three weeks. What did Hattie know of her background and history? Nothing. Hattie never asked for references. When someone came and wanted a place to sleep she just sized him up. Or her.

The other four current roomers had all been there longer—one of them, Raymond Dell, more than three years. In the thirties Dell had always had enough work to lunch at Sardi's twice a week, and in the forties he had done fairly well in Hollywood, but now he was down to a few television crumbs.

Noel Farris, a year and a half. A year ago he had been in a play which had folded in four days, and this season in one which had lasted two weeks.

Paul Hannah, four months. A kid in his early twenties with no Broadway record. He was rehearsing in a show that was to open next month at an off-Broadway theater, the Mushroom.

Martha Kirk, eleven months. Twenty years old. Was in *Short and Sweet* for a year. Now studying at the Eastern Ballet Studio.

That was what I had got when the taxi rolled to the curb in 47th Street. Tammy Baxter had said the house was a dump, and it was, like hundreds of others in that part of town. The wind whirled some snow into the vestibule when I pushed the door open. Hattie used her key on the inner door and we entered. I had told her that I would first take a look at the bookshelf, to see if the dust situation could furnish any information as to how long the package had been there, but as we were taking off our coats in the hall a voice came booming down the stairs.

"Is that you, Hattie?"

The owner of the voice was following it down. He was a tall thin guy with a marvelous mane of wavy white hair, in an ancient blue dressing gown with spots on it.

He was rumbling, "Where on earth have you been, or above it or beneath? Without you this house is a sepulcher! There are no oranges." He noticed me. "How do you do, sir."

"Mr. Goodwin, Mr. Dell," Hattie said. I started to offer a hand, but he was bowing, so I bowed instead. A voice sounded behind me. "This way for oranges, Ray! I got some. Good morning, Hattie—I mean good afternoon."

Raymond Dell headed for the rear of the hall, where a girl was standing in a doorway, and when Hattie followed him I tagged along, on into the kitchen. On a big linoleum-topped table in the center a large brass bowl was piled high with oranges, and by the time I entered Dell had taken one and started to peel it. There was a smell of coffee.

"Miss Kirk, Mr. Goodwin," Hattie said.

Martha Kirk barely looked her twenty. She was ornamental both above the neck and below, with matching dimples. She gave me a glance and a nod, and asked Hattie, "Do you know where Tammy is? Two phone calls. A man, no name."

Hattie said she didn't know. Dell looked up from his orange to rumble at me, "You're a civilian, Mr. Goodwin?"

It was a well-put question, since if I wasn't in show business my reply would show whether I was close enough to it to know that stage people call outsiders civilians. But Hattie replied for me.

"You watch your tongue with Mr. Goodwin," she told him. "He thinks he's going to do a piece for a magazine about me and my house, and that's why he's here. We're all going to be famous. There'll be a picture of us with Carol Jasper. She lived here nearly a year."

"What magazine?" Dell demanded. Martha Kirk skipped around the table to curtsy to me. "What would you like?" she asked. "An omelet of larks' eggs? With truffles?"

I was a little sorry I had suggested that explanation of me to Hattie. It would be a shame to disappoint a girl who could curtsy like that. "You'd better save it," I said. "This egg not only hasn't hatched, it's not even laid yet."

Raymond Dell was boring holes through me with deep-set blue-gray eyes. "I wouldn't have my picture taken with Carol Jasper," he said, "for all the gold of Ormus and of Ind."

"You can squat down behind," Hattie said. "Come on Mr. Goodwin." She moved. "He wants to see the house. I hope the beds are made."

I said I'd see them later and followed her out. Halfway down the hall she asked, not lowering her voice, "How was that? All right?"

"Fine," I said, loud enough to carry back. "They're interested and that'll help."

She stopped at a door on the left toward the front, opened it, and went in. I followed and closed the door. The window blinds were down and it was almost as dark as night, but she flipped a wall switch and light came from a cluster of bulbs in the ceiling. I glanced around. A sofa, dark red plush or velvet, chairs to match; a fireplace with a marble mantel; worn and faded carpet; an upright piano against the wall on the right, and beyond the piano shelves of books.

"Here," Hattie said, and went to the shelves. "I put the books back like they were." As I moved to join her the corner of my eye caught something, and I turned my head; and, seeing it, I turned more and then froze. It was Tammy Baxter, flat on the floor behind the sofa, staring up at the ceiling; and, as if to show her where to stare, the handle of a knife at right angles to her chest was pointing straight at the cluster of lights.

Chapter 3

To show you how freaky a human mind can be, as if you didn't already know, the thought that popped into mine was that Hattie had been right, a counterfeiter would have more clothes; and what brought it was the fact that Tammy's skirt was up nearly to her waist, exposing her legs. That took the first tenth of a second. The next thought was also of Hattie, just as freaky but for men only, based on the strictly male notion that women aren't tough enough to take the sight of a corpse. I turned, and she was there at my elbow, staring down at it.

"That's a knife," she said.

That plain statement of fact brought my mind to. I went and squatted, lifted Tammy's hand, and pressed hard on the thumbnail. When I released the pressure it stayed white. The dead hand flopped back to the carpet and I stood up. I glanced at my wrist; twelve minutes past one. "You'll see the cops now," I said. "If you don't want— Hands off! Don't touch her!"

"I won't," she said, and didn't. She only touched the skirt, the hem, to pull it down, but it was bunched underneath and would come only to the knees.

"It's your house," I said, "so you ought to phone, but I will if you prefer."

"Phone for a cop?"

"Yes."

"Do you have to?"

"Certainly."

She went to a chair and sat. "This is the way it goes," she said. "It always has. When I want to think I can't. But you can, Buster, that's your business. You ought to be able to think of something better than calling a cop."

"I'm afraid I can't, Hattie." I stopped. I hadn't realized she had become Hattie to me until I heard it come out. I went on, "But first a couple of questions, in case some thinking is called for later. When you came back here this morning to sew on the button did you see Tammy?"

"No."

"Did you see anyone?"

"No."

"The car that came up on the sidewalk and hit you. Did you see the driver?"

"No, how could I? It came from behind."

"The man and woman who helped you up, and the other man. Did they see the driver?"

"No, I asked them. They said they didn't. I can't think about that, I'm thinking about this. We'll go up to my room. Ray and Martha don't know we came in here. We'll go up to my room and you'll think of something."

"I can't think her alive and I can't think her body somewhere else. If you mean we forget we came in and saw it, then what? You said nobody comes in here much. Do you phone or do I?"

Her mouth worked. "You're no good, Buster. I wish I hadn't sewed that button on." She got to her feet, none too steady. "I'm going upstairs, and I'm not going to see any cops." She moved, but not toward the door. She stood and looked down at the corpse, and said, "It's not your fault, Tammy. Your name won't ever be on a marquee now." She moved again, stopped at the door to say, "The phone's in the hall," and went.

I looked around. There was no sign of a struggle. There was nothing to be seen that might not have belonged to the room—Tammy's handbag, for instance. I went and squatted by her for a look at the knife handle; it was plain black wood, four inches long, the kind for a large kitchen knife. It was clear in to the handle and there was no blood. I got erect and went to the hall, where I had noticed the phone on a stand under the stairs. Voices were coming from the kitchen. That it wasn't a coin phone, out in the open in that house, was worthy of remark; either Hattie's roomers could be trusted not to take liberties, or she could afford not to care if they did. Only now, evidently, one of them had taken the liberty of sticking a knife in Tammy Baxter. I dialed the number I knew best.

"Yes?"

I have tried to persuade Wolfe that that is no way to answer the phone, with no success. "Me," I said. "Calling from Miss Annis's house to report a complication. We went in the parlor to look at the bookshelf and found Tammy Baxter on the floor with a knife in her chest. The girl that came this morning to ask if Miss Annis had been there and that the T-man asked about. Miss Annis won't call the police, so I have to. I am keeping my voice low because this phone is in the hall and there are people in the kitchen with the door open. I have my eye on it. I need instructions. You told Miss Annis you would return her property to her, and you like to do what you say you'll do. So when I answer questions what do I save?"

"Again," he growled.

"Again what?"

"Again you. Your talent for dancing merrily into a bog is extraordinary. Why the deuce should you save anything? Save for what?"

"I'm not dancing and I'm not merry. You sent me here. In one minute, possibly two, it would occur to you as it has to me that it would be a nuisance to have to explain why we postponed reporting that counterfeit money. I could omit the detail that I inspected it and found it was counterfeit. If and when the question is put I could deny it."

"Pfui. That woman."

"It would be two against one, if it came to that, but I don't think it will. She says she's not going to see any cops and has gone to her room. Of course she'll see them, or they'll see her, but I doubt if they'll hear much. Her attitude toward cops is drastic. One will get you ten that she won't even tell them where she went this morning. But if you would prefer to open the bag—"

"I would prefer to obliterate the entire episode. Confound it. Very well. Omit that detail."

"Right. I'll be home when I get there."

I cradled the phone and stood and frowned at it. A citizen finding a dead body is supposed to report it at once, and in addition to being a citizen I was a licensed private detective, but another five minutes wouldn't hang me. Raymond Dell's boom was still coming from the kitchen. Hattie had said her room was the second floor front. I went to the stairs, mounted a flight, turned right in the upper hall, and tapped on a door.

Her voice came. "Who is it?"

"Goodwin. Buster to you."

"What do you want? Are you alone?"

"I'm alone and I want to ask you something."

The sound of footsteps, then of a sliding bolt that needed oiling, and the door opened. I entered and she closed the door and bolted it. "They haven't come yet," I said. "I phoned Mr. Wolfe to suggest that it would simplify matters if we leave out one item, that we knew the bills were counterfeit. Including you. That hadn't occurred to us. If you admit you knew or suspected they were phony, it will be a lot more unpleasant. So I thought I'd—"

"Who would I admit it to?"

"The cops. Naturally."

"I'm not going to admit anything to the cops. I'm not going to see any cops."

"Good for you." There was no point in telling her how wrong she was. "If you change your mind, remember that we didn't know the money was counterfeit. I'm sorry I'm no good."

I went, shutting the door, and as I headed for the stairs I heard the bolt slide home. In the lower hall voices still came from the kitchen. I went to the phone, dialed Watkins 9-8241, got it, gave my name, asked for Sergeant Stebbins, and after a short wait had him.

"Goodwin? I'm busy."

"You're going to be busier. I thought it would save time to bypass headquarters. I'm calling from the house of Miss Hattie Annis, Six-twenty-eight West Forty-seventh Street. There's a dead body here in the parlor—a woman with a knife in her chest. DOA—that is, *my* arrival. I'm leaving to get a bite of lunch."

"You are like hell. You again. I needed this. This was all I needed." He pronounced a word which it is a misdemeanor to use on the telephone. "You're staying there, and you're keeping your hands off. Of course you discovered it."

"Not of course. Just I discovered it."

He pronounced another contraband word. "Repeat that address."

I repeated it. The connection went. As I hung up a notion struck me. Hattie wasn't there to call me a bootlicker and flunky and toady, and it wouldn't hurt to be polite; and besides, it would be interesting and instructive to see how Stebbins would react to outside authority sticking a finger in his pie. So I got the phone book from the stand, found the number, and dialed it.

A man's voice answered. "Rector two, nine one hundred."

Being discreet. Liking it plain, I asked, "Secret Service Division?"

"Yes."

"I would like to speak to Mr. Albert Leach."

"Mr. Leach isn't in at the moment. Who is this, please?"

My reply was delayed because my attention was diverted. The front door had opened and a man had entered; and, hearing my voice, he had approached for a look. I looked back. He was young and handsome—Broadway handsome. The phone repeated, "Who is this, please?"

"My name is Archie Goodwin. I have a message for Mr. Leach. He asked me this morning about a woman named Tammy Baxter. Tell him that Miss Baxter is dead. Murdered. Her body was discovered in the parlor of the house where she lived on Forty-seventh Street. I have just notified the police. I thought Mr. Leach—"

I dropped the phone on the cradle, moved, and called, "Hey you! Hold it!"

The handsome young man, halfway to the parlor door, stopped and wheeled; and at the rear of the hall there were steps and Martha Kirk's voice, and she came trotting, the trot of a dancer, with Raymond Dell striding at her heels. As I crossed the hall a buzzer sounded in the kitchen, and I went and opened the door. It was two harness bulls. They stepped in and the one in front spoke. "Are you Archie Goodwin?"

"I am." I pointed to the parlor door. "In there."

Chapter 4

Two hours later, at twenty minutes to four, as I sat at the big table in the kitchen eating crackers and cheese and raspberry preserves, and drinking coffee, Inspector Cramer of Homicide West sent for me to ask me a favor. Very few people or situations had ever got Cramer to the point of asking a favor of me, but Hattie Annis had managed it.

With me at the table were two of the roomers, Noel Ferris and Paul Hannah. Ferris was the handsome young man who had appeared as I was phoning. Hannah was even younger, but not as handsome. He had chubby pink cheeks and not enough nose, and his ears stuck out. A dick had gone for him at the Mushroom Theater, where he had been rehearsing. At the moment Cramer sent for me he and Ferris were discussing the question, when had they last been in the parlor? Ferris said one evening about a month ago, when he had gone in to see if the piano was as bad as Martha said it was, and had found it was worse. Hannah said two weeks ago yesterday, when he had come downstairs to make a phone call and Martha was at the phone talking, and he had stepped into the parlor because he didn't want to stand there and listen. Before they had got onto that they had argued about the knife. Hannah said he had identified it as one from a kitchen drawer which he had often used, and Ferris said he shouldn't have identified it; he should have merely said it was similar. They had got fairly heated, paying no attention to a city employee who was on a chair by the door, taking it in.

I hadn't been allowed in the parlor, but I had seen the experts come and go, and some of them were still there. My first interview had been with Purley Stebbins, who had arrived in person only ten minutes behind the pair from the prowl car. That had taken place in the kitchen. My second interview had been in the room above the kitchen, Raymond Dell's room as I learned later, with Inspector Cramer and the T-man, Albert Leach. That was an honor, but I felt that I rated it because if it hadn't been for me they wouldn't have been there. My phone call to the Secret Service had brought Leach on the jump, and Leach's appearance had brought the Inspector. No doubt about it. So it was Cramer, not Stebbins, that I got to see reacting to outside authority, and it wasn't very instructive because he was mostly reacting to me as usual.

"You say Wolfe told her he would expect no fee and he wasn't interested in a reward, but he sent you here with her and you paid the cab fare. Nuts. I know Wolfe and I know you. You expect me to swallow that?"

Or: "You try to tell me that you don't know exactly how long it was after you found the body until you called Stebbins because you didn't look at your watch when you found the body. That's a lie. The way you've been trained looking at your watch would have been automatic. Raymond Dell and Martha Kirk say it was just a few minutes after one when you and Hattie Annis left the kitchen. You called Stebbins at one-thirty-four. Half an hour. What were you doing?"

Or: "Quit your clowning!"

Of course he was at a disadvantage, since at the

beginning he expected to be riled because he knew I knew how, and when he's riled his mind skips. So I got no bruises, and the one ticklish point was never mentioned. I gave him all the facts about the package from the time Hattie left it with me until I put it in the safe, excepting one detail, and he didn't even hint at the possibility that it might be queer, and neither did Leach. Leach horned in only once, when he got riled too.

"I warned you," he said, "not to try any fancy tricks with the Secret Service. And at that moment, when I was asking you if Hattie Annis had been there, she was in with Wolfe. You have just admitted it. You withheld information required by an agent of the Federal government in the performance of his duty, and you will answer for it."

"I'll answer now," I told him. "Why should I tell you anything about anybody? If you had any proper ground for asking me about Hattie Annis you didn't mention it. Inspector Cramer doesn't have to mention it. She and I found a dead body in her house, and it's his job to catch murderers, and it's possible that there is a connection between the murder and the package that Miss Annis found and brought to Mr. Wolfe. So I answer his questions. I can't think offhand of any question whatever that I owe you an answer to. Do you want to try?"

That was deliberate. Sooner or later someone was going to ask me if I knew that money was counterfeit, and I might as well get it over with and have it on the record. But he merely looked at Cramer, and Cramer resumed.

At twenty minutes to four, when a dick named Callahan entered the kitchen and said the Inspector wanted me, I supposed it had been decided that it was time to try me on the ten-thousand-dollar question, but when I saw Cramer's face I knew that wasn't it. Instead of being set to blurt a tough one at me, he was chewing on a cigar, and he does that only when he doesn't like the prospect. Lieutenant Rowcliff and another dick were with him, in Dell's room. Leach wasn't there. It didn't come easy for him. He took the cigar from his mouth, put it back, and rasped, "We need your help, Goodwin."

"I'd love to help," I said.

"Yeah." Not at all the right tone for asking a favor. "Did you tell that Annis woman to bolt herself in?"

"No. I have reported it as it happened."

"Yeah." He removed the cigar. "She won't open the door. She won't open her trap. We don't want to smash the door unless we have to. She's your client and if you tell her to slide that damn bolt she will."

"She is not my client. Nor Mr. Wolfe's."

"So you say. Wouldn't she open the door if you asked her to?"

"Probably."

"Okay. Ask her."

I allowed a grin to show. "Not the way you mean. Not with you at my elbow. I'm willing to try if I'm alone in the hall and the door of this room is shut, and I'll explain the situation to her. She has a personal attitude to cops. A cop shot her father."

"Yeah, fifteen years ago. Hasn't she got any sense?"

"No."

"She might know we'll bust the door if we have to. Will you tell her that?"

"Sure. With conditions as specified. You and yours stay here with the door shut. Rowcliff is slow in the skull but his feet are fast."

"Save the gags," Cramer growled, and stuck the cigar in his mouth. I went, closed the door behind me, walked down the hall, rapped on Hattie's door, and called, "It's me. Buster Goodwin. I'm alone. Let me in. I want to ask you something."

Footsteps and then her voice. "Where are they?"

"Still in the house but at a safe distance. I am not a flunky."

The bolt grated and the door opened. I entered, shut the door, and slid the bolt. The blinds were down and the lights were on. She had a magazine in her hand.

"You might have brought me something to eat," she said. "I haven't had any lunch. You're no good."

I faced her. "That's the second time you've told me I'm no good," I said. "Let's get that settled. If you really mean it why did you let me in?"

"I thought you had something to eat. When I say you're no good that's just for then, when I say it. I'm hungry."

"Okay. Actually I'm extremely good. If I wasn't, why would I bother to come and tell you to stay away from the door because they're going to bust it in?"

"No, they won't."

"Why won't they?"

"Because they know if they do I'll shoot."

I glanced around. A massive old walnut bed, a big old rolltop desk, dresser, chest of drawers, chairs, pictures of men and women all over the walls, actors from a mile off. "What will you shoot with?" I asked.

"Nothing," she said. "I haven't got a gun, but they don't know it."

I eyed her. "May I have permission to call you Hattie?"

"No. Not until I see what happens."

"Very well, Miss Annis. A cop named Cramer, an inspector, asked me to come and tell you they're going to break in. They can do that without getting in the line of fire, and they will. That's all he asked me to tell you, but I add this on my own, that if they have to smash the door to get to you it's an absolute certainty that they'll take you downtown, and they'll probably hold you as a material witness. They're investigating a murder that occurred in your house, and you're a suspect. Whereas if you let them in and answer the questions they have a right to ask, they probably won't take you downtown and you can sleep in your own bed."

She was staring at me. "You say I'm a suspect?"

"Certainly. When you came home to sew on the button, it could have been then."

"*You* suspect me?"

"Of course not. Even if I'm no good I'm not a halfwit."

Her tips tightened. "They'll have to carry me."

"They can. There's enough of them, and they have handcuffs."

"They'll need them." She cocked her head. A strand of gray hair fell across her eye, and she didn't bother to brush it back. "All right, Buster. I've never hired a detective. Do you want me to sign something?"

"Whom are you hiring, Miss Annis?"

"I'm hiring you. Call me Hattie."

"You can't hire me. I work for Nero Wolfe on salary."

"Then I'm hiring Nero Wolfe."

"To do what?"

"To show the cops. To make them wish they had never set foot in my house. To make them eat dirt."

"He wouldn't take the job. You might hire him to investigate the murder, and he might fill your order as a by-product. But he has exaggerated ideas about fees, and I doubt if you could afford it."

"Would you help him?"

"Of course. That's my job."

She shut her eyes, tight. In a moment she opened them. "I could pay him one-tenth of all I've got besides the house. I could pay him forty-two thousand dollars. That ought to be enough."

It took a little effort not to gawk. "I should think so," I conceded. "If you want me to put it to him, I have to ask a question that he'll ask. He's very realistic about money. What you've got besides the house, is it in something convenient? Would you have to sell something, for instance a race horse or a yacht?"

"Don't try to be funny, Buster. I'm realistic about money too. It's in tax-exempt bonds in a vault in a bank. Do you want me to sign something?"

"That's not necessary, now that I call you Hattie." I controlled an impulse to reach and brush the strand of hair away from her eye. "You may not be very available the rest of the day, so we'll leave it this way: you have hired Mr. Wolfe to investigate the murder, and if he doesn't take the job I'll notify you as soon as I can get in touch with you. And you'll leave—"

"Why wouldn't he take the job?"

"Because he's a genius and he's eccentric. Geniuses don't have to have reasons. But leave that to me. And if you're going to pay us I might as well start earning it. Have you got a stamp pad?"

She said yes, in the desk, and I went and found it in a pigeonhole. She said she had no glossy paper, and I took her magazine and found a page ad in color with wide margins in white, and tore it out. "I'll want all ten fingers," I told her. "First your right hand, the thumb. Like this."

She didn't ask why. She didn't ask anything. Either she knew why or she merely wanted to humor me, and your guess is as good as mine. When I had the set, the right hand on the right margin and the left on the left, I folded the sheet with care and put it between the pages of my notebook.

"Okay," I said. "You'll leave the door unbolted, and I'll tell Cramer—"

"No, I won't. If they break in that door they'll pay for it."

I explained again. I told her that anyone as realistic about money as she was ought to be able to be realistic about murder, but she wouldn't budge. I told her she didn't have to invite them in or let them in, just leave the door unbolted, and she said I was no good. So I left, and the second I was across the sill the door clicked shut and I heard the bolt go in. I walked to the rear and opened the door of Dell's room.

"Well?" Cramer demanded.

"No soap." I stood in the doorway. "If she has a brain I can't imagine what she uses it for. She wants to hire Nero Wolfe to make you eat dirt. I told her if you had to break in you would probably take her downtown and hold her, and she said you'd have to carry her. When I left she pushed the bolt."

"All right," Cramer said, "if that's the way she wants it." He turned to speak to Rowcliff, but I didn't stay to listen, because I had an urgent errand. Callahan, the dick who had brought me from the kitchen, wasn't in sight, and if I went downstairs unescorted I probably wouldn't be stopped. I backed off, made the landing, descended, asked the dick in the lower hall if it was still snowing as I got my hat and coat, took my time putting my coat on, opened the front door, and was gone.

The snow was coming down thicker and was an inch deep on the sidewalk. Outside were two harness bulls, four police cars double-parked, and a small group of unofficial criminologists. I headed east, found a phone booth in a bar and grill around the corner on Eighth Avenue, and dialed. It was after four and Wolfe would be up in the plant rooms for his afternoon session with the orchids, which is from four to six, so it was Fritz who answered, and I told him to switch it.

"Yes?" Wolfe is always gruff on the phone, but when it interrupts him up there he is even gruffer.

"Me again. From a booth on Eighth Avenue. I left the scene informally because I have something to report. We won't be contradicted about the money. Miss Annis, whom I now call Hattie, has buttoned her lip and will keep it buttoned. She is in her room with the door bolted and Cramer and Rowcliff are going to batter their way in. Stebbins isn't around. I was re—"

"He was here."

"Who? Stebbins?"

"Yes. I spoke with him at the door. He wanted the package of money. I told him it was not mine to surrender, since it had been left in your safekeeping. He said nothing about its being bogus. I didn't admit him. He was not pleased."

"I'll bet. I was requested by Cramer to persuade Hattie to let them in, and I tried—not through the door, she let me in. When I told her that if they had to bust the door to get to her they would take her downtown and hold her, she said she wanted to hire you to make them eat dirt. I said the only job you might take would be to investigate the murder, and dirt-eating, if any, would be a by-product, and your fee would be high. She said she could pay you twenty-one thousand dollars, one-tenth of the tax-exempt bonds she has in a bank vault. I said we would leave it that you are hired, and if you refuse to take it on because you're eccentric I'll notify her. The trouble is, how can I notify her if she's not accessible? Shall I ask Cramer to tell her you're too busy?"

"Yes."

"Naturally," I said sympathetically. "You would rather starve than work if only you had no appetite. The fact is, she wanted to hire me and I told her to get me she had to hire you. I'll hold the wire while you count ten."

"Confound you." It was a growl from the depths. "She may have no bonds. She is probably indigent."

"Not a chance. She's my favorite screwball, but she's not a liar. I'm under her spell and I'm in her debt. She made Cramer ask me a favor."

Silence. Then, more growl. "Come home and report. We'll see."

Chapter 5

One of the rules in that house is no business talk at meals, ever, and another is no business in the plant rooms except in emergencies. That winter day the emergency was not that some sudden development demanded immediate action or that an important case had reached a crisis; it was that Wolfe had to decide, to work or not to work, and he could get no pleasure fiddling with orchids with that hanging over him. He took my report not in one of the three plant rooms, with their dazzle of color, but in the potting room, perched on his made-to-order stool, at the bench. Theodore was washing pots at the sink, and I used his stool.

Wolfe keeps his eyes closed when I am reporting and

rarely interrupts with questions. When I finished he took in air clear down to his middle, let it out, opened his eyes, and grunted. "Any comments or suggestions?"

"Yes, sir, plenty. First, Hattie Annis is out. She couldn't possibly have been faking it when we went in and found the body. I wouldn't try to predict what she's going to do, but I know what she didn't do. She didn't kill Tammy Baxter. Second, their not asking if I knew the money is counterfeit is an insult to my intelligence and yours too. Leach had told Carmer not to mention it because what he wants is to find the source. He'd rather catch a counterfeiter than a murderer any day, and if counterfeiting was mentioned to me I might mention it to a reporter. Evidently he thinks we can't add two and two. A T-man coming to ask me about a woman who had left a package of bills with me, and the idea that they might be counterfeit wouldn't occur to me?"

"He didn't know she had been here and left a package."

"He did when I was being questioned. He heard me tell Cramer. Cramer must have been biting nails. He'd love to get us for being in possession of a stack of the queer. Ten to one Leach didn't know he sent Stebbins here to get it. Third, Tammy Baxter was a T-woman."

Wolfe made a face. "That mean something?"

"It does now. If there are T-men there can be a T-woman, though I've never heard of one. This morning Leach asked if she was here, and when I told him she had been and gone he asked if she had been back or phoned and then switched to Hattie Annis. Why didn't he ask what Tammy Baxter had said? Because he knew; she had reported to him. Also he knew the phone number of that house. Also Cramer. Why wasn't he more interested in my talk with Tammy Baxter only an hour or so before she was murdered? Because he already knew about it from Leach."

"Then she had been posted in that house by the Secret Service?"

"Sure. A good guess is that they knew someone who lived there had passed bad money. I doubt if they knew

which one, because if so they know who killed Tammy
Baxter, and I don't think they would dare not to tell
Cramer—but it's possible. Their big play isn't for the
passers, it's for the plant. Four, one of the four roomers
is it, on account of the knife. It came from that kitchen.
Raymond Dell, Noel Ferris, Paul Hannah, Martha
Kirk. If one or more of them have been crossed off by
alibis that would narrow it. Five, if Hattie Annis is your
client you probably want to speak to Parker, since you
are against leaving a client in the coop. I'll ring him."

"I haven't told you to."

"Do you tell me not to?"

He tightened his lips. He took a deep breath. "Confound you. Call him."

"Right. But first one more. Six, I see no reason why I
shouldn't try the package for prints, since it hasn't
occurred to us that the bills may be phony. I'm assuming that you don't intend to let loose of your client's
property unless a court orders you to."

"Certainly not. But there will be other prints than
yours. Hers."

"I've got hers."

"You have."

"Yes, sir. In case."

"So." He got off the stool. "So you make the decisions.
Let me know if you wish to confer. Go."

I went. It isn't easy to pass down the aisles of those
three rooms without stopping, even in an emergency,
but that time I stopped only once, where a group of
Miltonia roezlis were sporting more than fifty racemes
on four feet of bench. It was the best crop of Miltonias
Wolfe (and Theodore) had ever had. The display is
always harder to believe when snow is dancing on the
sloping glass overhead.

Since it was after office hours I dialed the home
number of Nathaniel Parker, the lawyer, got him, put
him through to Wolfe, and listened in, as I am supposed
to when not told to get off. He was a little doubtful
about springing our client before morning, since they
had had to smash a door to get to her and she wasn't

talking, but he said he would get on it immediately and do his best. That done, I went to the safe and got the wrapping paper and bills.

It was a two-hour job, and I took an hour out for dinner, so it was after nine o'clock when I finished. It took so long because (a) wrapping paper is a mean surface to lift prints from, (b) I had to check and double-check every print with Hattie's and mine, and (c) I had to be darned careful to leave the evidence intact if there was any there. During the last hour, after dinner, Wolfe was there at his desk in the only chair he really likes, reading his current book. Now and then he shot me a glance, of course hoping that I would announce that we had him, and his job would be simple. But at a quarter past nine I swiveled and spoke. "No. Positively. Seven good prints, twelve fair ones, and fourteen smudges. The only ones that can be identified are Hattie's and mine. Either he never handled it without gloves or he wiped it."

I'll say this for him, he never asks silly questions like Are you sure, or Have you tried the bills too. He merely growled, "It was too much to expect." He picked up his bookmark, a thin strip of gold that had been given him by a client in spite of the size of his bill, inserted it, and put the book down. "What do you suggest?"

Ignoring the sarcasm, I took the bills and wrapping paper, still handling them with care, and went to the safe and put them in. "Now," I said, returning, "it will take a brain, and you know where one is. I only run errands. I know you never leave the house on business, but if you—"

The doorbell rang. I offered myself three to one that it was Cramer, probably with Leach for company, stepped to the hall, and flipped the switch for the stoop light. It had been a bad bet. I stepped back in and told Wolfe, "All four of them. Dell, Ferris, Hannah, and Martha Kirk."

He glared at me. "You invited them?"

"No, sir. It's a surprise party. People have no consideration. They might at least have phoned."

"It's impossible! I'm not ready. I haven't prepared my mind." He ran his fingers through his hair. "It's impossible. Bring them in."

I went to the front and opened the door, and invited them to enter. Martha Kirk, first in, did not curtsy, and Raymond Dell didn't bow. When I turned after shutting the door she was sitting on the bench pulling off her galoshes and the men were removing their coats. "Have you written your piece?" Dell demanded.

That had been so long ago, eight whole hours, that for a second I didn't get him. "Oh," I said. "I had forgotten I was doing one. I got interrupted."

"We want to see Nero Wolfe," Martha Kirk said. "And you."

"Then you might as well have us together. This way." I went to the office door and stood aside, and they filed in. Wolfe arose, inclined his head an eighth of an inch as I pronounced each name, and sat. He never shakes hands with strangers. I was going to put Martha Kirk in the red leather chair, but Dell beat us to it, so I moved up a yellow one for her, next to me, and Ferris and Hannah moved their own, beyond her. Wolfe's eyes went from left to right and back again.

"Go ahead, Martha," Paul Hannah said. "This was your idea."

"No," Martha said, "it was Hattie's idea." She was still ornamental, and the dimples were still there, but she didn't look up to making an omelet of larks' eggs. She turned her face to me and then to Wolfe. "It's crazy," she said. "The idea that Hattie— It's just crazy."

"She doesn't mean," Noel Ferris explained, "that Hattie's idea is crazy, she means the idea that Hattie killed Tammy Baxter. Hattie's idea was that we should come and see you."

"According to Martha," Paul Hannah said.

"Idiot children," Raymond Dell rumbled. His hat had pressed his white mane down, but it was starting to unfurl. "Snapping and yapping in the face of tragedy."

"Death isn't tragedy," Ferris said. "Life is tragedy."

"Was it Miss Annis's idea," Wolfe inquired, "that you

should come and expound philosophy to me? Miss Kirk. I gather that she spoke with you?"

Martha nodded. "She spoke *to* me. She said she had hired you and Mr. Goodwin to make the cops eat dirt, and we must come and tell you everything we had told the cops."

"When did she hire you?" Hannah demanded. His chubby pink cheeks were a little saggy.

Wolfe ignored him and kept his eyes at Martha. "What else did she say?"

"Nothing. She couldn't. I was coming downstairs, and they were carrying her out, and she saw me and said that, and I said we would. Of course I couldn't tell the others then, they were still questioning us, but I did as soon as they left."

"They were carrying her literally? Bodily?"

"Yes. Two men."

"Had they forced the door of her room?"

"Yes."

Wolfe grunted. "Possibly actionable. For the record, Miss Annis is my client, but my job is not as she defined it. I have engaged to investigate the murder that was committed in her house."

"It wasn't committed by her," Martha declared. "But they've arrested her. It's crazy!"

"It was committed by a sex maniac," Paul Hannah said. "Twice last week a man followed her right to the door. When she told me about it I offered to ambush him, but she said no, if he did it again and came close she would handle him. She would, too."

Noel Ferris twisted his lip. "Lochinvar Hannah," he drawled. "These sex maniacs are damn clever. Of course getting in wasn't much, he could have a bag of assorted keys, but getting the knife from the kitchen was a real stroke. We know he did because you identified it."

"You keep harping on that." Hannah's cheeks were pinker. "Certainly I identified it, with that nick in it. I supposed you all would. I knew Hattie would."

"I did," Martha said.

Ferris turned a hand over. "Then I should have too. I was too sentimental, I always am. I had a vague notion that it would be better to leave it plausible that the knife was a stranger. Also I am too sensitive. I couldn't bear the thought that the knife I had sliced ham with had been . . ." He finished it with a gesture, an actor's gesture.

Raymond Dell snorted. "Adolescent imbeciles! All three of you! We came here to serve a friend in whose debt we are, not to prattle. Tammy Baxter was new in that house, not yet of us. For all we know, Hattie may have had reason to fear her beyond endurance. In a frenzy of fear, in the panic of desperation, she killed her. That is quite possible. We know that Hattie was not herself. We thought her incapable of guile, but she brought this man Goodwin, a professional detective— she brought him there and presented him to Martha and me in false colors."

Ferris's brows were up. "But you came here to serve her?"

"I did." Dell's boom would have carried to the gallery if there had been one. "Whether she killed or not, whether she was wise to trust her fate to this man Wolfe and this man Goodwin—we are not to judge. We can only ask, what can we do or say to help her?" His deep-set blue-gray eyes focused on Wolfe. "And we can only ask you."

Martha Kirk put in, "Hattie said we should tell him everything we told the cops."

Wolfe shook his head. "That may not be necessary. I hope not." He cleared his throat. "It has already been of some slight help to sit and listen to you; that is inherent in the situation. When four people are conversing in my presence and I know that one of them committed murder less than twelve hours ago, I would be a dolt to get no inkling at all. Look at you now—your reaction to what I just said. You are all staring at me. One of you opened his mouth to interrupt, but closed it. None of you glances at the others, or at any other. But I know that one of you is feeling the pinch. He is asking himself, are my eyes all right, how about my mouth, should I say something? He is aware, of course, that it will take more than an inkling to undo him, but an inkling can give me a start."

It wasn't giving me one. They all kept their stares at him. Martha's lips were parted, and Ferris's were twisted. Paul Hannah's jaw was working. Dell's chin was up and he was frowning. Ferris demanded, "You *know* it was one of us? How?"

"Not by an inkling, Mr. Ferris. There is the knife, and there is my conviction, on grounds that satisfy me, that Miss Annis didn't use it, but that isn't all. I prefer not to disclose why she took Mr. Goodwin to her house in masquerade; though one of you has certainly guessed why I'll leave it a guess." He flattened his palms on the chair arms. "And now we may proceed. Three of you came here to help a friend, and one of you came because he didn't dare to refuse; nor will he dare to refuse to answer my questions; and I expect him to expose himself. If he has already exposed himself to the police we are wasting our time, but I'll proceed on the assumption that he hasn't. If I fail, it will be because I haven't asked the right questions, and I don't intend to fail."

His head turned. "Mr. Dell. Have you paid your room rent for the past three months?"

Chapter 6

Raymond Dell's chin lifted another quarter of an inch. "We could all refuse," he said.

Wolfe nodded. "You could indeed. If you think that would serve your friend in whose debt you are. Shall I try the others?"

"No. As for that question, if Hattie is your client you could ask her. Perhaps you already have. I have paid no room rent for three years and she has asked for none."

Wolfe's head moved. "Miss Kirk?"

She was still staring at him. "The cops didn't ask me that," she said.

Wolfe grunted. "They have their technique and I have mine. That question applies to the problem as I see it. Does it embarrass you?"

"No. I have lived there nearly a year and I have paid five dollars every week."

"From current income?"

"I haven't any current income. I get a check from my father every month."

"I trust it doesn't embarrass him. Mr. Ferris?"

Noel Ferris passed his tongue over his lips. "How this applies is beyond me," he said, "but I don't dare to refuse to answer. I haven't figured how I stand on rent, but you can. I've had a room there for eighteen months. Last summer I was on television for thirteen weeks and I gave Hattie a hundred and fifty dollars. A show I was in flopped in November, and since then it has been television crumbs. Two weeks ago I gave her sixty dollars. You figure it."

"You're a hundred and eighty dollars short. Mr. Hannah?"

Paul Hannah was looking determined. "I'm not taking any dare," he blurted. "You may think your question applies, but I don't. You say you know one of us killed Tammy Baxter, but I don't believe it. I know damn well I didn't. You don't kill someone without a reason, and what was it? She had only been there three weeks and we barely knew her. The knife doesn't prove anything. Whoever killed her got in the house somehow, and if he was in the house he could have got the knife. I'm not taking any dare."

Wolfe shook his head. "Your spunk is impressive, Mr. Hannah, but it bounces off. If you are innocent the question whether you'll take a dare doesn't arise; the question is, what are you here for? To oblige a friend or parade your conceit?"

"I'm here because of what Hattie said to Martha and I wanted to hear what you had to say. And you asked if I've paid my room rent, for God's sake. All right, I have. I've been there four months and I've paid every week. That proves something?"

"Obviously. That you are not a pauper. You have an income?"

"No. I have money that I saved."

"So. That point is covered." Wolfe's eyes went to Martha. "Now, Miss Kirk, for what you have told the police—at least one detail. Your movements this morning, say from ten-thirty until one o'clock. Where were you?"

"I was in my room," she said, "until about a quarter after twelve. The police wanted to know exactly, but I couldn't tell them. I got in late last night, and I always do exercises for an hour when I get up. About a quarter after twelve I went down to the kitchen. There were no oranges and I went out and got some. I wasn't gone more than ten minutes. I was cooking bacon and eggs when Mr. Dell came in, and Hattie with Mr. Goodwin, and Hattie said he was going to do a piece for a magazine, and they went—"

"That's far enough. Which room is yours?"

"The third floor front, above Hattie's."

"And the others? Their rooms?"

"Ray's is the second floor rear—Raymond Dell's. The rear room on my floor, the third, is Tammy Baxter's. The one above mine, on the fourth floor, is Noel Ferris's, and the rear one on that floor is Paul Hannah's."

"Did you see any of them this morning?"

"No. Not until Ray came to the kitchen, and that was afternoon."

"Did you hear any of them moving or speaking?"

"No."

"Not even Mr. Ferris in the room above you?"

"No. I suppose he was up and gone before I woke up."

"Did you hear or see anything at all that might be of significance?"

She shook her head. "The police thought I must have, when I was in the kitchen, but I didn't."

Wolfe's head went left, to Raymond Dell in the red leather chair. "Mr. Dell. I know you came downstairs when Miss Annis entered the house with Mr. Goodwin shortly after one o'clock. Before that?"

"Nothing," Dell rumbled.

"Nothing?"

"Nothing. That was when I left my room for the first time. Until then I had seen no one, heard nothing, and seen nothing. I had been asleep."

"Then how did you know there were no oranges?"

Dell's chin jerked up. "What's that? Oh." He gestured. "That man Goodwin. I knew because there had been none when I went down for some in the early hours—the late hours. I don't sleep at night; I read. I was reading Sophocles' *Oedipus Rex*, and when I finished it, at five o'clock perhaps, or six, I wanted oranges. I always do around that hour. Finding none, I returned to my room and finally dozed."

"So that was customary? You rarely stir before twelve?"

"I never do."

"And at night you read. How do you spend your afternoons?"

Dell frowned. "Could that conceivably apply?"

"Yes. Conceivably."

"I want to be present when you apply it. That would be a revelation worthy of the Cumaean sybil. I baby-sit."

"You what?"

"The current abhorrent term is 'baby-sit.' I have a friend who is a painter, by name Max Eder, who lives in an East Side tenement. His wife is dead. He has a son and daughter aged three and four, and five days a week I am their keeper for five hours, from two till seven. For a stipend. Mondays and Tuesdays I am free to roam the market if I am so inclined. You frown. To offer my talents in television dens. I am so inclined only by necessity."

"What is Mr. Elder's address?"

Dell shrugged, an actor's shrug. "This approaches lunacy. However, it's in the phone book. Three-fourteen Mission Street."

"How long have you been—uh—performing this service for him?"

"Something over a year."

Wolfe left him. "Mr. Hannah. Since I am now merely asking for what you have already told the police, your whereabouts today from ten-thirty to one, I hope you won't be provoked."

"You do like hell," Hannah blurted. "Parading my conceit, huh? I'm sticking only because I told Martha I would. I left the house a little after nine o'clock and spent a couple of hours around the West Side docks, and then I took a bus downtown and got to the Mushroom Theater a little before twelve. We start rehearsal at noon. Around two o'clock a man came and flashed a badge and said I was wanted for questioning and took me to Forty-seventh Street."

"What were you doing around the docks?"

"I was looking and listening. In the play we're doing, *Do As Thou Wilt*, I'm a longshoreman, and I want to get it right."

"Where is the Mushroom Theater?"

"Bowie Street. Near Houston Street."

"Do you have a leading role in the play?"

"No. Not leading."

"How many lines have you?"

"Not many. It's not a big part. I'm young and I'm learning."

"How long have you been rehearsing?"

"About a month."

"Have you appeared at that theater before?"

"Once, last fall. I had a walk-on in *The Pleasure Is Mine.*"

"How long did it run?"

"Six weeks. Pretty good for off-Broadway."

"Do you favor any particular spot when you visit the docks?"

"No. I just move around and look and listen."

"Do you do that every day?"

"Hell, no."

"How many times in the past month?"

"Only once before today. A couple of times when I got the part, in November."

I was thinking that at least he had one of the basic qualifications for an actor. He was ready and willing to answer any and all questions about his career, with or without a dare, whether they applied or not. If Wolfe thought it would help to have the plot of *Do As Thou Wilt* described in detail all he had to do was ask.

But apparently he didn't need it. His head moved. "And you, Mr. Ferris?"

"I'm feeling a lot better," Noel Ferris said. "When the questions they asked made me realize that I was actually suspected of murder, and I also realized that I had no alibi, it looked pretty dark. Believe me. What if the others had all been somewhere else and could prove it? So I thank you, Mr. Wolfe. I feel a lot better. As for me, I left the house a little after ten and called at four agencies. Two of them would remember I was there, but probably not the exact time. When I got hungry I went back to the house to eat. I can't afford five-dollar lunches, and I can't eat eighty-cent ones. When I entered the house a man was at the phone telling someone that

Tammy Baxter had been murdered and her body was in the parlor."

"What kind of agencies?"

"Casting. Theater and television."

"Do you visit them daily?"

"No. About twice a week."

"And the other five days? How do you pass the time?"

"I don't. It passes me. Two days, sometimes three, I make horses and kangaroos and other animals. I go to a workroom and model them and make molds. Something on the order of Cellini. I get eight dollars for a squirrel. Twenty for a giraffe."

"Where is the workroom?"

"In the rear of a shop on First Avenue. The name of the shop is Harry's Zoo. The name of the owner is Harry Arkazy. He has a sixteen-year-old daughter as beautiful as a rosy dawn, but she lisps. Her name is Ilonka. His son's name—"

"This is not a comedy, Mr. Ferris," Wolfe snapped. He twisted his neck to look at the wall clock. "I engaged to act for Miss Annis only five hours ago and I haven't arranged my mind, so my questions may be at random, but they are not frivolous." His eyes moved to take them in. "Now that I have seen you and heard you I am better prepared, and I can consider how to proceed. I will leave it to Miss Annis to thank you—three of you— for coming." He arose. "I expect to see you again."

Martha was gawking at him. "But Hattie said to tell you everything we told the cops!"

He nodded. "I know. It would take all night. I'll go to that extreme only by compulsion; and if you told them anything indicative they are hours ahead of me and I would only breathe their dust."

Dell boomed. "You call this investigating a murder? Asking me if I had paid my room rent and how I spend my afternoons?"

It *was* a little odd, the four suspects coming uninvited to empty the bag and being told to go almost before they got started. Noel Ferris, his lip twisted, got up and headed for the hall. Martha Kirk, getting no satisfaction from Wolfe, appealed to me: didn't I realize that Hattie had been arrested for a murder she didn't commit? Paul Hannah sat and listened to us, chewing his lip, then got up and touched her arm and said they might as well go. Raymond Dell stood, lowered his chin, gazed at Wolfe half a minute, registering indignation, wheeled, and marched out. (Exit Dell, center.) I followed Martha and Hannah to the hall, but she preferred to put on her galoshes herself. When I opened the door for them a few snowflakes danced in.

Back in the office, Wolfe was sitting again, leaning back with his eyes closed. I asked if he wanted beer, got a nod, and went to the kitchen and brought a bottle and glass, and a glass of milk for me. He opened his eyes, took in a bushel of air through his nose and let it out through his mouth, straightened up, picked up the bottle, and poured.

He spoke. "Saul and Fred and Orrie. At eight in the morning in my room."

My brows went up. Saul Panzer is the best operative south of the North Pole. His rate is ten dollars an hour and he is worth twenty. Fred Durkin's rate is seven dollars and he is worth seven-fifty. Orrie Cather's rate is also seven dollars and he is worth six-fifty.

"Oh." I took a sip of milk. "Then you did get an inkling?"

"I got a conclusion: that it would be futile to go on pecking at them. Mr. Leach has been on their flanks for three weeks, and now Mr. Cramer's army has them under siege. My only chance of priority is to surprise him from the rear."

The foam was down to the rim of his glass, and he lifted it and drank, a healthy gulp. "It's a forlorn chance, certainly, but it's worth trying for want of a better. I am not familiar with the procedures of counterfeiters, but it seems unlikely that an underling would be entrusted with five hundred twenty-dollar bills. Ten thousand dollars. We know he had that large supply; and that permits the conjecture that his connection may be not with a mere go-between, but with the source. If so, the quickest way to settle it would be to locate the source."

"Yeah. It's barely possible that Leach has had that idea."

"No doubt. I assume that when Miss Baxter took a room in that house her primary mission was to search the premises for counterfeiting equipment. Obviously she found none. I also assume that, as you suggested, it was known that one of the inhabitants of that house had passed counterfeit money, but it was not known which one, and they were all under surveillance—by Miss Baxter in the house and by others outside. And if I were a Secret Service agent assigned to keep an eye on Raymond Dell I would suppose that any meeting he had with a supplier of contraband would be clandestine. That is how my mind would work. The first day I followed him to an East Side tenement I would of course make inquiries, with due caution, but when he went there five days a week and I learned from Miss Baxter what he did there, my attention would be diverted. But I am not a Secret Service agent. My attention is drawn to that tenement house, and specifically to Max Eder, a painter. An artist. I shall send Orrie Cather there tomorrow morning to reconnoiter. Fred Durkin will go to the shop on First Avenue—by the way, I want its address. Harry's Zoo." He made a face. "Saul Panzer will go to the Mushroom Theater. As I said, it's a forlorn chance, but what better can we do with tomorrow? Unless you have a suggestion?"

"I have," I said emphatically. "I respectfully suggest that you start thinking up something for day after tomorrow."

He grunted. He picked up his glass, took a gulp of beer, swallowed it, licked his lips, and put the glass down. "'Forlorn' was too strong a word," he said. "I have an expectation that is not wholly unreasonable. Twelve hours of the time of those three men plus expenses comes to more than three hundred dollars. I don't hazard that amount, even of a client's money, on a pig in a poke."

"Then you did get an inkling."

"Certainly."

"Fine. I hope it's not counterfeit." I swiveled and got the phone and dialed Saul Panzer's number.

Chapter 7

I was there at the beginning of the briefing session in Wolfe's bedroom at eight o'clock Tuesday morning, but when the phone interrupted us a second time Wolfe told me to go down to the office and take it there. The first time it was a *Times* reporter wanting to speak with Wolfe, and when I told him Wolfe was busy and would I do, he said no and hung up. The second call, which I took in the office, was from Lon Cohen of the *Gazette*, who preferred me to Wolfe any day. He wanted to know when he could send a photographer to take a picture of the dirt Wolfe was going to feed the cops. Evidently one of the two who had carried Hattie out knew a newspaperman. Lon had other questions, naturally, but I told him the answers would have to wait until I found out what they were.

I was considering whether to rejoin the briefing session when the phone rang again. It was Nathaniel Parker. He was sorry he hadn't been able to spring our client, but it had taken him three hours to find out where she was, and he hadn't got to see her until midnight. He expected to have her out by noon.

At nine o'clock the trio came down. One of the reasons they are better than most is that none of them looks it. Saul Panzer, under-sized and wiry, with a big nose, could be a hackie. Fred Durkin, broad and burly and bald, could be a piano mover. Orrie Cather, tall and trim and dressy, could be an automobile salesman. They stepped into the office, and Saul said they had been told to take three hundred dollars apiece in used bills. I said as I went to open the safe that even with inflation and even with janitors promoted to building superintendents, fifty bucks was the top price for one, and they would please return the change. Orrie said that if they had to buy clerks and elevator men and neighbors there wouldn't be any change. Saul said they would each give me a ring every couple of hours or so.

When they had gone I went on with the morning chores—opening the mail, dusting the desks, filing the cards of propagation and performance records which Theodore puts on my desk every evening. That was just for my hands and eyes; my mind was busy with something else. Of all the things I do to earn my pay, from sharpening pencils to jumping a visitor before he can get his gun up, the most important is riding Wolfe, and he knows it. Sometimes it's next to impossible to tell whether he's working or only pretending to. That was the question that morning. If he was only stalling, if he had sent for Saul and Fred and Orrie just to keep from starting his brain going, the thing for me to do was to go up to the plant rooms and go to work on him. It was the same old problem, and the trouble was that that time I would have nothing to say when he narrowed his eyes at me, as he would, and inquired coldly, "What would you suggest?"

That was what my mind was on, and was still on when the doorbell rang a little after ten o'clock and I went to the hall for a look. It was Albert Leach, with his snapbrim hat down even closer to his ears than yesterday. I went and opened the door.

"Good morning," he said, and slipped his hand inside his overcoat.

I supposed he was producing his credentials. "Don't bother," I said, "I recognize you."

But it wasn't credentials. His name came out with a folded paper. Extending it, he said, "Order of the Federal District Court."

I took it, unfolded it, and read. I read it through. "You know," I said, "this is a new experience. I can't remem-

ber that we have ever been served with an order from a
Federal court. Mr. Wolfe will be glad to add it to his
collection." I stuck it in my pocket.

"You note," he said, "that I am empowered to search
for the object specified if necessary."

"You won't have to. You heard me tell Cramer yesterday that I put it in the safe, and it's still there. Come
in." I gave him room.

He had excellent manners. He entered, removed his
hat, stood while I shut the door, and followed me to the
office. I swung the safe door open, got a corner of the
wrapping paper with my thumb and forefinger, carried
it dangling and put it on my desk, and went back and
brought the lettuce and the string. "There you are," I
said. "I didn't rewrap it after I lifted the prints."

His lips tightened. "You said nothing to Inspector
Cramer about lifting prints."

"No? I thought I had. Of course that was routine
after Miss Annis told us how and where she found it.
You won't find any except hers and mine. I couldn't, and
I was pretty thorough."

"You tampered with evidence."

"What was it evidence of—then?" My feelings were
hurt. "Anyway, the prints are still there. I'll give you a
bag to carry it in, but first we'll have to count it and I
want a receipt. It's still the property of Miss Hattie
Annis."

He opened his mouth and closed it again. It was a
situation. He knew that I knew that he knew that I
knew it was counterfeit, and therefore we both knew
that Hattie would never see it again, but he was still
keeping it off the record. "I'll make a concession," I
offered. "We'll weigh it on the postal scale. Put it on."

He picked it up and put it on the scale, and we looked.
Just under seventeen ounces. I brought a shopping bag
from the kitchen and gave it to him, got at the typewriter, and tapped out a receipt for 16-11/12 oz. of
twenty-dollar bills. I was tempted to add "in good condition," but remembered that he had warned me not to
try any fancy tricks with the Secret Service. As I

handed him the receipt and my pen the doorbell rang, and I stepped to the hall.

It was Inspector Cramer. I went and opened the door. He entered. I shut the door. When I turned his hand was emerging from inside his coat with a folded paper. He handed it to me. I read it through. It wouldn't be worth keeping as a souvenir—just the State of New York.

"You'll notice," he said, "that I can search for it if I have to."

"You won't have to. You know where it is."

He strode to the office door and on in. I stopped on the sill. Leach, at my desk, with the shopping bag in one hand and the bills in the other, turned.

"It's a problem," I said. "Leach has signed a receipt for it, but I can tear it up. Why don't you split it half and half?"

Cramer stood at arm's length from the T-man. A muscle in the side of his neck was twitching. "That's evidence in a murder case," he said. "I have a court order for it."

"So have I," Leach said. "From a Federal court." He put the bills in the bag, taking his time, and tucked the bag under his arm. "If you'll send a man to our office he'll be allowed to examine it, Inspector. We are always ready to cooperate with the local authorities."

He moved, detouring around Cramer. Cramer wheeled and followed him, and I stepped aside to let them by. As Cramer passed he gave me a glare that would have withered a lesser man. I didn't cooperate by going to open the door because I wasn't sure I could keep my face straight, and when they were out and the door had closed I quit trying. A whoop had wanted out the second Cramer produced the paper, and now I let it come. I laughed so loud and so long that Fritz appeared at the kitchen door to ask what had happened.

There was no point in disturbing Wolfe in the plant rooms, so I let it wait until he came down at eleven o'clock. He never whoops, but when I reported and showed him the court orders he allowed himself an

all-out chuckle and there was a twinkle in his eye. He
said it was just as well he hadn't been present, since
Cramer would probably have accused him of staging it,
and I agreed. I said I was glad the stuff was out of the
house, and he agreed.

Calls came from Saul and Fred and Orrie during the
next half hour. Nothing promising. Orrie had spoken
with Max Eder, the janitor of the building, and three
other tenants. Fred had bought a squirrel and a kanga-
roo and had spent an hour in the workroom in the rear
of the shop. Saul hadn't been inside the building that
contained the Mushroom Theater. From the outside it
looked as if it might collapse if you leaned against it. He
had spent the two hours covering the neighborhood.
When I relayed the reports to Wolfe, who was doing a
crossword puzzle in the *London Observer*, all I got was
a grunt. I had about decided it was time to go to work on
him when the doorbell rang and I went to answer it.

It was our lawyer and our client. I hadn't told him to
bring her. I was in no mood for her, and Wolfe certainly
wasn't. All I could tell her was that Wolfe either had an
inkling or hadn't, and he was spending her money at the
rate of fifty bucks an hour. I went and opened the door
but occupied the threshold.

"Greetings," I said heartily. "This is a relief! I'm
sorry we couldn't make it sooner, Hattie, but Mr.
Parker did his best. You'll take her home, Nat? I'm tied
up here."

"Don't call me Hattie," she said, "until I find what
you're up to."

"I brought her here," Parker said, "because she insisted." He looked harassed. "I'll be going. I've canceled
two appointments and I'm late for another one. Let me
know if you need me." He went.

"Every time I come here," Hattie said, "there you
stand. What good does it do to open the door if you fill it
up?"

I stood aside and she entered. She took off the gray
woolen gloves and stuck them in her coat pocket, and
unbuttoned her coat, and I certainly would have been

no good if I hadn't helped her off with the coat, so I did, and put it on a hanger. By the time I had it on the rack she was at the office door, entering, and by the time I got to the office she was in the red leather chair and Wolfe was glowering at her.

"About that lawyer," she said. "I'm not going to pay him too, and I told him so. When I told Buster I could pay forty-two thousand dollars that includes everything."

Wolfe looked at me. I nodded. "All right. I told you I was under a spell. I scaled it down."

He looked at her. "Very well, madam, I'll pay the lawyer. You came to tell me that?"

"I told you before not to madam me. First I want to see that counterfeit money, then I'll know I can trust you. Show it to me."

Wolfe looked at me. I have seen him handle many a crisis, but that was too tough for him. "Archie?" he said.

I opened my desk drawer, took out three sheets of paper, and went and handed her one of them. "A cop named Cramer brought that," I said. "Signed by a judge, ordering us to give him the bills and the wrapper. Cramer knows Mr. Wolfe and me and doesn't like us. When he handed me that he sneered."

"I thought so. You're no good. So you—"

"Wait a minute. We had been afraid that would happen. The cop was too late." I handed her another paper. "A man had already come with that, signed by a Federal judge, and I had turned the money over to him, so the cop was out of luck. I don't say we had arranged it, but facts are facts. The cop was so sore he marched out without a word." I handed her the third paper. "That's the receipt the man signed."

She hadn't even glanced at any of the documents. She handed them back. "I wish I had been here," she said.

"So do I, Miss Annis. You would have enjoyed it."

"Call me Hattie."

"With pleasure." I returned the papers to the drawer and sat. "Did you have a hard night?"

"Not too hard. There was a couch and I got some

naps, but the woman that stayed with me wouldn't turn the lights out, and every two hours they came back and started in again. Cops are too mean to live, and they're too dumb. They might have known I wouldn't speak to a cop."

"Didn't you speak at all?"

"No. Didn't I say I wouldn't?"

"Not a word?"

"No. The worst part was I was hungry. They brought some stuff twice last night and again this morning, but of course I wouldn't touch it. I don't know what kind of drug they had in it, something to make me talk."

"You haven't eaten at all?"

"Of course not."

Wolfe grunted. "That's ridiculous. We have a spare room that is comfortable. Mr. Goodwin will take you to it, and my chef will take you a tray. After your fast you should eat with caution. Have you a preference?"

She cocked her head. "You bet I have, Falstaff. Let the lady enjoy herself. I know about your chef. How about some lamb kidneys *bourguignonne?*"

Wolfe doesn't flabbergast easy, but that did it. He stared. "That would take time, mad—Miss Annis. At least two hours."

"I don't mind, I'll take a nap. Is there a bathroom?"

"Certainly."

"Then I can wash the smell of the cops off. But the other thing I want to know, what about the reward? We want that reward."

"That's problematical. I'll keep it in mind. We have a more urgent matter to deal with. After you are refreshed—"

"What matter?"

"The job you hired me for. Investigation of the murder committed in your house."

"I hired you to make the cops eat dirt, and you already have. The one named Cramer, is he a big one with a big red face and little blue eyes like a pig?"

"Pigs' eyes are not blue. Otherwise the description fits."

"Then you've already made him eat dirt. I wish I had been here. He was the first one in my room when they busted the door. That's part of your job, to make them pay for that door. The murder, that's their job. I'm surprised it was Tammy Baxter because I thought a counterfeiter would have more clothes, but of course when somebody came for the package and it wasn't there he thought she had taken it and he killed her, but she should have known I had it because I told her yesterday morning—"

The phone rang and I swiveled and got it. A female said that Mr. Mandel wanted to speak to me, and after a wait he came on.

"Goodwin? Mandel of the District Attorney's office. I want to see you. How soon can you be here?"

"Twenty minutes. If necessary."

"It's necessary. It's ten minutes past twelve. I'll expect you at twelve-thirty. Right?"

I told him yes, traffic permitting, hung up, and arose. "The DA's office," I announced. "I'm surprised it didn't come sooner. You don't need me anyway, you understand each other so well."

I left them.

Chapter 8

They kept me at 155 Leonard Street five and a half hours. All I got out of it was two corned beef sandwiches, a piece of blueberry pie, and two glasses of milk, on the house, eaten at the desk of assistant DA Mandel. What they got out of it was doubtful. In addition to Mandel, I had conversations with another assistant DA named Lindstrom, two detectives attached to the DA's office, and District Attorney Macklin himself.

Over the years I have been suspected of a lot of

things by various authorities, from corrupting a cop by buying him a drink to complicity in a murder, and that day they added a new one to the list. None of them came right out with it, but what was really biting them was their suspicion that I was in collusion with the United States government. Of course they covered other aspects of the case, all of them and thoroughly, but what they concentrated on was the package of phony lettuce. That was all the DA himself asked me about, and he put it to me point-blank: did I know the money was counterfeit? I told him point-blank no, and felt better; it's always a relief to get a lie off your chest. He said of course I was lying, that I would have been a nitwit not to suspect it. I said it didn't matter now anyway, since the Secret Service had it, and he blew his top. I admit it's hard to believe that he actually thought I had disposed of evidence in a murder case by arranging for Leach to beat Cramer to it, but I suppose a DA has as much right to be a damfool as the people who voted for him.

It was a quarter past six when I left the building and flagged a taxi. By the time it turned into 35th Street I had decided that I wouldn't wait until after dinner to go for Wolfe. He was too darned lazy to live. Since, thanks to me, Hattie had told him that he had already made Cramer eat dirt, he would consider that no matter what happened or didn't happen he could send her a bill for a modest hunk of the forty-two thousand, say five grand, and why should he strain his brain? She was out on bail as a material witness and in no real danger. We had got rid of the contraband. There was no great hurry. Nuts, I decided. He had to be poked. As I mounted the stoop and put my key in the door I was choosing my opening remark from three I had hatched.

But I didn't get to use it. The rack in the hall was so crowded with coats that I had to squeeze mine between two that I recognized—Inspector Cramer's and Saul Panzer's. Cramer's voice was raised in the office, and it was hoarse, as it always was when he was in a huff. As I reached the office door he was saying, ". . . not just to hear you spout! If you've got something let's have it!"

Wolfe, seated behind his desk with his fingers laced at the summit of his middle mound, had sent his eyes to me. "Ah," he said. "Satisfactory. I was concerned."

Sure he was. The bigger the audience the better when he is staging a scene. Before I headed for my desk I glanced around: Cramer in the red leather chair, Sergeant Stebbins at his right, Paul Hannah and Noel Ferris on chairs facing Wolfe's desk, Raymond Dell and Albert Leach, the T-man, behind them, and Martha Kirk and Hattie Annis on the couch to the left of my desk. Saul Panzer was over by the big globe. As I circled around Leach and Dell, Wolfe was speaking.

"You know quite well I have something, Mr. Cramer, or you wouldn't have come. As I told you on the phone, I had a stroke of luck, but I had invited it; and I knew where to send the invitation. True, I sent it to three addresses—an East Side tenement, a shop on First Avenue, and a building on Bowie Street which housed the theater—but my expectation was centered on the last. When my expectation was realized I was faced with the question whether to notify you or to notify Mr. Leach; and preferring not to choose, I asked you both to come and to bring Miss Kirk, Mr. Dell, Mr. Ferris, and Mr. Hannah. Miss Annis, my client, was here. I thought the first three had a right to be present; as for Mr. Hannah, since he is both a counterfeiter and a murderer, you and Mr. Leach will have to decide—"

"That's a lie," Hannah said, and was rising, but Leach, behind him, grabbed his arm. Hannah jerked, but Leach held on. "Who the hell are you?" Hannah demanded, and with his free hand Leach got his leather fold from his pocket and flipped it open, and by then Stebbins was there.

"Are you arresting him?" Stebbins said.

"No, are you?" Leach asked.

"Nobody's arresting me," Hannah said. "Turn loose of me."

"Sit down, Hannah," Cramer growled. He looked at

Wolfe. He had seen Wolfe perform before, and Leach hadn't. Not only had he heard Wolfe say that Hannah was a counterfeiter and a murderer, but also he saw the expression on Wolfe's face, and he certainly knew that face. He left his chair, put his hand on Hannah's shoulder, and said, "You're under arrest as a material witness in the murder of Tamiris Baxter. All right, Sergeant," and returned to his chair. Stebbins stood at Hannah's left and Leach stood at his right.

"That's prudent, Mr. Cramer," Wolfe said, "since I have no conclusive evidence. Up to three hours ago I had merely a surmise. Talking with these people last evening, I got nothing but faint intimations. Miss Kirk? Unlikely. She attended a ballet school regularly, she exercised an hour every morning, and she received a monthly remittance from her father, all of which could be checked. Mr. Dell? Also unlikely. He had paid no room rent for three years. Mr. Ferris? Possibly, but with a reservation. His statement that two of the agencies he called at yesterday would corroborate him made it improbable that he had followed Miss Annis here yesterday morning."

"So what?" Cramer rasped.

"So my attention centered on Mr. Hannah. He had lived there only four months. He had paid for his room every week. He had almost certainly lied when he said Miss Baxter had told him that a man had twice followed her to the door. Miss Baxter was an agent of the Secret Service of the Treasury Department, and she—"

"Who said so?" Leach demanded.

"No one. Mr. Goodwin inferred it. You have carried discretion to an extreme, Mr. Leach, in concealing the interest of your organization in the occupants of that house, but you will soon agree that it is no longer needed. So I did not believe that Miss Baxter had told Mr. Hannah that. Finally, Mr. Hannah's account of his movements yesterday left him completely free up to noon. He could have followed Miss Annis here and, when she left without entering, back to her house. He could have stolen a parked car and, when she left her house a second time, tried to run it over her; but, since he failed, that is of little consequence."

"There's damn little consequence in anything you've said," Cramer growled.

Wolfe nodded. "I'm only explaining why my attention centered on Mr. Hannah. I could indulge in speculation—for instance, why did he kill Miss Baxter there and then? Had she seen him try to kill Miss Annis with the car, and confronted him when he returned to the house? But you can speculate as well as I, and it will be your job, not mine, to screw a confession out of him."

"I've got nothing to confess," Hannah said. "You're going to regret this. You're going to regret it good."

"I think not, Mr. Hannah." Wolfe's eyes went to Leach, standing, and then to Cramer, sitting. "So when I sent three men to those addresses, with the invitations to luck, I sent Saul Panzer to the Mushroom. Mr. Panzer leaves less to luck than any man I know. He phoned four times to report progress. The third time, around three o'clock, he asked for reinforcements and I sent them. The fourth time, less than two hours ago, I told him to come and I phoned you gentlemen. Saul, will you describe the situation?"

Since Saul was over by the big globe, all but Wolfe and Stebbins and me had to twist their necks. "Just the situation?" Saul asked.

"Lead up to it briefly."

"Yes, sir. The first two hours I covered the neighborhood, but got no lead, so I went inside the building. I didn't tell the superintendent what I was after, just that I wanted to look around for something, and the way he reacted and the way he accepted forty dollars for his trouble, I decided he was honest. He showed me around the theater and the basement and the second floor. The third floor is occupied by a job-printing shop with two presses and the other equipment you would expect. He told the two men there what I had suggested, that I was an insurance underwriters' inspector looking for violations. From the way the men looked I decided I was hot, and I told the superintendent I would have to give the shop a good look and it would take a while, and he left. When I started looking behind things on shelves they jumped me and I had to get rough and pull my gun. I didn't shoot, but I had to knock one of them out. There was a phone on a table, and I rang you and asked you to send Fred and Orrie to help me search the place. You said they would be calling in soon, and you would—"

"That's far enough," Wolfe said. "And now?"

"They're still there. In behind stacks of paper on one of the shelves there are eight stacks of new twenty-dollar bills. In a compartment in the back of a cupboard are four engraver's plates that were probably used to make the bills. The two men are on the floor with their hands and feet tied. I don't know their names. There's only one chair in the room and Fred Durkin is sitting on it, or he was when I left, and Orrie Cather was sitting on a pile of paper. One of the men has a lump on the side of his head where I hit him with my gun, but he's not hurt much. I gave the superintendent another twenty dollars. That's the situation."

Paul Hannah had started to rise, but hands on his shoulders had stopped him—Stebbins on the left and Leach on the right.

"You might add one detail," Wolfe told Saul. "The name one of them mentioned."

"Yes, sir. That was after Fred and Orrie came and we had them tied and we found the plates. One of them said to the other one, 'I told you Paul would squeal. The goddamn murderous bastard. I told you we ought to clear out.' Do you want to hear the rest of it?"

"That will do for now. You will of course report in full to Mr. Cramer and Mr. Leach." Wolfe's head moved. "As you see, gentlemen, I was faced with a dilemma, since he was both a counterfeiter and a murderer. Preferring not to choose, I asked you both to come, and I leave the question of priority to you. Since Mr. Cramer has him under arrest—"

The movement that interrupted him was by Paul Hannah, but it wasn't much of a movement. Apparently his idea was to lunge at Wolfe, but Stebbins and Leach had him pinned. They glared at each other and Hannah glared at Wolfe, and Hattie Annis's voice came from the couch.

"You see, Falstaff? Didn't I tell you?"

She had told him absolutely nothing.

Chapter 9

O ne day three weeks later Wolfe and I were in the office disagreeing about something when the doorbell rang. It was Hattie. I escorted her in, and she sat in the red leather chair, opened her handbag, and took out a little package wrapped in brown paper. Wolfe made a face. I thought, Good Lord, she's found another one. But she reached into the bag again and came out with an envelope that I recognized.

"This check you sent me," she said. "You say in your letter it's for my share of the reward, a hundred dollars. So you kept your share?"

"Yes," Wolfe lied.

"Did you get yours, Buster?"

"Yes," I lied.

"Then that's all right. But what about this bill? Five thousand dollars fee for services and $621.65 for expenses. What did I tell you that day, Buster? Didn't I say I could pay forty-two thousand dollars?"

"You did."

"Then here it is." She tossed the package onto Wolfe's desk. "A man at the bank helped me pick those bonds and he says there's none better. These are transferred to you. This is the first time I ever let any of them go, and I hope it's the last, but it was worth it. That was a day, the best day I've had since my father died. I didn't like it when I saw in the paper that he had confessed, but that wasn't your fault. I've got no use for anybody that confesses anything to the cops. That Paul Hannah was no good. He even told them how he stole the car and tried to kill me with it because he thought I had the package and knew who put it in my parlor, and he saw Tammy across the street and knew she saw him, and when he went back to the house she was at the phone dialing a number and he got the knife from the kitchen, and when he got near her and she stood up he stabbed her, and then he carried her in the parlor and left her there with her skirt up to her waist. He was no good. I'll have to be more careful about people that want a room."

Wolfe was frowning. "I can't accept those bonds, mad—Miss Annis. Not all of them. I prefer to evaluate my services myself. I did so and sent you a bill."

She nodded. "I tore it up. The day I told Buster that, that settled it. I hired you and I said what I could pay. Now you say you won't accept it. That's no way to do."

Wolfe looked at me. I grinned. He pushed his chair back and arose. "I have a matter to attend to," he said. "I'll leave you with Mr. Goodwin. You understand each other." He marched out.

It took me half an hour to talk her around, and she told me twice not to call her Hattie.

The World of
Rex Stout

Now, for the first time ever, enjoy a peek into the life of Nero Wolfe's creator, Rex Stout, courtesy of the Stout Estate. Pulled from Rex Stout's own archives, here are rarely seen, never-before-published memorabilia. Each title in "The Rex Stout Library" will offer an exclusive look into the life of the man who gave Nero Wolfe life.

HOMICIDE TRINITY

Rex Stout—A Lizzie Borden supporter? Indeed, he was a defender of her good name. Shortly after the 1962 publication of HOMICIDE TRINITY, Stout was awarded this certificate (from an organization of doubtful legitimacy).

Would Wolfe have been able to clear her name?

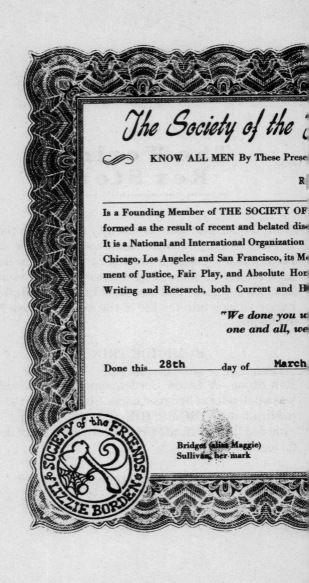

The Society of the ʃ

KNOW ALL MEN By These Prese

R

Is a Founding Member of THE SOCIETY OF
formed as the result of recent and belated dis⸱
It is a National and International Organization
Chicago, Los Angeles and San Francisco, its M⸱
ment of Justice, Fair Play, and Absolute Hor⸱
Writing and Research, both Current and H⸱

"We done you u⸱
one and all, we⸱

Done this ___28th___ day of ___March⸱

Bridget (alias Maggie)
Sullivan, her mark

SOCIETY of the FRIENDS of LIZZIE BORDEN

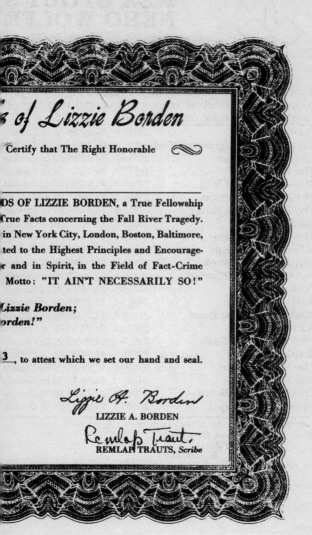

s of Lizzie Borden

Certify that The Right Honorable

_____

DS OF LIZZIE BORDEN, a True Fellowship

True Facts concerning the Fall River Tragedy.

in New York City, London, Boston, Baltimore,

ted to the Highest Principles and Encourage-

r and in Spirit, in the Field of Fact-Crime

Motto: "IT AIN'T NECESSARILY SO!"

Lizzie Borden;

orden!"

3, to attest which we set our hand and seal.

Lizzie A. Borden
LIZZIE A. BORDEN

Remlap Trauts.
REMLAP TRAUTS, *Scribe*